D1670487

BLOODCRY

FAITH BIRMINGHAM

Published by BookBaby.

Cover illustrated by Roger and Makenzie Pemberton.

Edited by Sarah Wessman.

Print ISBN: 978-1-66783-626-3
eBook ISBN: 978-1-66783-627-0

Visit @bloodline_trilogy on Instagram for further information.

To Bart and Vicki Baker. I'm the Christian, the student, the teacher, and the leader I am today largely because of you two. May God bless you both wherever He takes you, just as you bless everyone you meet. Especially me.

Contents

chapter 1

Raiden

*W*hzzzzz. *Smack!*

The sound of his arrow hitting its mark sent a feeling of pleasure through Raiden's mind. The familiar feeling of practice gave him a sense of peace. And in the yard of the small cabin that he and Sir Macarius shared, there were plenty of dead and dying trees to target.

The cabin was located just off of the dirt street that led into the village. In the distance, Raiden could even see the market square, teeming with early morning life. The cabin was located in the northeastern corner of the Maith grounds. Raiden had a view of the castle wall through some of the trees. The men who had been charged with building Maith's walls years ago had apparently only cut down the trees that stood in the way of the wall. The trees surrounding the cabin marked the very edge of the woods where Raiden had spent what was possibly the most stressful and dangerous week of his life, only a few months ago.

Raiden glanced at the road behind him. A pleasant faced man was passing by. Raiden waved in greeting. The man returned the action, smiling. Raiden sighed and turned back to the trees, firing a few more arrows. As usual, every arrow hit its mark. Years of practice didn't come without reward. Even with his mind not completely focused on the task, he could hit the center of a tree. Eventually, however, he ran out of arrows.

Again, he turned to the road. For a moment he thought he spotted Sir Macarius walking toward the cabin, but as the man approached it became evident by his clothes that he was just a common farmer. Disappointed, Raiden moved to the trees to retrieve his arrows. As he walked, he studied the bow in his hand.

Raiden's bow was his favorite possession. It was a simple recurve bow, designed so that the ends curved away from its user. Such a weapon was known for being light and easy to carry, but also powerful. There were other types of bows, of course, and Raiden had been trained to use all of them. The longbow, notorious for its ability to shoot extremely far, required more strength. There was also the crossbow, one that Raiden hated deeply. It shot several hundred meters at its best, but took a painfully long time to load.

The diversity of the bows in which Raiden had been trained was what marked him apart from the average Rathús archer. Despite training with all of these bows, however, the recurve bow gave Raiden the most comfort and confidence.

It wasn't just the type of bow that Raiden liked. The advantages of being a bowmaster would suit him well one day. He had learned firsthand, while they had fought Kuvira's forces in the woods, that being an archer allowed him to fight from a distance, away from the hectic chaos of the battle. And while Raiden felt that he was slowly improving with a sword, he knew the bow would always be his source of skill.

He gathered his arrows and returned to his spot beside the road.

Raiden's bow was the best style for an environment such as Rathús too, he thought. There weren't many areas in the kingdom where a longbow or crossbow would be needed. Most confrontations would take place in a semi-flat area, with occasional hills to shoot from. His recurve bow allowed him to shoot closer targets.

Unlike most simple wooden bows, Raiden's bow had a dark brown, almost black color to it. He wasn't sure why, but the uniqueness made the bow feel more special. Something that was his own.

"Hullo there," a male voice called from behind Raiden, pulling the boy from his thoughts. He turned hopefully, but was disappointed by yet another passerby.

"Hullo," he called back, not wanting to be rude.

"Pleasant morning, isn't it?" the man asked.

Raiden frowned. He had never seen the man before, much less spoken to him. It was odd, he thought, how friendly he was being.

"I suppose it is," Raiden replied, trying not to sound too skeptical.

The man stood awkwardly, looking at Raiden for another minute or two. Finally, Raiden could take it no longer.

"Do I know you?" he asked, his tone slightly irritated.

The man didn't seem to notice. "I was wonderin' the same thing," he said. "Only I think I've figured it out now."

"What's that?"

"You're Timothy's boy, aren't yuh?"

Raiden blinked, taken by surprise.

"I am," he answered slowly. The man nodded eagerly.

"I've just taken on a job at the stables. Your Pa's been showin' me how things work. You look a lot like him."

Finally content that the man was not a threat, Raiden slung his bow around his shoulder and turned to face the man full on.

"I see," he said in a more cheerful tone. He walked to the road's edge and held out a hand to the man. He shook it gladly.

"Your Pa is mighty proud of ya," the man bragged. "He's been talking nonstop about all the things you can hit with that bow of yours. An archer, are ya?"

"Well, I'm a bowmaster in training," Raiden corrected humbly. "But an archer nonetheless."

"Tim says you're due to complete your trainin' soon!"

At that, Raiden's smile wavered. Truth be told, Raiden had no clue when his training would end. Of course, it was due to be soon. But with Sir Macarius absent so often, and with their trip into the woods months ago, in the spring, Raiden's training hadn't been given the attention it required.

"I'm hoping so, sir," Raiden managed. The man nodded in approval.

"Well, I might as well get on with it," he said, turning back toward the road. "It was sure nice to meet you."

"You as well," Raiden replied as the man walked away.

He turned back to the trees, more determined now than he had been moments before. Perhaps if he could impress Macarius with his shooting, he could convince the man to let him take his final assessment sooner.

He scoffed aloud at the thought.

"Sooner," he muttered. "More like 'on time.'"

Since, after all, it was Macarius's absence that had delayed Raiden already. It wasn't Raiden's fault at all.

Drawing his eyebrows together in focus, shaking the negative thoughts away, he drew the bow back and aimed for a nearby tree.

"Hello."

Raiden jumped at the sound of a sudden voice, making his shot fly sideways and into the woods. The boy cursed, turning to see Sir Macarius squinting back at him.

"Now why on earth did you miss your target?" the bowmaster teased.

Raiden frowned. "Where have you been?"

"Alright, alright," Macarius conceded, chuckling. "Go and fetch your arrow. Meet me inside and I'll tell you all about it."

Raiden obeyed, taking plenty of time to make sure his arrow hadn't been damaged before he replaced it in his quiver and moved inside the cabin. Sir Macarius gestured for Raiden to sit at the wooden table in the kitchen. As he did so, the older man set a cup of tea in front of Raiden. The boy drank gladly. Eventually, Sir Macarius joined Raiden at the table. The two drank their tea for several minutes. Finally, Raiden broke the silence.

"Is there something you were going to tell me," he asked moodily, "Or were you simply interrupting a good practice?"

Macarius snorted. "Did you see that last shot? I would hardly call that a *good* practice, my boy."

Raiden raised an eyebrow, unamused. Macarius, in turn, cracked a grin.

"Okay," he said, holding his palms up in a show of surrender. "You are right, I have been absent far too much lately."

Raiden made a sound of agreement.

"And I apologize deeply for that," Macarius rushed onward. "I haven't said it, or even shown it, but I was beyond worried when I had to let you go off with Lord Hightower into those woods. And when you returned? When Lord Hightower told me of all you had done? Why, I was beyond *proud!*"

Despite his annoyance at his master's constant absence, Raiden felt himself blush slightly at the praise. Still, he remained silent as Sir Macarius continued.

"After the fire, especially, I hadn't meant to be gone so much. I remember that day vividly."

"Believe me," Raiden commented dryly. "So do I."

Macarius was silent for a moment, and Raiden wondered if his last words were ill considered. But before he could think about apologizing, Macarius continued in a softer, more heavy voice.

"I had gone out to grab a meal and to gather some food to restock our cabinets, and I was met by Luca and some woman running like their lives depended on it. In moments, I was updated on the situation and ran home, praying that your life be spared."

Raiden tried to imagine his master acting so hastily in worry for his life. It made him feel awkward, so he pushed the mental image aside.

"But after the fire, I was informed of your friend Rayla's … ah … situation, and I found out that you would be alright, so I began trying to help Carrow."

Raiden leaned forward slightly. "Why would the scribemaster of Maith need help from a bowmaster?"

Macarius frowned.

"It … It's just a small task that requires some traveling. Carrow couldn't get away from his duties here, which is why he asked me to help him with the issues that required travel."

Raiden frowned.

"Carrow couldn't be bothered by his duties, but you could afford not to train me?"

A small part of Raiden couldn't believe he had actually said what he'd been thinking for so long now. But he didn't regret it. Not even when guilt and perhaps a small touch of hurt passed over Macarius's face.

"Raiden, I didn't mean for you to–"

"It's alright," Raiden said stiffly. "It doesn't matter now, anyway. Go on with your story."

Macarius hesitated, that injured look never leaving his face. But Raiden didn't relent, and finally Macarius continued, if somewhat quieter than before.

"Well, I didn't want to overwhelm you with questions after the fire. That seemed to be taken care of by every other human alive."

Raiden scoffed. "I will admit, it probably would have only served to annoy me if you had been asking if I was alright every time I walked through the door," he said. Macarius nodded before continuing.

"As I said, I have been traveling. Digging into this legend with a few of my colleagues from Rathús Province."

Raiden sometimes forgot that his master was originally from the capital province, and had only moved to Maith temporarily to train Raiden.

"These were people Carrow wouldn't know, of course," Macarius was saying, "Seeing as how he spends so much of his time up in that library. That's another reason he thought of bringing me in on the project."

Macarius glanced at Raiden, almost as if he was seeking approval. Guilt stirred in Raiden's gut for making his master feel so badly, and Raiden decided to nod his understanding.

"While you were in the woods on what was *supposed* to be a simple scout party, I was traveling to Riraveth. I've found a man who thinks he may know not only where Rayla comes from, but also has inside information about Kuvira's troops and their location."

Raiden stared blankly at his master, trying to take in what the man was saying.

"You know where Rayla came from?" he asked hopefully. "You know who her family is?"

Macarius shook his head.

"Not exactly. He only mentioned having some small lead to that information."

All thought of resentment and anger against his master was left behind as Raiden's heart raced toward this new information. If Macarius had found a way to track down Rayla's parents, it would mean everything to his friend.

"That's still more than we've ever had before! What was his lead?"

Macarius winced. "I don't know."

"What?" Raiden exclaimed. "You didn't ask him for that information?"

"Of course I did," Macarius assured him quickly. "But this man had never heard of Rayla by name. He'd only ever heard what Kuvira and the other men had mentioned of a specific girl with a specific gift."

Raiden frowned thoughtfully.

"So you both knew two different sides of the same story," he concluded.

"Exactly. But he agreed to ask some men he could trust for more information to give me later. We will see what he can give me. In the meantime, I still have to handle the matter of Kuvira's forces themselves."

Raiden, only just now remembering that Macarius had mentioned this earlier, sat back in his seat in shock.

"Where are they?"

"According to him, they are in Riraveth. He wouldn't say where specifically, but he seems to believe their forces were too large to have moved very much."

Raiden shook his head.

"But how would this man know about Rayla's bloodline when she doesn't even know herself? And how does he know so much about Kuvira's forces?"

"Well, the answer is simple," Macarius warned, "But it's not pleasant."

"What do you mean?"

Macarius sighed. "He was one of Kuvira's men."

Raiden felt his body tense. He swallowed hard.

"Was?"

"Yes. He left after he learned of Kuvira's true plan. It was along the lines of attacking Maith and overthrowing Lord Hightower. But anyone could have seen that coming. We've always known that Kuvira hates Lord Hightower."

Raiden took a shaky breath.

"But I don't understand," Raiden said slowly. "Why would he leave? If it was so obvious that Kuvira hates Lord Hightower, why didn't this man already have a guess of what Kuvira had planned?"

Macarius shrugged.

"Kuvira knows how to mislead his men. Many are too young to remember when Kuvira and Lord Hightower lost their family. It was years ago, and it was an internal affair. Think about how much you know of the other provinces' lords and captains of the guard."

Raiden considered the point.

"Very little," he admitted.

Macarius nodded. "Exactly. So many of the men following Kuvira now aren't even aware of the history between their leader and the lord of Maith. And as I said before, Kuvira is a good leader. Good, that is, in the sense that he knows how to rally his men. It's likely he isn't coming right out to say he wants to overthrow this province. And if he is, he has probably spun a masterful lie in as well. My informant simply found out the truth."

Raiden accepted his master's logic, but pressed forward with another question. "But wouldn't this man know Kuvira would hunt him down?"

Macarius shrugged. "He figured as much. According to him, he has begun using a different name, dyed and cut his hair, and taken to hiding within the castle walls. It is beyond crowded in Riraveth. If anyone wanted to hide, that would be the place to do it. Either there, or the isolated hills. But this far into the year, the hills are a death sentence."

"Why?"

"There's no food. And unless you want to survive by begging from farmers and surrounding village people, your only hope for food is the land, which is hopeless in the winter, or Castle Riraveth, which is at least two days away from the hills themselves."

Raiden pursed his lips.

"So he chose to hide in the castle walls."

Macarius nodded. "And as for why he left, he didn't go into much detail. I assume he knew that attacking Maith was madness. The rest of the kingdom would be at Kuvira's doorsteps before he even settled into Castle Maith. And that's assuming Kuvira managed to win against our forces."

"Okay," Raiden said, nodding slowly. "But I still don't get how this man would know about Rayla's heritage?"

"Well, that's a simple answer too, although, again, not pleasant."

Raiden waited for his master to continue.

"See, one thing about Kuvira is that whatever he knows, he likes to share with his inner circle. I've no clue if he's just smart enough to ask for advice – although I doubt that very much – or if his inner circle is a way to make up for the lack of companionship he has in life. The point is, if Kuvira knew something about Rayla, he would have shared it with these men to get their input."

"So you're saying that Kuvira himself knows where Rayla came from?"

"My informant seemed to think so," Macarius agreed.

"And this man was a member of Kuvira's inner circle?" Raiden asked.

Macarius considered the question. "I suppose you could say that," the bowmaster said. Raiden frowned.

"What do you mean?"

"Well, he wasn't just any member of Kuvira's council," Macarius said. "Before he left, this man was the commander of Kuvira's troops."

chapter 2
Rayla

Rayla hated this time of year. Everything started to get cold and all the plants died. The beautiful greens and reds and yellows turned to brown and gray and brown. Perhaps it was a lasting hatred from when she had lived without a home as shelter, and the cold weather meant miserable nights of no sleep and lots of shivering. Whatever the reason, the late autumn and early winter made Rayla feel dead inside.

She was sure that part of her misery had nothing to do with the cold air. In fact, she knew exactly why she had been so unhappy for the last few months.

Even after occupying herself with lessons and training, she couldn't put Finn out of her mind. At night, when she closed her eyes, she could see herself running to the man again in slow motion. She could remember when she had, at first, thought the fallen guard was someone she didn't know. She could recall feeling mildly concerned for the unknown man only to feel her entire world come crashing around her when she recognized his face. She could recall wishing to go back just a few moments in time, before everything changed so quickly. Could feel the helplessness, the uselessness, as she was stuck in reality.

And when she woke again, nothing that anybody could say would give her peace. Finn's death was her fault. She had gotten captured. She had led them deeper into the woods. She had guided them back to Kuvira's camp. And in the end, she had failed to revive him.

In the long run, any more deaths that took place at the hands of Kuvira and his troops would be Rayla's fault. She couldn't get that thought out of her mind. Who would be next? All of this was happening just because she was cursed with some legendary power. All because she was born of a mysterious, lost bloodline that she knew nothing about.

As she walked along the dirt path, she kicked a pebble as hard as she could. It sailed down the street.

She hadn't asked for her gift. In fact, she wished she could give it away to someone who would use it better. It seemed ironic that she would be born with the gift to only heal the people she had good memories of. She was the most closed off and introverted person in the kingdom. What good was her gift if she had no memories of anyone to heal them with?

Finally, she arrived at the arena, where the once green grass had begun to turn brown. Already, several of her fellow battle students had gathered around, all shifting uncomfortably. She felt their pain. Her nerves were on edge as well. Only the familiar bump on her left hip that came from her beloved sword gave her comfort. She could never express to Sapphire how much it meant that the young blonde girl had retrieved the sword for Rayla when she had entered Kuvira's camp during the battle in the spring.

Rayla took a deep breath, trying to steady her shaking hands.

Today was the day of final lessons. It was only natural for her to be nervous.

As she reached the arena, she passed a large cluster of battle students. Shying away, she made a wide circle around them. They were her age, here to be tested as well, and she knew them to be decent young men. Still, she hated to be around anyone, especially these days.

Since their return from the woods months ago, everyone in the school had seemed to come up with their own explanation as to why Rayla and Raiden were suddenly getting such special treatment. One group had decided that Lord Hightower had already chosen them out as future Maith guards. Rayla supposed that wasn't completely false. Lord Hightower had offered her a position the day they had packed up to head home in the woods, promising her that it would be waiting when she passed her final lessons. Still, that hadn't been why she'd gone as part of the scout party. Before the battle, Lord Hightower knew little of Rayla's swordsmanship.

Other, more imaginative students had decided that she and Raiden had mastered dark magic and bewitched Lord Hightower, convincing the lord to give them such privileges. The suggestion was of course absurd, and very few students chose to believe the story. Still, the mention of any type of magic in the same context as Rayla's name made the girl nervous. It was just too close to the unbelievable truth.

"Nervous?" A voice from beside her asked. Rayla jumped slightly, turning to look at the young man who had spoken. She had seen him before, she realized, although she had never spoken a word to him.

Not wanting to engage in conversation, she only nodded.

"At least you don't have to go first," he joked lightly. Rayla nodded again.

The boy grinned mischievously. "Come on," he said. "You can't be that worried? It's just a little lesson."

Rayla snorted in disbelief before she could stop herself, and the boy frowned.

"What?" he demanded, suddenly looking annoyed.

"Nothing," Rayla said, shrugging.

"It sure sounded like something."

"Just that I'm not so sure that you've taken this seriously if you think it's just like any other lesson."

To Rayla's surprise, the boy's face grew red with sudden rage.

"I'm plenty prepared," he insisted. "My father was one of Lord Hightower's own personal guards, so I've learned plenty about swordsmanship."

Rayla knew she should probably be disgusted at the boy's tone. In fact, on another day, she might have even spat back. But something that he had said had caught her attention, wiping away any anger she might have felt.

"Was?" she asked softly.

"What?"

"You said he *was* one of Lord Hightower's guards."

The boy's face contorted. Rayla recognized the expression immediately. It was something she felt herself, every day. Pain.

"Yes," the boy snapped, clearly trying to maintain his tough attitude. "That's what I said."

"I'm sorry," Rayla replied evenly. To her own surprise, she meant it.

The words seemed to shock the boy as well. His expression softened slightly.

"Yes, well… " he muttered, struggling for words. "You shouldn't be. It doesn't matter."

"I'm sure it feels better to think that way," she said. It was strange, but Rayla felt completely comfortable speaking to this boy. She wasn't sure why she wanted to help him. She didn't even know him. But she knew how he felt.

"But the truth is, it does matter," she continued. She didn't meet his eyes, which made talking easier. "And it hurts, and it's going to hurt for a long, long time. But eventually, you learn to live with it. It won't go away. But you'll become numb to it."

After she finished, she looked up at the boy. There were tears in his eyes.

"How did he die?" she asked gently.

"He–" the boy choked. "He was killed in the woods. In the spring."

Rayla felt a lump form in her throat. It was already happening. She was already destroying other people's lives.

"I … " she tried, but her voice failed.

"His name was Ron," the boy said in a shaky voice. "He was one of the scouts that Lord Hightower took with him. And he just … didn't come back."

Rayla felt her heart racing. She wanted to tell him what happened. She wanted to take responsibility for Ron's death, if for no other reason than to give this boy someone to blame. Somewhere to direct his anger. But she couldn't bring herself to speak, and the boy walked away.

Rayla pursed her lips and lowered her head in shame. For months, she had been ignoring the pain in the back of her mind. The memories that flooded her head every time she thought of the woods were enough to bring Rayla to her knees if she dwelled on them for too long.

It had been nearly five months since Rayla had discovered her gift. She still couldn't believe all that had happened. She had spent seventeen years of her life disconnected from her family and her past. Not only was she disconnected from them, she didn't have a desire to reconnect at all. At an age before she could remember, Rayla had been torn from her family. She had made her way to Castle Maith when she was still fairly young, and had learned to grow up alone and independent, sometimes going for days without eating. The only source of dependence she'd had was her best friend, Raiden.

At some point in her late childhood years, Sir Luca, the battle master of the province and Lord Hightower's captain of the guard, had seen her fending off several rotten boys and had suspected her natural skill with a sword. Once she had proven herself, he had enlisted her as the battle school's first female student. The man had gifted Rayla with her beloved blue-gray sword, the only thing she possessed of real value. Her skill with the sword had become the thing she focused on most, and she had learned to use that skill to build a hopeful future for herself.

Until, Rayla remembered bitterly, Kuvira had appeared and altered that reality. Rayla could vividly recall the panic in her mind as she had rushed into Raiden and Sir Macarius's cabin the night that Kuvira had set it ablaze. She remembered Raiden's injuries, and how still he had been. She remembered dragging his motionless body out of the house. And she remembered healing him.

That had been the incident that set everything else in motion. From then on, Rayla's life had been a whirlwind of confusion and chaos. She had been changed, and not necessarily for the better. Rayla's back twinged from the whiplashes that scarred her back, and her heart rate involuntarily sped up as she remembered what it was like to be in Kuvira's clutches.

But even after being in Kuvira's camp for only a few days, Rayla had no clue as to why Kuvira had wanted her in his possession so desperately. Her gift was for healing, and all Kuvira seemed to want to do was destroy, and to exact his revenge on Lord Hightower, who Rayla had only just learned was Kuvira's brother-in-law. Kuvira had blamed Hightower for his wife's death, forgetting that while he had lost a wife and children, Hightower had also lost a sister, a nephew, and a niece.

Still, of all the confusion that had come in the spring, none of it compared to the aftermath of the battle itself. Rayla hid her face with her hair now, letting the tears fill her eyes as she remembered Finn. The guard that had escorted her and Raiden to and from her lessons with Carrow – an escort that had always been the bright part of each day as Finn had teased her and laughed with her. The guard who had gone with them to take Sapphire on her first walk through the woods, and had patiently explained what each bird and flower was to the bubbly young girl. And who had leapt to Rayla's aid when she had fallen down the hill and twisted her ankle later that same day. A lump formed in Rayla's throat, making it nearly impossible to breathe, as she remembered how Finn had looked out for her for months, becoming a brotherly figure to her. And finally, how he had given his life fighting the men who were threatening both Rayla and Maith as a whole, ever the noble man of honor.

The image of Finn would forever feel like a stab in the heart. And losing him would forever haunt Rayla's mind.

She would never get to be as carefree as she once was.

Around her, the idle chatter settled, bringing Rayla out of her miserable thoughts. Across the arena, Sir Luca had emerged from a door. Immediately, the trained battle students fell in line. Rayla, as always, made sure she was on the far end and away from as many people as possible. She blinked away the tears that had surfaced to her eyes, shook her head to clear it, and forced herself to focus.

Luca walked slowly in front of the students, sizing each of them up. He began at the end opposite of Rayla, studying each student's armor. Nervously, Rayla glanced down.

Her armor was, of course, perfect. Her loose breeches were tucked into her perfectly tied boots, and leg guards covered her shins. Her white shirt was tucked into her belt, which held her sheathed sword and a small knife. Her leather breastplate, which would be swapped out for a metal one upon her completion of training, was strapped to her chest flawlessly. Her close helmet sat on her head, her visor pushed up so she could see better for the time being.

Still, the girl felt uncertain. Once Luca reached the middle of the line, he caught her eye momentarily to shoot her a glance of encouragement. Rayla felt some of the tension in her chest disband.

Ten students away. Nine. Eight.

"What is this?" Luca suddenly asked. It was Luca's professional voice, the one he used when instructing, but never when he was having a simple conversation with Rayla or any of the captain's other close friends. Rayla winced, pitying the boy her instructor was frowning at.

"I'm sorry, sir?" the boy asked, clearly confused.

"If even the smallest detail in one's armor is uncared for," Luca began, quoting himself. Rayla mouthed the words as the swordmaster finished the sentence. "A soldier may lose his life for that one mistake."

Rayla leaned forward, wondering what part of his armor the poor boy had neglected.

"Go home, son," Luca said bluntly. "An additional month will be added to your training. Next time, don't skip the little details."

The boy nodded once before trudging away in shame.

Finally, after several grueling minutes, Luca reached Rayla. The man carefully looked over her breastplate, her leg guards, and her helmet. Then he closely examined the laces of her boots, making sure she had tied them securely. Standing up, Luca looked her in the eyes, giving a single nod.

Rayla exhaled. She'd passed the first half of the exam.

Sir Luca returned to the front of the group, clearing his throat.

"Congratulations, you have successfully donned the armor of a Maith guard. Now, we will proceed to the assessment of hand-to-hand combat. Each of you will be fighting a skilled swordsman. For your final lesson, you will be sparring with someone who will challenge you deeply. You will be fighting me."

Rayla's heart plummeted. Sir Luca was renowned for his advanced skills with the sword. He would make even the best of them look like fools.

She watched in curiosity as the first boy stepped forward. With a small pang of guilt, she recognized him to be the boy who had spoken to her earlier. As he and Luca began to spar, Rayla found herself silently cheering for the younger opponent. She watched as he made mistakes and then corrected himself just in time to deflect one of Luca's blows.

For about a minute, the two men fought furiously. But Rayla could see the outcome from the beginning of the fight. Exhausted from Luca's hard strikes and quick movements, the boy eventually found himself at the mercy of the swordmaster.

Still, Rayla reasoned, it could have been worse.

"You are dismissed," Luca announced, barely out of breath. "Stay tuned for your results."

With that, the boy retrieved his sword and scuttled away, shooting Rayla a quick glance before he disappeared. Rayla swallowed hard.

She felt her knees shaking as, one by one, Luca faced each student. After each duel, he dismissed the students, telling them to stay tuned for their results. Rayla watched each duel carefully, making mental notes of the mistakes made by her fellow students. One boy held his sword too low when there was a break in the fighting. This gave Luca the opportunity to strike up high before the boy could raise his sword in defense. Another boy focused too much on looking impressive, spinning and twirling his sword any chance he got. The action slowed him down and took his focus from what Luca's next move might be.

Too soon, it was Rayla's turn.

"Marcus," Luca said to the boy he had just finished sparring with. He kept his eyes on Rayla, regarding her with interest as he spoke to the other student. "Stay behind, please, as a witness to the duel. I don't want to be accused of any unfairness."

"Yes, sir," the boy next to Rayla said. He was sweating and out of breath from his recent duel. He had performed somewhat better than the other students. Rayla cleared her throat as the boy flopped down on the grass, wiping the sweat from his brow. She closed her eyes, taking a deep breath before turning back to face Sir Luca.

As with the other students, and as with any Rathús tournament duel, Luca and Rayla faced each other straight on. First, they touched their blades together gently, then brought their own weapons back, touching the flat of their blades to their foreheads. They stood that way for several seconds. Finally, Rayla leapt into action.

She knew it would be smarter for her to initiate the duel rather than allow her master to gain the starting head on her. If Luca got an advantage, the duel would be over before it began.

Luca blocked her first blow easily. Still, Rayla kept her footing, refusing to let the stronger opponent knock her backward or to the side. The two whirled into action, a combination of blocking and attacking. It was a difficult art, fighting without harming. They had to be sure that they only exerted the right amount of force, in case they got the better of the other opponent. They hadn't used blunted blades. Luca wanted his students to show skills with a real sword.

Rayla's blue-gray blade rang against Luca's silver one as she blocked his overhead stroke. They had been fighting hard for several minutes. Rayla was sweating, but so was Luca. The balance tipped from her favor to Luca's and back again. Once, Rayla felt her foot slip. She managed to roll to the side and come back up on her feet before Luca could make a strike at her. Another time, Luca nearly fell for a fake right cut from Rayla, managing to block her surprise left cut just in time. The spar continued this way for a few more minutes.

In the back of her mind, Rayla knew that if she allowed the fight to continue like this, she would tire before her master would, and she would lose the battle.

With the last ounce of strength she had, Rayla sent a vicious strike towards her master. Forced to block the blow, Luca lost his offensive position. In the break of the battle, Rayla kicked off the ground, spinning in a complete circle. With the momentum of the spin, she sent her sword downward, ringing a blow so hard on the crosspiece of Luca's sword that it vibrated in his hand.

Before the swordmaster could gain control of his sword again, Rayla landed. Quickly, she switched her sword from her right hand to her left. She closed the space between herself and Luca, using her free hand to take hold of Sir Luca's sword hand. She pulled it up and to the right, away from her body. At the same time, she brought her own sword, now in her left hand, behind Luca's neck.

They both froze, sweating and breathing with difficulty. Rayla kept her muscles taunt, waiting for any sudden escape that Luca may try to make. She looked her master in the eyes.

"Holy heavens," Marcus gasped from behind the two opponents.

Luca glanced from his sword, now held firmly in Rayla's hand and away from the two of them, to Rayla. He did this several times. Finally, the swordmaster spoke.

"I think," he said between breaths, "you may like your results."

Rayla felt a massive sigh heave from her chest.

chapter 3
Rayla

"Are … are you sure?"

Rayla couldn't believe what she'd just heard. The two were still standing in their fighting positions. Neither had made a move to leave yet.

Sir Luca nodded, sending sweat dripping into his eyes.

"Quite sure," he said.

Rayla stayed frozen in shock. She had done it. She had passed her final lesson.

Sir Luca cleared his throat, pulling Rayla from her thoughts.

"Although if you don't release me soon," the swordmaster said calmly, "I may be apt to change my mind."

"Oh!" Rayla quickly released Luca's sword arm. Carefully pulling her own sword back around to her body, she stepped away from Luca. Her sword hung low in exhaustion as she took several deep breaths. "Sorry."

Luca chuckled, although it was strained from his own exhaustion. "It's alright."

They stood still for several minutes to regain their strength. The boy that Luca had asked to stay behind was staring at Rayla with such intensity, she could feel his eyes boring into her. She tried to ignore him. Once she and Luca had begun to breathe regularly again, Luca sheathed his sword and considered Rayla.

"Congratulations, Rayla," Sir Luca said, laying a hand on her shoulder. "You are now an official Rathús warrior. No matter what position you have or where it is held, you will have this title wherever you go."

Rayla could do nothing more than look at Luca's grinning face in shock.

"You do, however, have much to consider," he added.

"I do?"

"Yes. With your skill level, you likely have several options. The most guaranteed position is as a Maith guard, of course. But there are other options. You could travel, searching for a position in the other provinces. Or you could seek to directly become one of Lord Hightower's personal guards. He already knows and trusts you, so I'm sure the offer would be open."

Rayla's mind whirled. She'd never thought of anything but becoming a simple Maith guard. At least, not since her silly childhood fantasy of becoming a knight. Of course, Lord Hightower had offered her a position as his guard in the woods after their battle with Kuvira's men, and part of Rayla had wondered all this time what he had meant by the phrasing. Had he been offering her a position as one of his personal guards, or just amongst the Maith ranks? Either way, she had never considered what it would be like to actually be given the honor.

"Of course," Sir Luca continued, "your being female may restrict you in some areas. Not all provinces are as accepting as I am of the idea of a female warrior."

Sir Luca paused, as if thinking deeply about his next words.

"That being said," he added slowly, "With a letter from both Lord Hightower and I, there is a small chance that, despite your gender, you could achieve knighthood in Rathús Province."

Rayla's eyes widened. "Me? A knight?"

"Yes," Sir Luca said without humor. "You just bested the captain of the Maith guard and the sword instructor of the most renowned battle school in the land. I believe that with further training, you would be able to reach knighthood."

"If they would accept me at all," Rayla clarified.

Luca nodded. "If they would accept you," he agreed. "But a letter from men in high positions can go a long way."

Rayla shook her head, not believing what she was hearing. Being a knight was something almost every child in the kingdom dreamed of. And very few men ever reached that goal. A young orphan like herself would never make it, she reasoned. She had no connections to the higher officers in the kingdom, aside from Lord Hightower and Luca. And to top it all off, she was a woman.

She couldn't imagine the faces of the Rathús knights when she came strolling up asking to be trained. They would probably laugh and kick her out of the province. The idea was simply impossible.

Besides, becoming a knight meant leaving Maith. And Raiden.

"Lord Hightower has already offered me a position as a Maith guard. It would be rude to refuse," she said decisively.

Luca frowned. "Lord Hightower would hardly be offended–"

"I would like to become a Maith guard. Perhaps with time, I'll look into becoming my lord's personal guard. But I think it's only fair that I start in a humble place."

Rayla looked into the eyes of Sir Luca, the man she had strived to impress for so many years. She felt a twinge of sadness at the disappointment in Luca's face. Still, she stood her ground. This was the right decision. It *was*.

"Very well," Luca finally said. "In three days, you are to meet me in Castle Maith for your ceremony. Of course, it is usually a more special occasion, seeing as how it should be the first time you would see the castle. However, I think you are quite accustomed to the structure by now."

Rayla managed a small smile, still in shock of what was happening. It seemed too good to be true. All she had worked for in her life was finally coming together.

"Thank you, Sir Luca," she said, offering a hand. The swordmaster took it, but shook his head as he did so.

"You are a Rathús warrior with impressive skill. Address me as Luca from now on."

Rayla balked at the thought of such a casual title for the man before her, and the honor of addressing him in such a way. She blushed, nodding quietly. Luca turned to leave.

"Sir–" Rayla called after him, correcting herself at the last minute. "Er … I mean, Luca." The name felt weird in her mouth without the proper title in front of it.

Luca smiled encouragingly. "Yes?"

"Why did you tell me what my results were, but not any of the others?"

Luca considered the question.

"Well, for one thing, none of the others bested me," he said with a rueful grin. Rayla blushed again. "And for another," the man continued, "I've always told my students their results in private. It helps them avoid embarrassment in the case that they did not meet my expectations." Luca paused. "I don't want any of my men to feel ashamed for having to repeat a few months of training. For some, it just takes a little more time to master their skills. That doesn't mean they should be embarrassed in front of their peers."

Rayla nodded her understanding, and Luca took his leave. Rayla turned to do the same.

To her surprise, Marcus was still standing in shock, off to the side of the arena.

"It's Rayla, right?" he said almost shyly.

"Yes," she replied shortly.

"That was … " he tried. His voice was full of disbelief. "Well, that was incredible. Was your father a swordmaster?"

Rayla winced. None of the other students knew her full story. It was hard enough for Rayla to be the only female in the battle school. She didn't want her fellow students to know she was an orphan as well.

"Not quite," she said quietly, hoping Marcus wouldn't press the subject any further. Unfortunately, he did.

"A guard, then?" he asked excitedly.

"No," Rayla said, slightly annoyed now.

"Well surely he must have–"

"Let me save you some time," Rayla interrupted. "I can fight because I learned the skill from the same man that you did. The only difference is that I spent every free moment practicing. I don't know what my father did. And to wrap this all up, I don't know what he did because I never knew my father at all. Or my mother, for that matter."

Marcus was silent, and Rayla immediately regretted her outburst. She sighed.

"I'm sorry," she said half-heartedly.

"No, I'm sorry," Marcus replied, his voice was more mellow than it had been earlier. "I had no idea."

Rayla pursed her lips.

"Very few people do," she replied.

"Well, I do hope you have the best of luck," Macrus said in a more cheerful tone. "That spin move toward the end of your duel was amazing."

"Thanks," Rayla said. "And good luck to you, too."

With that, they went their separate ways.

o o o

"Are you serious?" Raiden exclaimed. Rayla felt a grin spread across her face as she nodded.

She felt herself swept into a massive bear hug as Raiden lifted her off the ground, spinning her in a circle. She couldn't help but laugh.

"I knew you could do it, Ray! I always did. You're going to be the best warrior this kingdom has ever seen!"

Rayla rolled her eyes, squirming against Raiden's arms.

"Alright, alright, put me down," she said, though her voice was still light with joy.

Raiden released her, stepping back with a smile on his face.

"I'm so proud of you, Ray."

"Thanks," she said, smiling in return.

The two began to walk down the road again. Suddenly a thought struck Rayla.

"How is your training going?" She looked over to see her friend frowning.

"That's kind of why I rushed to meet you after your lessons," he said slowly.

"Oh, so it wasn't because you were so eager to know how I did?" Rayla teased. "And here I was, thinking you cared."

Raiden laughed softly. "I already told you, I knew you would do great."

Rayla turned to smile at her friend, but saw that he seemed distracted.

"So … " she pressed. "Your lessons?"

Raiden hesitated.

"Sir Macarius has been absent a lot recently," he finally admitted.

Rayla wrinkled her nose in annoyance. She was somewhat perturbed at Macarius for leaving Raiden in the middle of his final year of training. It seemed very inconsiderate and unprofessional.

Raiden cleared his throat.

"And because of that, I think I may need an extended time of training," Raiden continued.

A stronger feeling of anger flared inside Rayla. It wasn't fair. It wasn't Raiden's fault that Sir Macarius wasn't doing his job. Rayla looked over, ready to argue on Raiden's behalf, but the boy had noticed her expression and was holding up a hand to stop her.

"That's not the reason I needed to see you, either," he said. Rayla shut her mouth, willing to at least hear her friend out before she began to spit out her opinions on the matter.

"Sir Macarius told me earlier today why he has been gone so much," Raiden explained. "And why he didn't go on the scouting mission with us."

Rayla's heart twisted at the mention of the scouting party. She shook her head, suddenly realizing that Raiden was still talking, and refocused her attention to his story.

"–He managed to start a fight in the tavern and slip out, but he said it was close," the boy was saying. "Anyway, he found a man in Riraveth Province. He wouldn't say his name, but the man apparently has inside information on Kuvira's troops and their location. Not only that, but he says he knows about your bloodline. Rayla, he knows where you and your gift come from."

Rayla's steps faltered to the point that she nearly tripped over her own feet. She steadied herself before simply freezing in place. Raiden stopped beside her, watching her closely.

Rayla swallowed thickly, her mouth suddenly dry. She tried and failed to speak several times before she finally managed to find her voice again.

"We need to go to Lord Hightower," she said huskily. She wasn't sure how she felt about some stranger claiming to know about her past, but if this man knew something about Kuvira's troops then they needed to tell Lord Hightower immediately. The troops posed a threat to Maith. She could handle the information about her past later.

Raiden was nodding in agreement.

"Sir Macarius is planning to go to the castle in three days. He wants to have a full plan to present instead of 'just a little bit of information,' as he put it."

"That's good. I can meet you both there. My ceremony is in three days, too."

Raiden nodded.

"And we should go tell Sapphire about what Sir Macarius said," Rayla added as an afterthought. She glanced sidelong at Raiden, curious to see what his reaction would be.

Raiden was frowning, deep in thought. "How much should we tell her?"

Rayla didn't hesitate with her answer.

"Everything."

"Even about the troops in–"

"Everything, Raiden," Rayla insisted. "Sapphire is part of our group. And she has proven herself in these types of situations already. She was an asset to us in the spring. She deserves to know."

Rayla watched as her friend sighed, knowing she was right.

"Okay," he said finally. "Let's go."

chapter 4
Raiden

The door in front of Raiden swung open, and a plump, middle-aged woman stepped out.

The sight warmed his heart. Her gray hair was tied back and damp with sweat. The apron that hung around her waist was stained and dirty.

"Hi, Mother," Raiden said with a smile. The woman grinned up at Raiden and tackled him in a hug.

"Oh, honey, how lovely to see you! How are you?" She began fussing over Raiden's clothes, straightening his shirt and standing on her toes to fix his messy hair. Raiden gently eased her hands away.

"I'm well, Mother," he said, trying not to laugh. "You haven't been working too hard, have you?"

Raiden guessed, by her attire, that his mother must have just started cooking a meal for his father and Sapphire. Raiden's father, he knew, would still be working in the stables four another half hour.

"Oh, no. Of course not," Mistress Browne replied breathily. "Come in, won't you? There, that's better."

Raiden and Rayla let the woman usher them through the hall as they listened carefully to her story.

"I met a very nice couple when I was out getting food for the house. They were rather young, and I wanted to ask if they were new to the area, but of course I shouldn't be nosy. Haven't seen them around before, though. They were very good company with their smiles and laughs. I rather liked them."

As soon as she had finished speaking, the woman shifted her attention to Rayla. Raiden grinned at the expression on his friend's face as Mistress Browne fussed over Rayla's hair.

"You really should have it trimmed up a bit. Surely it's getting too long for you to handle? There, nice and braided and out of the way." She stepped back and glanced toward the kitchen. "Would you two like a snack?"

Raiden caught Rayla's eyes and they shared a smile.

"Yes please, Mistress Browne," Rayla replied.

"Oh don't mention it, sweetheart. And call me Molly, please." With that, she left for the kitchen.

Raiden glanced over at his friend. He knew that Rayla wasn't hungry at all. She hardly ever ate. But they needed to talk to Sapphire without Raiden's mother hovering over them and quizzing them about their safety. Eating a meal together was a good excuse for privacy.

They loved her, but she was a mother, after all.

"Where is Saph?" Raiden called, using the affectionate little nickname he had acquired for his sister.

"She's out back, dear," Molly called back.

Raiden drew his eyebrows together in confusion.

"Why is she out back?" he muttered.

"I have a guess," Rayla replied, a small smile on her lips.

The two made their way to the back of the house and glanced around. A jolt of shock went through Raiden as he saw Sapphire in the corner of the small yard area, practicing with a one-handed sword. She was hacking away at an innocent nearby tree.

"That's really not good for the blade," Rayla whispered. Raiden ignored her. He watched as Sapphire practiced several moves. Beginner moves, but moves that she had obviously put a lot of time into learning. From the corner of his eye, Raiden saw Rayla nod in approval. Pride suddenly glowed in him. If Sapphire was able to get Rayla's approval on her skill with the sword, then she must have been doing something right.

Eventually, Sapphire stopped for a break. She turned to see the two of them standing behind her, and she jumped in shock. A small blush appeared across the young girl's cheeks. Raiden cracked a smile.

"How are lessons going?" he asked casually. Sapphire's face glowed with delight as she approached her two older friends.

"Oh, Rayla, thank you *so* much for getting me a spot in the battle school! I love my lessons!"

"I simply asked Luca to take a look at you," Rayla insisted. "You got in on your own."

It was true. Rayla had told Raiden all about Sapphire's success. Apparently, Sir Luca had taken one minute to watch Sapphire duel a dummy before he had immediately enrolled her as the battle school's second female student. Luca had allowed Sapphire to live at home with her and Raiden's parents, and she attended classes everyday, but with two days to rest every week.

"Most of the other students my age ignore me," Sapphire continued, pulling Raiden from his thoughts. "I think it's because I'm a girl. That's okay, though. It gives me more time to focus on my lessons. There is one boy that's rather annoying, but I can handle him."

Raiden set his jaw, knowing what this boy was likely after. He felt Rayla place a hand on his arm. He glanced over to see her looking back at him, one eyebrow slightly raised.

"I'm sure you can," Rayla said in response to Sapphire, without looking away from Raiden. For several seconds, the two stared at each other until Rayla finally rolled her eyes and looked back to Sapphire.

"The lessons are so amazing," the girl continued, oblivious to the exchange. "Everything just feels right once I finally master it. But I think I like using knives best."

Raiden looked at Rayla and saw that she was frowning. "Knives? I never used knives, beyond learning a few simple tricks to defend myself in close quarters."

Sapphire beamed as she explained herself. "Sir Luca has been staying late after lessons so that I can get in some extra practice. He says knives are not a very common weapon, but I've learned to use throwing knives pretty well. I like the way they balance in my hand."

"That's really impressive, Sapphire," Rayla told the girl, patting the her shoulder affectionately.

Again, Raiden felt a surge of pride toward his sister.

The three moved to an area near the center of the yard, sitting in a circle.

"In other news," Rayla casually said, "I passed my final lessons today."

"You did?" Sapphire exclaimed, nearly jumping back to her feet. "I knew you would, Rayla! I just knew it!"

She threw her hands around Rayla's neck. Raiden smiled at the sight.

"Thanks, Saph," Rayla said. She, too, had taken to using the nickname.

"And what about you?" Sapphire said, turning to look at Raiden. He felt his heart drop.

"Ah, I still have a little while to go," he said slowly, trying desperately to avoid a prolonged conversation on the subject. "I've missed a few lessons, with Sir Macarius being so busy lately."

"That's alright," Sapphire said, shrugging. "You'll probably still finish super fast. I've never seen a target that you can't hit."

Raiden smiled, grateful for his sister's confidence in him.

After about a half hour of small talk, Molly came out and distributed fresh slices of bread. They thanked the woman, who smiled and left them to their business.

"Mother is such a good cook," Sapphire commented between bites. Raiden smiled warmly. He liked that Sapphire had taken to calling his parents "Mother" and "Father" so easily.

"Yes, she is," Rayla agreed, shoving a large bite of bread into her mouth as she spoke.

Raiden rolled his eyes.

"You two have awful manners," he teased. Sapphire shrugged.

"What can you expect," she answered. "We grew up living off scraps."

Even Rayla burst out laughing at the joke.

After they had eaten, Sapphire became suddenly serious.

"So," she said bluntly. "What exactly are you two up to now?"

Raiden frowned, looking at Rayla. His friend seemed to be just as confused as he was. She shrugged.

"What do you mean?" Raiden asked.

"Oh please," Sapphire said, rolling her eyes. "I knew as soon as you started trying to make small talk that there was something going on."

Raiden and Rayla shared another look. Sapphire sighed, stretching out on the ground in front of them.

"This is going to be a long story, isn't it?"

"Not too bad," Rayla promised.

"Alright, take it away."

Raiden did. He plunged into the story, explaining why Sir Macarius had been gone more than usual in the past few months. He told Sapphire everything, just as he and Rayla had discussed. Occasionally, Rayla would jump in when Raiden forgot an important detail. Sapphire listened closely. She kept her eyes focused on her hands, but somehow Raiden knew that she was paying close attention to his words.

"Until Sir Macarius goes to Lord Hightower with a plan," Raiden finished, "that's about all we know. We can't do anything without Lord Hightower's approval, and he certainly needs to be updated on the situation anyway."

Sapphire silently considered all that Raiden had said. Raiden was content to give the girl plenty of time to think. It was a lot to process, he knew.

"Well," she finally said, looking up at Raiden. "Whenever Sir Macarius gets a plan together, I want to be a part of it."

"We'd been counting on that," Rayla replied.

Raiden felt torn between wishing his sister would have simply asked if she could sit this one out, and feeling proud of her for being so willing to help. He had learned months ago that she was beyond capable of taking care of herself. Shutting her out would only make it more dangerous for her, because she would try to follow anyway. He had learned that lesson the hard way.

Besides that, Sapphire was not only tough, but also smart. Part of Raiden knew that he should consider the fact that she might be vital in whatever mission they embarked on.

"So it's decided," he announced. "Anything that Lord Hightower and Sir Macarius come up with has to involve us. All of us."

Rayla and Sapphire nodded.

"Saph, I can stop by on my way to the castle in three days, and you can go with me. You'll get to see my ceremony, and you'll already be there for the meeting when Raiden and Macarius arrive."

"Really?" Sapphire cried. "I get to watch your ceremony?"

Raiden chuckled at his sister's excitement, but he noticed that Rayla was suddenly frowning.

"What's wrong?" He asked the girl. Rayla turned hesitant eyes to him.

"I just forgot that … " She chewed her bottom lip. "I'm only allowed to bring one witness."

Raiden felt his heart drop slightly at the thought of missing such an important moment in his friend's life. But then he remembered the excitement in Sapphire's voice.

"Oh," the young blonde girl was saying. "I can just arrive after–"

"No," Raiden said, forcing a light tone. "You should go. I'll be arriving with Sir Macarius. And besides, it might do you some good too, Sapphire. You'll get to see what you're working toward for yourself one day."

Raiden looked at Rayla, and the two seemed to share the same moment of disappointment. But Sapphire couldn't seem to hide her hopeful expression.

"Are you sure?" She asked, trying to sound hesitant. Raiden smiled softly.

"I'm sure," he said, ignoring the ache in his chest. "I'll meet you both there after the ceremony."

After a small moment of silence between the trio, Sapphire stood, brushing the dirt off her breeches.

"We'd better go inside," she said. "Before Mother becomes too suspicious."

Rayla managed a tight laugh.

"If I know your mother at all, she already is."

chapter 5
Raiden

The walk to Castle Maith was silent for Raiden and Sir Macarius, which was fine with Raiden. After the morning he'd had, he didn't feel like making conversation.

As they walked, he decided to let his mind wander to his training earlier that morning. If it could even be called "training" at all.

Sir Macarius had brought Raiden to the stables. It had been a rather uncomfortable experience. Raiden's father had been working, and Raiden had been slightly worried that his father would embarrass him in front of Sir Macarius if he decided to make conversation. Thankfully, Sir Macarius had avoided idle chatting. The bowmaster had seemed to have other plans.

As it turned out, he and Raiden had spent the morning revisiting Raiden's skills on horseback.

Raiden had grown up feeling comfortable around horses. As a young boy, he would often go with his father to work. He had helped clean stalls, feed the horses, and sometimes he would exercise them by riding them around the small pasture. This had come in handy when Sir Macarius had told Raiden a few years into his training that he would need to learn to shoot from horseback.

Raiden was an excellent archer, although he would never say so himself. Shooting from atop a horse, however, was a far more advanced skill. Over the years, Raiden had learned to do so. He had spent several of his days off in the stables, practicing his archery while atop whichever horse was available that day. But it had been quite a long time since Raiden had practiced the skill. Now, in light of their upcoming journey, Sir Macarius had seemed to think Raiden needed a refresher.

Raiden hadn't wanted to train with his father watching nearby. It distracted him, knowing that the man was there. He couldn't help but worry about what his father was thinking every time he failed to hit a target. Still, Sir Macarius had told Raiden long ago that he couldn't afford to worry about outside distractions when he was shooting. It was a lesson Raiden had always struggled with, but one he had eventually learned to accept. Now, he could control his focus enough to drown out most distractions.

Most, but not all.

From the beginning of the training session, Raiden had known that Sir Macarius wasn't doubting his ability to shoot while mounted. He had been tested for something else that morning.

Macarius was testing him to see if his father's presence would crumble Raiden's focus.

Unfortunately, it had.

Raiden had missed too many of his shots, and Sir Macarius had shaken his head each time in disappointment. Even when Raiden's shots had hit their mark, the bowmaster hadn't seemed satisfied. Raiden hadn't been either. Though they might have hit the target, they certainly weren't centered.

Now, as they walked in silence, Raiden frowned to himself. He knew better than to let himself get distracted. He'd simply gotten into his own head. He had put too much thought into each shot and target.

For the past several weeks, the only thing Raiden had been worried about was convincing Sir Macarius that he didn't need any extra training, despite whatever lessons he had missed while Macarius had been absent. Instead, in one morning he had done the exact opposite, proving to his master that he needed much more time before his final assessment.

"What are you thinking?" Sir Macarius asked in a calm voice, pulling Raiden from his thoughts.

It was something Sir Macarius said often. Over the years, Raiden had come to expect the question. Any time he was silent for too long, his master would ask what he was thinking. It was both a blessing and a curse. Raiden enjoyed sharing his thoughts and questions with his master almost as much as he enjoyed Macarius's wise answers. Still, it also meant that Raiden was never able to hide his disappointment or concern from his master.

"I'm thinking about my training," he admitted. "I did terribly today. I've been trying so hard to catch up with my lessons where I have been falling behind. I was trying to prove that I was ready. But today I failed. Miserably. I proved that I *do* need extra training."

He glanced over and saw Sir Macarius frowning.

"I think I know why I was so nervous," Raiden continued quickly, hoping to ease some of the disappointment that he thought must have been going through his master's mind. "I didn't want to mess up in front of my father."

Macarius gave Raiden a curious glance.

"Raiden, your father–"

"I know he is proud of me," Raiden rushed on. "But I was afraid that if he saw me fail, he would think that I had wasted years of my life trying to learn something that I couldn't." Raiden shifted uncomfortably. "I didn't want him to think that he had made a mistake in letting me take up archery, that he should have trained me as a stable boy like he had always planned to. I–"

"Raiden," Sir Macarius said, stopping the boy from explaining any further. Raiden watched in shame as the bowmaster shook his head.

"I knew exactly why you were nervous," Sir Macarius said slowly. "In fact, I had been expecting it."

Raiden slumped his shoulders in disappointment. Macarius had been expecting him to fail.

"You *knew* I would be?" he asked quietly.

"Yes," Sir Macarius said. He hesitated, sighing before he continued. "The fact of the matter is, even with you missing several months of training, there's not much left for me to teach you."

Raiden frowned. "What do you mean?"

"Everything I have to offer, I've already shared with you. Every skill, every technique, every trick – you've already learned. You may not be as seasoned as I am, but the rest of your skills will only come with experience."

"I don't understand," Raiden said slowly. Sir Macarius smiled.

"I plan to ask Lord Hightower to announce that you have officially finished your training with me. Today."

Raiden stopped in the middle of the road. Sir Macarius noticed and stopped as well, a grin on his face.

"What?" Raiden managed.

"You've learned everything that I have to teach you, Raiden."

"But I–I'm not ready. I haven't even had my final assessment yet. There's still a lot–"

"Raiden," Sir Macarius said patiently. The boy stopped stammering and looked at the bowmaster.

"You are ready."

Raiden felt his mouth drop open to protest further, but no words came out. He didn't know what to say. Did Sir Macarius really think he was ready? After his horrible performance today?

Unsure of what to say, Raiden stood in silence for several seconds. Eventually, Macarius turned and began walking toward the castle again. Raiden quickly followed. He drew a shaky breath.

"You really think I'm ready?" he asked. Sir Macarius nodded encouragingly.

"I do."

Raiden turned to look at Macarius again, but something else distracted him.

To his surprise, they had arrived at the castle doors. One of the guards, seeing Sir Macarius, quickly moved to let them through. A twinge of pain shot through Raiden, and he hesitated in the doorway as he remembered another guard that used to open the castle doors for him and Rayla only a few months ago.

The loss of Finn was a pain that came in waves at unexpected times, and stayed until it wanted to leave.

Raiden shook the thought aside. Dwelling on the past wouldn't do him any good now.

He forced himself to walk through the door, and it shut behind him with a loud thud. Raiden waited until his eyes adjusted to the much darker lighting before he looked around for Sir Macarius. His master was standing, looking at him in concern.

"What is it?" he asked. Raiden attempted a confused look.

"What do you mean?"

"The look on your face," Macarius elaborated. "The flinch that you made halfway through the doorway?"

Raiden dropped his eyes.

"It's the guard, isn't it?"

Raiden didn't answer. He hadn't spoken of Finn at all to Sir Macarius. It had been too painful to even think about his late friend. Macarius must have heard about him from someone else. Perhaps Sir Luca had told him. Or Lord Hightower himself.

"Raiden," Macarius said softly. He moved forward, laying a hand on Raiden's shoulder.

"We only knew him for a short time," Raiden admitted, fighting to keep the emotion out of his voice. Unfortunately, he seemed to be losing that battle.

"That doesn't mean that you cared for him any less," Macarius reasoned. Raiden looked up, surprised that his master seemed to understand so well.

"We often form connections in strange ways," the bowmaster continued. "The more serious the circumstance, the stronger the bond seems to be."

Raiden hesitated to respond. Macarius pursed his lips.

"I'm terribly sorry that you have been subjected to such horror so early in your life."

Raiden swallowed thickly.

"I wasn't the only one that had to go through it," he stated.

Macarius nodded.

"Maybe not," he said. "But no man as young as you should have to witness such a thing. And I know from experience that this feeling won't go away. Losing people before it was their time is a tragedy that will follow you for the rest of your life."

Briefly, Raiden wondered what loss Macarius had experienced that allowed him to understand how Raiden was feeling. Raiden had always assumed that his master had simply chosen to never start a family. Perhaps he had been wrong.

"But I do think," Macarius continued, "that this has matured you. I think it's part of the reason that you are ready to finish your training."

"I guess," Raiden replied half-heartedly. Macarius glanced behind him, clearly not ready to drop the conversation but knowing that they needed to head forward.

"We had better not keep Lord Hightower waiting," he said. "But Raiden, don't let this consume you. It's alright to feel upset. Overwhelmed, even, at times. But you must find a way to cope with the loss. Otherwise, it will drag you down before your life has even begun."

Raiden nodded, still feeling hollow inside but comforted by how much his master cared.

"Yes, sir," he managed.

Macarius turned and started down the dark hallway. Raiden allowed himself a moment to regain his composure before following.

The two emerged into the bright throne room. Raiden blinked several times to adjust his eyes once more to the change of lighting.

Lord Hightower was easy to spot, tall and burly as he was. He was standing several meters to the right of his throne, speaking to Sir Luca and, to Raiden's delight, Rayla. Sapphire was also standing nearby, although she didn't seem to be engaged in the conversation. She was standing quietly behind Rayla, looking uncomfortable and bored.

As Sir Macarius and Raiden approached, Sir Luca and Lord Hightower broke their conversation off.

"Well, look who has arrived," Lord Hightower said with a welcoming smile on his face. "And how are the infamous Maith bowmasters today?"

"Might I remind you that I am no property of Maith, my lord?" Macarius replied with a smile.

Raiden knew that as a seasoned bowmaster and old friend of Sir Luca's, Sir Macarius had become Lord Hightower's friend as well. In fact, the lord, the bowmaster, and Luca, being Maith's captain of the guard, had spent plenty of time together, both in times of peace and conflict. In a way, they were a timeless trio. Still, Raiden would never be able to make himself comfortable with the idea of his master teasing Lord Hightower.

Eager to escape the circle, he slipped away and gravitated toward Rayla. The girl was beaming.

"I take it the ceremony went well?" Raiden asked. A part of him was still upset that he hadn't been allowed to watch the ceremony. He had asked Sir Macarius if they could try to arrive early for the event in hopes that Lord Hightower might make an exception, but the bowmaster had shaken his head, explaining that while Lord Hightower wasn't as strict as other lords on some customs and procedures, one thing that he held in high esteem was the Maith guard initiation ceremony.

Rayla smiled at him now, but a hint of Raiden's disappointment was mirrored in her expression.

"It did," she said.

"When do you get to know where you will be assigned first?"

"I start on the wall tomorrow morning," she whispered excitedly. Raiden could tell by the look on his friend's face that she was desperately trying to conceal her joy so as not to make a scene. Still, he could see the excited energy bubbling up inside of her, and he couldn't help but laugh.

"A little excited, are we?"

Rayla frowned. "I'm sorry," she said sarcastically. "Is this better?"

She slumped her shoulders, faking a bored look.

Raiden rolled his eyes. He opened his mouth to retort, but never got the chance.

"Well, we've got business to attend to!" Lord Hightower suddenly announced. His voice was so loud, even the servants across the room froze and turned to look at him. One man who had been sweeping the floors even dropped his broom. The wooden handle made a ringing *ping* that echoed through the halls. Lord Hightower seemed unfazed by this. He was staring directly at Raiden, who gulped.

Macarius and Luca each took a step back, respectfully, as Lord Hightower made his way to the younger members of their group. Sir Macarius was smiling at Raiden, and the boy felt his stomach churn. He got the sudden feeling that when his master had said that he planned to announce Raiden's completed training today, he must have meant as soon as they entered the castle.

"I'm told that there's a second graduate here," the lord exclaimed, confirming Raiden's suspicions. "Raiden Browne, please step forward."

Raiden swallowed hard and obeyed the order, somehow managing not to stumble over his own two feet. Nervously, he glanced around the room. Everyone, even the servants and the guards, were watching him closely.

"As lord of Maith Province, and in front of these witnesses," Hightower boomed, stealing Raiden's attention back, "I hereby decree you are an official Rathús bowmaster."

Raiden heard Rayla gasp behind him. He wanted to turn and look at his friend, but he was frozen in shock at what was happening.

"You will be allotted two weeks to decide where you would like to serve," Lord Hightower continued. "And to give you a head start, I would like to offer you a position as a Maith archer and the official bowmaster of this province, as Maith has not had one in several years."

Raiden balked at the offer. He knew that the demand for bowmasters was diminishing quickly. In fact, as far as he knew, none of the remaining bowmasters, aside from Macarius, were training anyone. Macarius would soon be traveling back to Rathús Province now that Raiden's training was finished, which would leave Maith as one of two provinces without a permanent bowmaster. In Raiden's mind, to be offered the position was the greatest honor he could receive.

Lord Hightower had not taken his eyes off of Raiden as the boy considered his words. The lord took a step forward, placing a hand on Raiden's shoulder.

"I have seen you in battle, and I believe you would make an excellent Maith warrior. But please, do not give me an answer until you have thought the matter over thoroughly. And Raiden," the lord added as an afterthought. "Congratulations."

Raiden felt his cheeks flush. Behind him, he could hear Sapphire begin to cheer. Sir Macarius clapped him on the shoulder. Even Sir Luca seemed to approve. Raiden couldn't help but smile.

"Thank you, my lord," he managed.

"You're quite welcome, my boy."

"Raiden," Rayla said quietly, whispering over his shoulder. A chill went down Raiden's spine as her breath touched his neck. "That's amazing!"

He only smiled wider.

"I told you!" Sapphire exclaimed, rushing up to tackle Raiden in a hug. The momentum sent the boy staggering forward several paces. Luckily, he was able to regain his footing before he crashed into Lord Hightower.

"Thanks," Raiden replied through a chuckle. "But I'm not sure what good it'll do me if you crush me to death now."

Sapphire didn't relent.

"I knew you were going to do it! I told you so. You're going to be the best archer this kingdom has ever seen!"

From one side, Sir Macarius cleared his throat.

"Second best," the man added.

Raiden gave his master a look of amusement. Finally, Sapphire released Raiden and returned to Rayla's side, although the girl was still clearly overflowing with energy.

"Now then," Hightower said, requiring the group's attention. "Let's take this party up to the library. From what Sir Macarius tells me, Carrow should be involved in this next conversation."

chapter 6
Raiden

The library had become familiar to Raiden over the past few months.

Although at first the room only represented the constant slicing of his palm while Rayla frowned over his bleeding hand for hours, it was also the room where she had finally discovered how to control her gift. It was where she had first healed him. At least, it was where she had healed him while knowing what she was doing. In a way, the room marked the beginning of this new journey of theirs.

Now, there were seven of them standing around a table, waiting for Carrow to speak.

Raiden's mind flashed momentarily to the first time he had been in this very spot when they had only just begun to learn about Rayla's magical blood-line. They'd known so little of what would happen. Of who they would lose.

The sudden reminder of Finn and his absence from the group hit Raiden like a blow to the stomach, and he was forced to shove his feelings aside. He glanced sideways at Rayla, and could immediately tell that she, too, was remembering the guard. Her lips were tight and her eyebrows were drawn together in a way that told Raiden that she was concentrating hard on fighting her emotions.

Slowly, so as not to attract the attention of anyone else, he bumped her shoulder softly. Rayla looked up, momentarily letting her pain shine through her eyes. Raiden gave her a small nod, hoping that she would feel comforted. Then he turned back to the table.

He, Rayla, and Sapphire were standing on one side of the rectangular table facing Lord Hightower and Sir Macarius, who were standing on the opposite side. Sir Luca and Carrow stood at the head of the table, bent over a letter. So far, everyone but the three youngest members of the group had read the letter. Raiden's nerves were on edge. He had no idea what was written on the parchment, but the expressions of the older men weren't comforting.

He wanted to ask what was written there, or request a chance to read the note himself. A more mature part of him, however, kept his curiosity at bay. Sir Macarius had written the letter himself, so Raiden assumed that it contained a suitable course of action. And if Raiden needed to know, his master would tell him.

"I'm not so sure about this," Luca finally said. Both he and Carrow had furrowed their eyebrows together. "I don't know if every part of this plan is a good idea."

Across from Raiden, Lord Hightower nodded in agreement.

"I'm skeptical as well," the lord admitted. "But you have to admit that it is the only logical course of action that has been suggested so far."

Sir Luca shrugged.

"There's no getting around it," Lord Hightower continued. "I think this is the only option we have."

Raiden's curiosity spiked again, wondering what that could mean.

"You're right," Carrow said. "But there are just too many holes. Too many places for something to go wrong."

"Do you have a better plan?" Macarius spoke up, not at all offended but determined to defend his idea.

"No," Carrow admitted, shifting his weight from one leg to the other.

"The entire plan is based on the words of one man, who could very well be lying," Luca pointed out. Macarius nodded, conceding the point.

"That is true," the bowmaster said. "But what he said made too much sense to be a lie. Every part of what he told me matched up with what we already know, plus some new information that filled a few holes in our understanding of Kuvira and his plans."

"Forgive me, Macarius," Carrow began bluntly, "but I'm not too eager to risk so much on your personal opinion of this man. Let's be reasonable, he is one of Kuvira's trusted officials. How honest can he be?"

"He *was* one of Kuvira's officials," Macarius retorted, stressing the past tense. "And honest enough to have left Kuvira's army and risk being caught and punished in order to give me information."

"Okay, wait," a voice beside Raiden piped up. He looked over to see Rayla, clearly flustered, holding a hand up. "Are you planning to share any of your plans with us, or are we simply here for looks? Because if it's the latter option, then I could be practicing with my sword right now instead of standing here and letting my mind be filled with all this nonsense."

Raiden glanced around the table, worried that his friend's outburst would meet disapproval. Instead, he saw Lord Hightower turn an amused gaze to the young girl.

"Fair enough," Lord Hightower said. His lips twitched at the corners as if he was trying not to smile.

"Sir Macarius is proposing a mission, that would include you and Raiden, to meet with his informant once again in Riraveth while also sending Carrow to warn the lord of Riraveth about the potential danger in his province."

"What potential danger?" Rayla asked. "And why would Carrow have to go with us to talk to the lord? Can't one of us do it?"

Raiden glanced nervously at Carrow, afraid the man would have taken offense to Rayla's words. Instead, he seemed to agree with her.

"I thought that too, at first," the scribe agreed. "But then I considered the nature of Lord Dunnman and Riraveth Province as a whole. It's very possible that the lord would refuse to see anyone that he deemed to be 'unworthy' of his time. As the high scholar of Maith and a close advisor of Lord Hightower, I would have one of the best chances of being admitted into the castle."

Raiden frowned. "The nature of the province?" he repeated curiously. "You mean because of the crime that takes place there?" Carrow shrugged.

"Partly. But there's a reason there is so much crime in Riraveth. It didn't just magically appear overnight."

Rayla leaned forward, placing both her palms on the table.

"You're saying that Lord Dunmann is responsible for Riraveth's crime?"

This time it was Lord Hightower that answered.

"As the lord of a province, part of our duty is to manage the crime and enforce appropriate punishments. Lord Dunmann has been the lord of Riraveth Province for some time now–"

"And he doesn't do his job well," Rayla finished. Lord Hightower winced.

"I don't like to speak ill of other lords … "

Raiden watched as Lord Hightower chewed his lip. "But?" Raiden pressed.

Lord Hightower sighed.

"But no," he admitted. "Lord Dunmann does not do his job well, in my opinion. In the years that he has overseen Riraveth Province, the crime there has only gotten worse."

The group was silent for several seconds, reflecting on the words of their lord. Finally, Raiden cleared his throat.

"So … This mission … "

Lord Hightower nodded. "Yes, the mission. You are both able to set off on the journey, seeing as how you will not have to miss any training. I, of course, will have to remain behind. I cannot leave the province without a leader for a second time. I will, however, agree to send Carrow with you. Luca and Macarius will join as well. There are plenty of other seasoned guards to take over lessons for the younger students at the battle school in Luca's absence. I will also send twenty Maith guards as your escorts."

At Lord Hightower's last words, Macarius perked up, apparently meaning to protest. However, Lord Hightower anticipated the action and stopped the bowmaster with a raised hand.

"I am aware that you want your party to be small," the lord said. "But I will not send so many valuable members of my province away without proper protection. Especially not if you're wanting to take *him* with you."

Raiden watched as Macarius settled, willing to accept the terms. Rayla, however, had already formed another question.

"Him?" she asked.

"Yes," Hightower replied. "The plan proposes that the five of you, plus your escorts, will travel to Riraveth province, and that you will take Kuvira with you."

Raiden immediately glanced at Rayla, who balked at the words.

"Why?" she asked, failing to hide the disgust and fear in her voice. Raiden knew that she hated to even think about being near Kuvira. He couldn't blame her, after all that she had gone through at his hands.

"He will be used as leverage," Lord Hightower explained.

"Leverage for what?" Raiden asked, nonchalauntly laying a comforting hand over Rayla's. The girl had begun to breathe harder as the conversation moved forward.

"Macarius is proposing that if his source is correct, and Kuvira's men are in Riraveth, you should attempt to lure Tenabris from their camp and force his surrender by threatening his father's life. If Kuvira does not go with you, Tenabris will never believe that his father is still alive. He will assume that we killed him quickly. Don't worry," the lord added. "With more than half a dozen men at arms, I am confident that Kuvira will not try anything foolish. He knows better than to fight a losing battle."

Raiden's heart began to pound.

"You're going to send half a dozen men to meet with Kuvira's entire army?" His voice shook with the words. "We'll be killed immediately!"

Sir Luca rushed to shake his head.

"Not his whole army," he clarified. "We will demand that Tenabris meet us alone, or we will kill his father anyway. We won't, of course, but hopefully the threat will convince Tenabris to meet with us."

"And you're going to trust that Tenabris will do as you say?" Rayla demanded. "He's vile! He was raised by a monster. He killed Finn!"

Rayla's voice broke, and Raiden swallowed hard at the pain that was laced through his friend's voice.

"Rayla," Sir Luca said gently. "Sir Macarius has thought this through. We will send scouts out to watch for any sign of an army approaching. We will be in an open field, so there is no way they will be able to sneak up on us."

"And," Sir Macarius added, "We will be staying within the walls of Castle Riraveth. Lord Dunmann may not be eager to help us, but he will have to defend his own home if Tenabris marches on it."

The conversation in the room paused, as if the men were waiting to see if Raiden or Rayla had any further questions. When neither spoke up, Lord Hightower continued with his explanation.

"Once you reach Riraveth, Carrow can use his title as my primary advisor to get an audience with Lord Dunmann and inform him of these intruders in his land. I will also send a messenger to Castle Rathús to inform the king."

As Lord Highower finished, Raiden and Rayla shared a look. Raiden wasn't exactly sure what he had been expecting. A strong force of action? Perhaps he had hoped that Lord Hightower would call a great army down and they would march out to destroy Kuvira's camp at once. This, however, was a much less exciting plan. In fact, it seemed to be more for the purpose of gathering intelligence than solving the problem.

The men were all watching Raiden and Rayla closely.

"I understand that you may not be interested in going–" Sir Macarius began.

"We will go," Rayla said, her voice somehow calm and collected compared to the rattled expression on her face.

Unable and unwilling to leave Rayla alone, Raiden nodded in agreement.

"So will I," Sapphire chipped in, speaking for the first time since they had begun the meeting. If Raiden was honest with himself, he had almost forgotten the young girl was there.

The men around the table shared a look.

"Ah," Lord Hightower began uncomfortably. "You are quite young–"

"All due respect, my lord," Rayla interrupted. "She goes where we go. We are in this together."

Raiden watched nervously as Lord Hightower considered the three of them. Finally, he sighed.

"Very well," he conceded. "But I feel it is necessary to make it known that I think that is a very, very bad idea."

Rayla nodded respectfully.

"Noted," she said plainly. Lord Hightower frowned, as did the other men, but no one argued any further.

"Macarius," Carrow finally said from the head of the table. "There's still one thing that bothers me."

The bowmaster motioned for Carrow to continue.

"What makes you so sure that Tenabris will even consider wagering with us? After all, he was raised by Kuvira, and as we know, Kuvira is not the most compassionate man alive. Likely, he will have taught his son that nothing is worth risking the main goal. Not even his own life. How can we wager so much on Tenabris's feelings for his father?"

Raiden raised his eyebrows. It was an excellent point, and one he hadn't thought of. Curiously, he turned to Sir Macarius. The bowmaster scrunched his face up in thought.

"That's the tricky part," he admitted. "Someone will need to manipulate Kuvira himself. They will have to trick him into talking about his relationship with his son without him realizing it. And that won't be easy. Kuvira is smart."

"Manipulate him? How so?" Luca asked.

"They're going to have to get Kuvira to talk about Tenabris and see if the man trusts him. If Kuvira shows any sign of doubting the boy's ability or drive, then we will simply have to keep him talking until we can confirm that he believes Tenabris may be willing to make a deal with us."

"And what if Kuvira doesn't cooperate?" Carrow suggested.

Nobody answered.

After a moment or two of awkward silence, Rayla spoke up.

"Well I for one like the idea of at least having a plan," she said. "Even if it is risky. Even if it has holes in it. I'm tired of sitting around, waiting for something else to happen."

"If Kuvira doesn't cooperate, we will just have to find another plan," Sir Luca said. "Until then, let's take things one step at a time."

"In the case that he *does* cooperate, we should allow ourselves plenty of time to prepare," Macarius said, moving on. "And to make arrangements where they are necessary."

Lord Hightower sighed heavily. "Well, we have a plan for now … " he said in a voice that hinted at closure.

"Aren't we forgetting something?"

All eyes turned to Raiden, except Macarius. The bowmaster only nodded.

"You are correct," he said.

"What exactly have we forgotten?" Luca asked.

Carrow, who had also caught Raiden's point, cleared his throat.

"Someone has to be appointed with the task of talking to Kuvira," the scholar clarified.

Again, nobody spoke. Raiden glanced nervously at his master, who sighed. He could see in Macarius's eyes that the man knew who should go, but he was reluctant to say it. Still, he lifted his eyes slowly to look at someone across the table.

"Rayla does have the best chance," the bowmaster admitted solemnly.

"Absolutely not," Luca cut in.

"She knows him better than anyone here," Macarius argued weakly. "Aside from Lord Hightower. But if Kuvira saw him, his guard would go up immediately. I'm sorry, but Rayla is the best option."

Across the table, Lord Hightower ran a hand over his face.

"Macarius is right," he admitted. "I hate to say it, but I believe Rayla must be the one to talk to my brother-in-law."

"Can she take someone with her?" Luca suggested.

"That would only alert Kuvira that something was out of the ordinary," Hightower pointed out.

"Won't he already be alerted by the fact that Rayla is visiting him?" Sapphire questioned.

"Perhaps," Lord Hightower admitted. "But he has an overwhelming desire to understand Rayla and her gift. More than likely, that curiosity will win out over any reasoning he would otherwise have. A chance to gather any extra information on Rayla would be too much to pass by."

Raiden turned to look at his friend. Her complexion had paled considerably as the rest of them had been speaking.

"I'll do it," she choked. Raiden desperately wanted to stop her, but he knew Macarius had been right. She was the only option.

"Although," the girl added, "I'd rather do it now. I don't want this to be hanging over my head."

Across the table, Lord Hightower nodded.

"Of course," he said gently. "I'll have someone take you to his cell right away."

chapter 7
Rayla

Nervously, Rayla followed the guard down the dark, damp stairwell. It smelled of musty dirt and sewage. The scent, mixed with the knot in her stomach, made Rayla feel sick.

The guard hadn't said a word to Rayla, but she didn't mind. She was too busy worrying about how she was going to get Kuvira to let his guard down without him realizing. How was she going to distract him? He was clever. Rayla was all too aware of that.

As they reached the bottom of the staircase, the ground leveled out. Their footsteps echoed on the stone floor. Water droplets could be heard from somewhere in the dungeon. A few torches held in place by brackets on the walls dimly lit the open room. Cells were easily visible on both sides of a long hallway. As they made their way along the hall, the damp stones caused Rayla to nearly slip. Her guide, Rayla noted, didn't even turn to check on her. She curled her lip in disgust and began to follow him again as her boots made a loud, squeaking noise with every step.

At the end of the passageway, another cell marked the end of the dungeon. This cell, Rayla noticed, was somewhat larger than the others. It had more sturdy-looking bars and several extra locks on the door. Appropriate, she thought, that they would put Kuvira in such a cell. Four guards stood by the door, two on either side. The rest of the cells were empty, and Rayla allowed herself to consider how crime-free her province truly was.

She stopped abruptly as her guide turned and jerked his head toward the guarded cell.

"He's in there," the man said, none too kindly.

"I couldn't tell," Rayla replied matter-of-factly. She allowed herself a small smirk as she saw the guard's eyebrows come together in annoyance.

Ignoring the man's deadly glares, she passed him to approach the cell door. The four guards stationed beside the cell said nothing. They didn't even move to question her, she noticed. It seemed odd, but she decided not to dwell on it too much. She had more important things at hand.

She peered closely through the cell bars. In the center of the dark cell, she could see the silhouette of a man sitting cross-legged. His shoulders were relaxed as if he was completely unconcerned that he was imprisoned. His face and most of his body were hidden in the shadows, so Rayla couldn't make out any of his features. He had the audacity to whistle a jaunty tune to himself. The sight of him annoyed Rayla to her core. A sudden wave of anger so intense it made Rayla see red washed over her. Not only anger, but also fear. Before her was the man who had beaten her raw, who had stolen so much more than her pride from her. Of course, he had been locked away the moment they had returned home from the woods. But he hadn't received any other punishment yet. And now, here he sat, receiving two, well-rounded meals a day with what could only be described as a smug look on his face.

Rayla swallowed her hatred with obvious difficulty.

"Kuvira."

Her voice was gruff and filled with emotion, shaking with the fear of being so near to him, but there wasn't much she could do about that.

The man stood, slowly making his way toward her. As his face came into view, she couldn't help but fall back a step. He was skinnier, and weak-looking. His skin had somehow gotten even more pale than it had been before. But his hair and beard, grown out as they were, remained a dark contrast to his complexion. And his eyes, Rayla noticed with a gulp, seemed to be full of both curiosity and a burning passion for something Rayla didn't understand, and quite frankly, didn't want to understand.

Still, despite her feelings, Rayla forced herself to move forward again, even as her legs wobbled. She would not be intimidated.

As Kuvira watched her approach, his hands twiddled at his sides. Once she reached the cell bars, she successfully managed to stare back at him in resolve.

Suddenly, a loud ringing sound echoed through the dungeon.

Kuvira had brought his hands up, grasping the bars so quickly that it had shaken the door of his cell.

Rayla flinched, scrambling back several paces. Behind her, she could hear all five guards drawing their swords. Despite the adrenaline that was now coursing through her veins, she kept her eyes on Kuvira, who rolled his own in exasperation.

"Oh relax," he said in his usual gravelly voice. The sound made Rayla shiver. "I'm not going to hurt her. How could I? With all this iron between us. Honestly, you guards are too on edge … "

Rayla noted the carelessness in Kuvira's voice. These guards, while they were not a part of Lord Hightower's personal circle, still held high authority. They also held sharp swords, and the power to use them if Kuvira gave them a reason. Still, the criminal before Rayla didn't seem to care one lick about their authority or their threats. It was just like Kuvira, Rayla thought, to be so arrogant.

Rayla took a deep breath, drawing herself up and crossing her arms over her chest. Her skin crawled with the closeness of Kuvira, but she forced herself to stare into his eyes with determination.

"Please leave us," she said in a soft voice, wishing she could make herself sound stronger. She turned, seeing the guards glancing uncertainly at each other.

"I'll be fine," she added, gesturing to her own sword at her hip.

"Our duties are to remain here," one of the guards grumbled. Clearly, they weren't as concerned for her wellbeing as much as they were about receiving orders from a woman.

Rayla flared her nostrils. "Perhaps I should speak with the person who gave you those orders."

Mumbling to one another, the five guards walked down the hallway and well out of earshot, although none of them actually ascended the stairs.

They can't hear us, Rayla reminded herself. *That's all that matters.*

She turned back to the cell to see Kuvira grinning coldly at her. Again, a wave of sickness ran through her. She took a deep breath and let it out with a huff, hoping to appear annoyed.

"Already pulling strings as Hightower's favorite little princess, are you?" Kuvira taunted. Rayla ignored him, blinking once before looking him up and down in disgust.

"I hope your food is at least soggy," she said. She didn't bother to hide the hatred in her voice or her expression. There was no point. Kuvira would know she was up to something if she acted innocent and forgiving. Besides, she wasn't sure she could pull that off anyway.

"Not at all," Kuvira replied with a smile. "I think they send it down before Cormac gets his own plate, because it's always steaming hot and delicious."

"A shame," she admitted, ignoring the disrespect that Kuvira had given toward Lord Hightower by using the man's first name. "I'll have to talk to someone about that."

"Oh, you've been promoted? See, I just knew that with that fancy sword you drag around everywhere, Cormac would eventually see your potential as kitchen overlord. Right where a woman belongs, if I do say so myself."

Rayla bit the inside of her lip, forcing herself not to react to the taunt.

"Well," Kuvira continued in a proud voice, "if you're truly in charge of my meals, then I have a few suggestions of what you could send me to eat. I'm particularly tired of the stew–"

"Oh believe me," Rayla cut in, hoping she sounded just as arrogant as Kuvira. "I've been learning a lot more than how to cook a meal. More to do with my … special talent."

On her way down the stairwell, she had been mulling over something that Lord Hightower had said about Kuvira's overwhelming curiosity, and how it always got the better of him. Now, she was counting on this.

Satisfaction filled her as she saw a split second of confusion in Kuvira's eyes. It was working. Kuvira was obviously taking the bait. The man leaned closer to the cell bars, his eyes narrow with open curiosity.

Despite her steel will, she felt her pulse quicken as Kuvira leaned closer. The sound of a whip slapping itself against bare skin echoed in her mind, and she flinched away from him. Rayla swallowed.

"But of course, you know all about that, don't you?" she said. She meant the question to sound teasing, but it came out stiff and awkward. Still, Kuvira huffed an amused breath, smirking.

"Refresh my memory," he retorted.

"You know," she said. "About my *gift*. About why you think I'm so important."

"A gift," he repeated, leaning forward even further so that his face was practically pressed against the bars. "Every gift is different, you know. What exactly *is* yours?"

Rayla's breath caught in her throat.

"It's my little secret," she said.

Kuvira sneered. "You could always choose to use whatever you've learned for a cause greater than yourself," Kuvira hissed.

"Lord Hightower told me that I am doing just fine with how I choose to use my gift," Rayla cut in.

Kuvira growled, and Rayla felt as if she couldn't breathe at the familiar, menacing sound. She stared at the bars, suddenly terrified that they would break and there would be nothing between her and Kuvira. She began to shake.

"Hightower doesn't know how to use the tools at his disposal," he said carefully. "He wastes what is given to him."

Rayla cocked her head to the side. She suddenly understood how to get Kuvira to talk about Tenabris, but she would have to be careful not to seize the opportunity too abruptly.

"And you think that you are so good at using the tools at your own disposal?" she pressed. "Really?"

Kuvira's eyebrows shot together in annoyance. "I'm an excellent delegator."

"I'm sorry," Rayla said, finally managing to stop her body from shaking in fear. "I just don't believe it."

"My forces are well organized–"

"And who is maintaining that order now that you are gone? Your 'star warrior?'" Rayla rolled her eyes at the nickname. "No, surely not him. He seemed too young and inexperienced when I last saw him."

When you had me tied to a post and whipped, she thought, but she pressed on.

"And considering how smart you are, I'm assuming you've probably been looking for one of your more seasoned men to take up your role in case you were ever …" she smirked. "Well, captured."

"Why are you down here, girl?" Kuvira spat. Clearly, he was getting angry with this little game.

"To make your life miserable," Rayla growled. "You've taken more than you should ever be allowed to take without penalty. If it were up to me, you'd already be dead. But, since your dreadful life is being spared, it's the least I can do to give you something to think about while you're behind those bars."

"As if I need something to think about, with all the lovely company I have," Kuvira muttered through clenched teeth. He gestured to the guards at the end of the room.

"I am curious though," Rayla asked, ignoring his comment. "*Was* Tenabris your plan for a replacement? Do you really believe that your precious 'star' is ready to lead all of your troops? You're gone now, so there are one of two things happening as we speak. Either your forces are fighting each other to see who gains control in your place, or your little protégé has stepped up prematurely, obviously before you had planned, and assumed power. In which case, it's only natural to wonder if he is ready. Or if he is even the right man for the job."

"He is," Kuvira responded quickly. Too quickly, she noticed. Not only that, but the stone cold man had let slip a show of emotion. It was almost imperceptible, but Rayla had managed to catch sight of it, only because she had been looking for it. A gleam in his eyes as he had spoken. It resembled pride, but it was something more. Something deeper.

Responsibility.

He actually *cared* for Tenabris. The realization shocked Rayla, but she didn't let it stop her from reaching her goal.

"Is he?" she asked innocently.

"I think I would know who to trust with my troops, *girl*," he spat the last word as an insult.

"Oh I'm sure you do," she said sarcastically.

Kuvira raised his chin.

Rayla snorted. "I suppose you think you know everything?"

Kuvira frowned. "I'm not so ignorant to think that I know everything. But I am no fool."

"Well here's a question. What if your warrior fails? What happens to your precious army then?"

"Then I suppose the commander of my troops would take over!" Kuvira growled. "Either way, Maith *will* fall! Cormac will get what he deserves, and you will be at my command!"

He was pressed up against the bars as closely as he could get now, his face centimeters from Rayla's. She flinched again. The smell of his breath and his clothes made her tremble. She closed her eyes, and an image flashed before her. An image of Kuvira leaning over her, forcing her to meet his eyes with a rough hand under her chin. The same smell of Kuvira, only in her mind, it was mixed with the scent of her own blood.

The guards at the end of the room had moved to run to Rayla's aid. She could hear their armor and swords clinking together.

She wanted nothing more than to be whisked away from Kuvira, taken to Luca or Raiden or anyone that could protect her. But she wasn't finished yet.

She held up a hand behind her and the noise stopped.

She stared at the man before her. Sweat was beaded on his forehead. His face was twisted in an attempt to control his rage. Rayla smiled.

To Kuvira, it had been a simple question, meant to taunt him and annoy him. But in answering so quickly, and with such an answer, he had confirmed Rayla's suspicions.

Clearly, he had thought about this before, and considered the commander of his troops as Tenabris's backup. Which meant that Kuvira had considered the fact that Tenabris might need a backup. That he could very well fail. And, Rayla supposed, if he was ill prepared to be a leader, he would be desperate to regain the approval of his father again.

She'd done it.

"It's impolite to yell in the presence of a lady," Rayla said, attempting to ease her way out of the conversation. She watched in satisfaction, a small smile on her lips, as Kuvira struggled to regain his composure.

Kuvira sneered. "Shouldn't you be returning to the kitchens soon?"

"Oh yes, of course," she said, turning to leave. As an afterthought, she turned once more and smirked.

"Enjoy your cold stew this evening, Kuvira."

And with that, she walked back down the dark hall, not bothering to wait on her guide as she ascended the stairs. She kept her shoulders back and her head high as she reached the throne room.

Raiden was waiting for her at the top of the stairs, having promised to stay until she returned from the dungeon.

"How did it go?" He immediately asked. "Are you okay?"

Rayla ignored him, making her way to the castle yard. Raiden followed quickly. Once outside, the fear of being in Kuvira's presence for so long finally caught up to her. Trembling, she braced one hand on the cool stone of the castle wall and doubled over, retching.

chapter 8
Rayla

It had only taken Luca two days to find Rayla a spot among the Maith guards.

No week off for her to adjust. No time to take in the fact that a major chapter of her life had just come to a close.

She remembered the feeling of excitement that had gone through her body when Lord Hightower had offered her the position again at her ceremony. She had known it was coming, of course. The lord had already offered to give her a place among his ranks a few months ago, in the woods. Still, she hadn't fully believed her luck until Hightower had announced that she was an official guard.

She had simply bowed in respect and gratitude, unable to speak. Now, she wished she had replied strongly or bravely, or at least mustered the voice to thank him properly. But she couldn't change the past. At least, she thought, Lord Hightower had been amused by her response. She assumed that was why he had laughed so hard at her pale expression, just before Raiden and Sir Macarius had joined them.

Now, Rayla stood at the top of Maith's southeastern wall. It was a relatively easy spot to guard. She could see miles in front of her, beyond the vast field that covered the horizon. Slightly to the east and out of the corner of her eye, she could see just a sliver of the edge of the woods. Less than a year ago, the sight would have warmed her heart. Now, it turned her insides to stone.

Their journey in the spring had taken a much deeper toll on Rayla's mind than she had ever thought it could. After years of living and surviving alone, Rayla was sure that she had become calloused to anything else that life could throw her way. But when Kuvira had captured her, when he had tied her to a post and whipped and beaten her, she had experienced more fear than ever before in her life.

Worst of all, seeing Finn's dead body and knowing that she couldn't heal him had sent her backsliding more than she cared to admit. For a few short months, she had allowed herself to open up. Not just to Raiden, but also to Finn, and Sapphire, and Luca, and Carrow.

But when Finn had died, when she had felt that gaping hole in her heart, she had felt more pressure than ever before to close herself back up. She had fought with her desire to hide her pain and fear and her desire to be comforted by her new friends. The ones that were left.

Rayla sighed, shaking her head to clear the depressing thoughts. She forced herself to return her thoughts to her new position as a Maith guard.

In addition to the relatively boring view, Rayla's job was little more than uneventful. She was charged to stand in her spot, scanning the area until another guard was sent to relieve her for the day. That was all she had been told when she had arrived around sunrise that morning. There were no instructions for what she should do in case of an attack. Nothing about how she should respond to an emergency. Simply, "Stand here and keep watch."

Part of Rayla was still completely overjoyed. She had been dreaming of this day since Sir Luca had given her the familiar blue-gray sword that was still at her side now. Becoming a guard of one of the most renowned provinces in the kingdom was an extremely high honor. Although more and more students graduated from the battle school each year, and this resulted in a surplus of Maith guards, the respect for their position didn't decrease. Despite their abundance, each student had put years of hard work into his, or her, training, and that included Rayla.

Still, despite the honor and the feeling of great accomplishment, Rayla felt at a loss. This, she thought, was not how she had imagined her position to be. She had imagined herself fighting battles, righting wrongs, defending the weak, and saving the day. Instead, she was stationed on a wall, with nothing to do but stare at the distance. It was boring. It was somewhat demeaning. At times in the day, Rayla even thought it was a joke. All in all, it was simply disappointing to Rayla. She had trained for years ... for *this*?

Rayla glanced to her left. Several meters away, another guard was posted. He was staring out toward the woods. Below him, Rayla knew, was the outhouse.

At least I didn't get that spot, she thought to herself.

It occurred to Rayla that she had overlooked a major point in her new position. She was the only female Maith guard.

As far as she was concerned, Lord Hightower had been extremely open to the idea of treating Rayla the same as any other male guard. She was offered the same pay, given the same duties, and welcomed into the position by the same ceremonial process.

Of course, Lord Hightower did offer Rayla a more comfortable living condition. Most of the Maith guards, once given the position, were also given two living choices. They could live at home with their families or, if they had no family or little money, they could live in the barracks at Maith Castle.

However, since Rayla was the only female, Lord Hightower refused to give her such a horrible fate as living in the Maith barracks with numerous men. Instead, he offered Rayla the option of remaining at her current home, which Luca had so graciously purchased for her years ago. Rayla had gladly accepted the offer, and secretly vowed to repay Luca for his investment once she had earned enough silver coins from serving as a guard.

Rayla glanced to her left again. The other guard hadn't moved, and Rayla thought he might be asleep despite his standing position.

It was clear from the way the Maith guards acted that nobody expected anything to happen anytime soon. Most of the guards, she had noticed, also gave her a wide berth. They were none too eager to make any kind of contact with her, almost undoubtedly because she was a woman and they didn't approve of her position as a guard. Despite how upsetting it was to be dismissed for her gender, she was slightly relieved at the lack of interaction. She didn't want to be pressured into joining them in their leisure activities.

The Maith guards, for all their honor and dignity, were known to spend their free time in brothels and taverns getting drunk. Rayla was in no way interested in such things. However, she worried about what the future would hold for her if she never formed any connections with the guards. Would it make for a boring and lonely life? Being alone was all fine and well with her for now, but what if she eventually grew to resent that space between her and the other guards. Not to mention the fact that she couldn't help but feel that she wasn't just being left alone, but possibly ignored or avoided.

Rayla sighed, rolling her head around to loosen the muscles in her neck. Nearby, one of the other guards coughed.

It was a quiet day. The field before her was slowly draining in color as autumn rolled by. Only patches of green were left in both the grass and the trees of the forest. Rayla blinked, forcing her eyes to focus. She was learning that it was easy to lose focus when she stared at one spot all day. She was even starting to see things. She could imagine an entire force of hooded men marching out of the forest.

She wanted so badly to tell the other guards to snap out of their lazy moods. They *had* to understand why being a guard was so important, especially at a time like this.

Still, she knew that she couldn't say a word. Lord Hightower had been very specific about not letting on about the danger of Kuvira. So far their involvement with him was a secret, and Lord Hightower wanted it kept that way.

So much of their plan was so weak. Rayla felt her own mind was stretched as thin as their plan, as if one tiny pebble tossed onto a tripwire could ruin the whole thing. One wrong move, and they would lose their only chance to gain the upper hand. And Rayla would lose her only chance at revenge.

To Rayla's right, there was a glimpse of movement. One of the guards had inched his way closer to her. Carefully, she watched out of the corner of her eye. The guard slowly continued to make his way closer and closer. Finally, he stopped with only a few meters in between them, but said nothing.

Rayla waited. For several minutes, she stood still, listening for any sound the guard might make. When he continued to remain silent, Rayla's curiosity got the best of her. She sighed and turned to look at the man head on.

"What exactly is it that you're trying to do?" she asked in an exasperated tone.

To her surprise, the man seemed embarrassed. His cheeks flushed and he refused to meet her eyes. Her breath caught as she noticed that he was rather young, probably only a few years older than she was.

Mentally chastising herself for being so rude, she took a deep breath and relaxed her face, creating a more inviting look. The man seemed to notice.

He was tall, she realized, and well-toned. Slowly, he turned to face her, finally meeting her eyes. *Brown*, she noted. Brown eyes to compliment his short, sandy hair and facial stubble. If Rayla felt like being honest, he was rather attractive.

"I … just wanted to say," he began uneasily, stopping to clear his throat, "that I heard about what happened in the woods a few months ago."

Rayla's heart plummeted. She hadn't been expecting that.

"I figure most of it is an exaggeration?" he asked confidently. Rayla couldn't speak around the knot in her throat, so she shrugged.

"I do know that at least one thing is real, though," he said softly. "Finn died in those woods."

This time, Rayla audibly choked. Tears sprang to her eyes instantly. Nobody had actually spoken to her about Finn since the battle, and she hadn't spoken about him to anybody. She hadn't wanted to. She wasn't sure if she was ready to. And now she *knew* she wasn't ready.

Terrified of her own emotions, she dropped her eyes to the stone floor of the wall beneath her.

"When … When I first got placed as a guard a few years ago," the man continued, his voice thick with emotion, "I was completely lost. Everyone was so rude, and they made me feel stupid because I was so young. But Finn … Finn helped. He was the only encouraging person I ever met. He … he taught me how to place my things near my bed, so that I could reach them quickly when I woke up. He told me who to avoid while on duty. He even told me a few secrets on how to sneak a couple extra meals in on a particularly long day."

Rayla felt herself craving to hear more. More about what Finn was like as a fellow guard. More about his legacy as a good person. And yet, her breath seemed to be taking more and more energy to control.

It didn't matter how much she *wanted* to hear. She couldn't take much more without breaking down.

"I don't know how you knew Finn," the man said in a concluding tone. "But all the talk about what you did for him, the ceremony you held for him in the woods, it got around pretty quickly. It was more of a romanticized story around the barracks, but to me . . . well, I think Finn would have absolutely loved it."

The man fell silent. Rayla swallowed hard. She refused to look up, but she spoke nonetheless, her voice raspy and uneven.

"Did . . . " she choked out slowly. "Did he have any family?"

Her eyes remained on the ground as she waited for a reply.

"No," the man finally said. "It was just him. He did have a wife, but she died a few years back. Right before I joined the guard, actually. Fever got her, I think."

Rayla took a deep, shaky breath.

"He was a good man," the guard mused. "He didn't deserve all the dirt he got in life. None of it. Life's unfair like that. But I just wanted you to know that I think he would have appreciated what you did."

With that, Rayla heard the sound of receding footsteps as the man returned to his post along the wall.

The tips of her shoes, she noticed, were wet with her tears. Her body was shaking from silent sobs. Eventually, after several minutes of deep breathing and wringing her hands together, she turned back to her own post.

Her mind whirled in a million different directions. Until now, it had never occured to Rayla that Finn might have had an impact on more than just her own life.

What would it have been like, she wondered, if Finn hadn't died? If he was here now, giving her advice like he did for this man? What would it have been like to see Finn in action, not only as a guard, but as a human being? To see him cheerfully combat every sarcastic comment with a smile and a nod.

She couldn't help but imagine how much more joy she might have felt at her ceremony with Finn by her side. She wondered if Finn would have gone with her to the dungeon as her escort as she talked to Kuvira.

Rayla closed her eyes momentarily, picturing the guard's face. She recalled the warm smile that he welcomed her with every morning as he had knocked on her door to escort her and Raiden to their daily lessons with Carrow. She remembered the pride on his face when she had told him of her first successful lesson when she had finally mastered her healing gift.

Pain washed over her as she opened her eyes, facing the reality that she would never experience those things again.

Heartbroken, Rayla lifted her head to look back out across the field. Only this time, the ground before her seemed blurred from tears.

chapter 9
Raiden

Raiden sniffled, shrinking farther into the chair that sat just inside his and Sir Macarius's cabin. The autumn weather, it seemed, was starting to affect his health.

If he closed his eyes, he could picture the vivid image of the Tacktan Sea. Raiden had never seen it himself, but Macarius had, and he had described it to Raiden many times before.

The sea served as the southern border of Rathús and lay far to the south of Maith Province. It gave Seol, the coastal province, an easy port to ship goods and materials out to other kingdoms. It was a beautiful sea at certain points in the year. In the summer, especially, the water was a bright blue from a distance, but up close one could see through the clear liquid to the bottom of shallow water.

As for now, however, Raiden could only think of the cold air that the body of water was sending north, to his home. It made him shiver despite his being indoors. The action felt odd. Shivering was something he hadn't done often in the warmer province of Maith.

Aside from the cold air, Raiden loved this time of year. The leaves in the woods to the east were changing colors. Even the trees that ventured into Maith's walls and surrounded his cabin home had turned yellow and red. Some had browned and fallen from their branches. They made a satisfying crunch when he walked across them.

In spite of the fact that the vivid colors of plants and the variety of active animals decreased at this time, Raiden found beauty in autumn. It gave him a sense of completion. As if every plant and animal had run its course for the year and was ready to rest. He could relate to that. Not that he felt like he had lived his life to the fullest yet, but he could relate to feeling the need to rest after a particularly hard time in life.

The more Raiden's mind roamed, the more he began to think that maybe the colder weather wasn't so bad. It was better than the muggy, sweaty heat of summer. The cold air might give him chillbumps, but it was also refreshing.

Not that Raiden was enjoying such fresh air at the moment. He had been pinned up in the cabin with Sir Macarius for the past two days. Usually, the small two bedroom cabin felt cozy to Raiden. He loved the warm sitting room with its small fireplace. Their old cabin didn't have a fireplace. It did seem rather ironic that the first home was burned to the ground. Still, the crackling wood relaxed Raiden, even if he did catch himself continuously glancing over to make sure the fire remained in its place.

The bedrooms that faced each other near the back of the cabin were just as cozy. The beds were slightly softer than the straw mattresses his parents could afford back home. Their thicker winter blankets had only just been brought out from their trunks that sat at the foot of their beds. In all, the small room that Raiden had occupied for the last few months already felt special. It was his own. He couldn't help but feel a small twinge of sadness at the idea of having to leave the cabin when he chose an assignment.

But even more pressing than choosing an assignment was the upcoming mission involving Kuvira. He and Macarius had been preparing for their journey.

They had two saddle packs lying on the floor, a few meters to the right of the door and propped up against the sofa. Each was filled with dried fruit preserves and jerky. Two canteens of water were also stored inside, as well as an extra bowstring in each. Their bedrolls were also propped up near the door. They would be gone for at least two weeks. Sir Macarius had gone over the plan, looking for any holes or mistakes. He'd done this about five times already.

The previous morning, Sir Macarius and Raiden had taken a trip to the castle stables to see some of the horses that had not been deemed battle horses. These were smaller and less muscled mounts. Macarius had explained to Raiden that he wanted to take as many regular horses as he could. Lord Hightower had already given his scholar and twenty of his guards, not counting Rayla and Sir Luca. The bowmaster didn't want to put the lord out of force any more than he already had. Also, Carrow had suggested that the less bulk that was in their group, the less likely they would be to draw unwanted attention to themselves. And battle horses were considerably bulky. "In a province as crime stricken as Riraveth," Macarius had explained, "the wrong kind of attention could be disastrous for our mission."

Raiden thought the attempt was futile. After all, twenty-six armed escorts guarding a prisoner would be easily noticed, with or without battle horses. Still, it was Sir Macarius's journey, and he seemed to agree with Carrow.

On this particular day, the bowmaster had been mumbling to himself for hours on end, stooped over in a chair as he studied the notes strewn across the kitchen table. The parchments were filled with Macarius's own writing. He had jotted down any and every detail of their mission, carefully lining out the specific conversation they would have with Tenabris, if the man showed himself. But there was one particularly large parchment that Macarius kept coming back to. Each time, he would shake his head. As Raiden watched him from the sitting room, he couldn't decipher what was on the parchment, and he wasn't too keen to ask.

For the vast majority of the day, Raiden had been lounging on the chair. Each time he had asked Macarius if he could slip away to practice his shooting, the bowmaster would shake his head and mutter a chore for Raiden to do. So far, Raiden had polished and organized their trunks and packed away anything that could be taken with them. He had used the straw broom to sweep out the cabin.

The last chore had been the worst. Macarius, obviously tired of Raiden's constant interruptions, had sent the boy on a task that took nearly three hours. He had asked Raiden to clean out the shelves in the kitchen, where the spices, bowls, utensils, and pots were kept. The job seemed simple to Raiden, at first. He quickly learned that Sir Macarius's definition of putting the dishes away was simply throwing everything into the shelf that was the most empty at the time. As soon as Raiden had removed one pot, an avalanche of other items came tumbling down on top of him.

After that, Raiden learned to simply stop asking Sir Macarius any questions at all. Now, however, he was tired of feeling useless.

He sat up in the chair, clearing his throat to get Macarius's attention. The man didn't notice. Awkwardly, Raiden shifted in the chair and cleared his throat louder. The action sent him into a fit of coughs, taking him by surprise. When he finally managed to stop coughing, he looked up to see Macarius watching him in concern.

"Are you getting sick?"

Raiden thought of the unusual shivers he had felt all day. It was the cold air, he reasoned.

"No."

Macarius narrowed his eyes. "Come here."

Raiden sighed, standing. He made his way to the kitchen, hoping to steal a glance at the large parchment that had taken so much of Macarius's time. He didn't get the chance. Macarius stood, blocking his view. As Raiden came to a stop in front of the man, Macarius raised a hand to Raiden's forehead.

"Hmm," the bowmaster said thoughtfully. "I think you might have a fever."

Raiden ignored his concern. "Have your notes changed at all since the last time you stared at them?"

"Your cheeks are flushed."

"What's on the larger parchment?"

Raiden waited patiently as Macarius sized him up, eventually accepting that the boy wasn't going to admit that he was sick. Finally, the older man turned to sit back in his chair.

"It's a map," he said shortly, leaning over to stare at the paper again.

"Why is it so interesting? You know Rathús like the back of your hand."

It was true. Not only that, but Macarius had demanded that Raiden also memorize the layout of the kingdom. Now, Raiden could confidently trace the borders of the five provinces in the dirt with his eyes closed. Rathús Province was in the middle, surrounded by the other four: Maith to the north, Riraveth to the west, Seol to the south, and Tiri to the east. He could even name the details of each province. Maith had the forest on the eastern side of its castle walls. Riraveth had a series of hills to the southwest, and a bordering kingdom called Saodda just beyond the hills. The Tacktan sea bordered the southern edge of Seol, and to the east of Tiri was the Marfoch desert.

This map, now that Raiden could get a full view of it, showed just that. Nothing seemed to be different.

He leaned forward, frowning.

"It's not the map that has me confused," Macarius said, pulling Raiden from his thoughts. "It's something else."

"Okay," Raiden said, leaning forward even further. Unfortunately, the action sent a wave of dizziness through him. He swayed, grabbing the table for support.

"Raiden," Macarius demanded, grabbing the boy's biceps to steady him. "What is going on with you?"

"Nothing," Raiden lied, blinking several times to keep the room from spinning. After a few seconds, the dizziness passed.

"You cannot go on this journey–"

"Yes I can."

"If you are unwell," Macarius finished, pushing Raiden down into a chair.

Raiden sighed, letting his head fall back.

"I'm not sick," he began slowly. "I'm just exhausted."

"You haven't been sleeping well?" Macarius asked, pulling up a chair to sit down across from Raiden. The boy jerked his head up to stare at his master in disbelief.

"No, I haven't been sleeping well!" he exclaimed. "How on earth could I be sleeping at all? Rayla might discover where she is from, which could either drag her away to some new place or bring her even more pain than she's already been through. Sapphire just *has* to come along on every life-threatening journey we take, which is already two more than it should be at our ages, by the way."

"I know that," Macarius added gently, but Raiden wasn't finished.

"And this plan has a better chance of failing than it does of succeeding. It isn't even really a plan at all. We have to travel around with Kuvira outside of his cell, and his being behind bars was one of the only things helping me sleep at all."

At this, Macarius frowned. "You should have asked me about the plan if you were–"

"I have to watch as Rayla and Sapphire go through the pain of missing Finn each day, and I can't help because I feel just as much pain," Raiden continued, not hearing Sir Macarius at all now. "And now, instead of killing Kuvira like we should have that day in the woods after the battle, instead of ending this as soon as possible, we are going to march up to the doorstep of his army with twenty-something people and politely request that Tenabris give up the fight, which is basically asking for him to kill us where we stand! So no, sir, I am definitely not sleeping well."

By the time he had finished, he was sitting straight up, sweat pouring down his face, and his breaths were coming in gasps. Macarius had leaned back to watch in contemptment.

Raiden, suddenly aware of the fact that he had yelled at his former master, squirmed uncomfortably.

"I'm sorry, sir," he said between breaths. "I didn't mean to–"

"It's alright, Raiden," Macarius replied evenly. To Raiden's surprise, the bowmaster seemed to mean the words.

"It is?" Raiden asked quietly.

"Yes," Macarius assured. "I know all of these things have been keeping you up at night. Better yet, I know you have been hiding them from everyone you come into contact with. You are trying to make things easier on your friend and your sister by withholding your own pain."

Tears began to rise behind Raiden's eyes. He blinked them away in annoyance.

"I–" he said through emotion. "I don't want them to have to deal with my pain. My problems. They have their own, and it's already too much for them. If I show them that I'm hurting too, it will only add to their problems."

Macarius leaned forward, patting Raiden's knee softly.

"I know you think that," the man said gently. "But you are wrong. What you are doing is running from your pain because you are afraid of it. You're afraid to show it. And in the end, you have made it worse by shoving it deep down inside of you. It has built up, and now it has exploded."

Raiden took a deep breath, knowing that his master was right but hating the fact nonetheless.

"You've allowed yourself to grieve alone, when you are supposed to be sleeping. It's unhealthy. It's dangerous. And it's starting to take a physical toll on your body."

"What do I do?" Raiden asked, desperation clear in his voice. He looked up to see Macarius looking back at him with deep sympathy in his eyes.

"My boy," he said, "You need to grieve with your friends. With those who are feeling just as lost and hurt as you are. It will comfort you *and them* to know that you're not alone. It won't make the pain go away, but it will make it bearable."

Raiden squeezed his eyes shut, allowing a few tears to fall down his face. When he opened his eyes again, his breathing had finally calmed down some, though he still felt light-headed.

"Okay," he said. "So we march up to Tenabris's doorsteps. Then what?"

Macarius leaned back again, a small smile on his lips.

"Not exactly," he corrected. "See, Carrow and Lord Hightower want to trust the fact that Tenabris will love his father enough to give up the fight to spare Kuvira's life. They want to believe that he will show us his hands, tell us what forces he has left, what plans his father left him."

"But you don't think that?" Raiden asked.

Macarius shook his head. "I think that, though he doesn't mean to, Lord Hightower is allowing his vision to be clouded. Tenabris is his nephew, after all. I think Lord Hightower wants to believe that there is still some good in the boy. That Kuvira didn't completely corrupt him."

"But this is no time for guesses," Raiden concluded.

"No," Macarius agreed. "It's not."

"So what's the plan?"

"Well, I agree that Kuvira will have to come with us, like it or not. But I intend to keep his identity a secret. We should only need to use him as a defense mechanism. *If* Tenabris comes after us."

"I thought we were going to Riraveth to find him?"

Macarius considered the question, making a face.

"The main purpose of us going on this journey is to meet with my informant again."

Raiden frowned. "But why can't you do that on your own?"

"Because this time, when my informant tells me exactly where Kuvira's forces are hiding, we will be prepared to rally the first of many forces to combat the enemy. And because he believes they might be hiding in Riraveth, the first line of defense will be Riraveth's men."

"And since Lord Dunnman is so difficult—"

"We need Carrow, and possibly Kuvira, to prove that this is a serious matter. Only then will we stand a chance of Lord Dunnman listening to us."

Raiden considered his former master's words.

"And … " Raiden thought aloud. "The plan of luring Tenabris out comes in … where?"

Macarius grimaced.

"I'm in a slight disagreement with the others on that subject," he admitted. "At first, I thought luring the boy out was a good idea. But now I'm wondering if it might be better for us to rally the provinces and simply attack Tenabris's forces. I don't believe we should lure Tenabris out, but we can certainly use Kuvira if Tenabris and his troops find us."

"That sounds a little better," Raiden said, feeling as if he could breathe easier now. "Won't you have to get the others to agree to that?"

"Already done," Macarius said. His face told Raiden that the conversation had not been a pleasant one, but Raiden was glad that Macarius's plan had won out. It made more sense to Raiden.

"But there's still something I don't get," Raiden said hesitantly.

"What's that?"

"You've been studying these notes all day," he explained. "But you said you weren't bothered by the map you've been looking at. If it isn't the map, then what is bothering you?"

Macarius sighed, running a hand through his hair.

"This man that I met," he began slowly. "He had too much information to not be part of Kuvira's circle." He paused. "And he had proof of his identity – of being the commander of Kuvira's troops. He had to. Otherwise, I would have dismissed him as a lunatic. He showed me his cloak. The hooded ones that Kuvira's men wear. He told me that only those who are in Kuvira's inner circle have silver fabric that lines their cloaks. His cloak had this mark. Of course, at first I thought that he could be lying, but the cloak resembled the one that Kuvira wore, that you described, too much. There is no way the man could have had a piece of clothing made specially to mirror Kuvira's cloak that well. The cloak only proves his previous position in Kuvira's army."

"That all sounds like it only confirms what your informant told you. Which is *good* news," Raiden pointed out. Macarius, however, shook his head.

"What I don't understand is why he wanted to wait to give me some of the information, like where exactly Tenabris is hiding, and what he knows about Rayla. It makes no sense for him to request a second meeting. The logical thing to do in his position was to give me all the information and get out before Tenabris could find him."

"I thought you said he wanted to go gather some of that information before he gave it to you," Raiden commented. "Wouldn't that explain why he wanted you to meet him again?"

Macarius nodded. "He did, and it would. Only … "

Raiden looked up at his master as dread pooled in his stomach.

"Only you're not confident that he won't double-cross us?" he asked.

Macarius looked up, and the expression in his eyes made Raiden shiver again.

"Not completely, no."

Raiden chewed his lip.

"And what do we do if he does?"

Macarius leaned back in his chair.

"I have an idea," he admitted, "but it is not a full plan. Not yet."

Raiden let the words sink in. Now, he thought, not only were they headed on an already questionable journey with a stretched-thin plan, but they were also headed to possible confrontation. This man could quite possibly return to Kuvira's forces and lead the troops to attack Raiden and his friends. And despite how excessive their small group had seemed earlier in the week, it would be nothing compared to Kuvira's army.

"Sounds fun," Raiden said grimly. "When do we leave?"

Macarius quickly stacked his notes and moved to pack them away in his saddle pack.

"If all goes well," he said, "we should be ready to leave by the end of the week."

chapter 10
Rayla

Exhausted, Rayla climbed down the set of stairs that led away from her post at the top of Maith's wall. For the past ten hours, she had been standing in the same spot, staring at the field as the chilly autumn air had blown around her. Now, her feet and back were aching. It was strange, she thought, how tiring it was to do nothing.

Not just physically, but mentally too. Her mind was stretched from the boring work of looking at an empty field for hours on end. She wanted nothing more than to go home and lie in bed. To sprawl out on her mattress, stuff her face into her soft pillow, and sleep. But she couldn't have that pleasure. Not quite yet.

The previous day, Raiden had startled her half to death on her way home. She had just finished a particularly rough post, where she had accidentally bumped into an older guard on her way up the stairs. Unfortunately, she ended up positioned directly beside that same guard, and the man seemed to be an expert at holding a grudge. He had used his seniority to demand she switch him positions so she was standing in the cold wind, no longer protected by the small structure that covered the entrance to the stairs. The wind had been eerie, and she couldn't help but envision Tenabris sneaking out from the treeline and shooting her down with his bow.

As she had been walking along the dirt path on her way back to her house that night, Raiden had come running up behind her. She had been too preoccupied with her thoughts to hear him, but as he had laid a hand on her shoulder, she had effectively jumped a foot into the air and let loose a string of choice words.

As it turned out, the boy had only wanted to ask her if she would meet him and Sapphire in the local tavern the following night, after her guard duty.

She had agreed immediately, not thinking of how exhausted she would be after keeping watch all day. It had been four days since they had met at the castle to make the plans for their upcoming journey. Despite how tired she was, Rayla couldn't help but feel excited to see her two favorite people again.

There were very few people out at this time of night. The sun had already sunk below the horizon. Only a faint red glow was left in the sky as proof that the day had ever existed. In just a few short minutes, Rayla found herself at the door of the tavern. Grunting slightly at the energy required, she pushed through and into the building.

She blinked as her eyes adjusted to the bright light coming from several lanterns that were hanging from the ceiling. Rayla squinted and glanced around. In the center of the room was a small circular table with four chairs around it. Two of those chairs were occupied.

A smile played on Rayla's lips. She quickly found a seat on the other side of Sapphire. Raiden, who was directly across the table, smiled in greeting.

Before the two siblings could start much of a conversation, Rayla waved to a nearby waitress.

"A stew and a glass of water, please," Rayla said. The waitress nodded before leaving with the order. Rayla sighed, turning back to her friends.

"Well you certainly wasted no time," Raiden mused, his eyebrows slightly raised. Rayla wrinkled her nose in mock annoyance.

"You try standing on a wall all day," she replied. "You'd be famished, too."

"How was it?" Raiden asked after laughing at her retort.

Rayla paused, suddenly realizing the nasally tone of Raiden's voice. She squinted at him.

"Are you getting sick?" She asked him. Raiden sniffled.

"No," he lied. Rayla raised an eyebrow.

"Right." She dragged the word out to show just how unconvinced she was. Raiden shifted uncomfortably in his chair.

"It's just the weather," he assured her. "And you didn't answer my question. How was the wall?"

Rayla considered the question. She knew that Raiden was still strongly considering Lord Hightower's offer of a position among Maith's ranks, and selfishly, she hoped he would accept.

Still, in the four days since Raiden's completion of his training had been made official, no changes had been made in his status, and Rayla knew that everyone was pressuring Raiden to consider his options fully.

Of course, he had been given a parchment with Macarius and Lord Hightower's signatures on it, signifying his completion of training. But he had remained in the cabin with Sir Macarius. Both Macarius and Lord Hightower had continuously asked the boy to take his time in making the decision. Rayla knew all of this. She could remember Luca's face when she had made her own decision so quickly. He hadn't even tried to hide his disappointment.

But Rayla couldn't help but hope that her friend would ultimately decide to stay in Maith. After all that they had been through in the last few months she couldn't imagine her friend leaving the province.

"Rayla?" Raiden pressed, pulling the girl from her thoughts. She shook her head to focus.

"Oh, sorry," she replied quickly. "It was, uh … amazing."

It was a straight out lie, and Rayla was hoping against all odds that Raiden wouldn't notice. But she was afraid that if she told Raiden the truth, he would rethink the idea of becoming a Maith warrior and leave the province after all. If she could make the position sound exciting …

"That's great," he replied, evidently clueless to Rayla's lie.

Rayla felt her cheeks flush slightly. The fact that she had just lied to her friend didn't settle well with her.

"Your stew, miss," a nearby voice said, saving Rayla from her guilt.

"Oh, yes, thank you," Rayla replied, moving to allow the waitress to set the bowl down.

After a few bites, it occurred to Rayla that she was the only one who had ordered anything.

"Did I miss the meeting where we all decided to skip dinner," she said between bites, "or are you both just that amused by watching me eat?"

Sapphire laughed.

"No," she replied smoothly. "We ate with Master and Mistress Browne."

"Oh," Rayla nodded.

She didn't mind being the only one eating. She was too hungry to care.

"Rayla, guess what? My lessons are going great!" Sapphire announced, suddenly full of excited energy. "I've improved my knife skills *so* much in the last few days, and my sword strokes are getting stronger."

"That's great, Saph!" Rayla replied, allowing a rare grin to spread across her face.

The action felt foreign. Rayla didn't smile often, and hardly at all since Finn had died. But she wanted Sapphire to know that she was proud of her.

"Not only that," Sapphire continued eagerly, "But Sir Luca says I may even have a head start on the next lesson if I work with him in our free time while we are on the mission. Plus, I've been practicing every afternoon at home until sundown."

Across the table, Raiden chuckled.

"She's going to beat you out of your title as best female warrior before she breaks thirteen," the boy laughed.

Rayla smirked. "At least I can still swing my sword without tripping over my own feet."

Raiden's smile faded. Rayla fought a laugh.

After Rayla had finished her meal, she leaned back in her chair to stretch.

"So what is it that we need to discuss so urgently?" she asked.

Raiden frowned. "I didn't say it was urgent."

"No?" Rayla said in a tone of mock confusion. "Well I guess I just assumed it must be, seeing as how you scared the–"

"Rayla!"

"–out of me and I couldn't go home and rest first."

Sapphire suppressed a laugh. Rayla felt her own lip curl slightly at the expression on Raiden's face. He seemed completely baffled.

"I didn't mean to make you to go out of your way, I just thought–"

"Oh for goodness sake, Raiden, she's messing with you," Sapphire said, rolling her eyes to the ceiling dramatically.

Raiden blinked. He turned his gaze to Rayla, seeming to ask a silent question. *Are you?* Rayla winked.

"Okay," Raiden continued awkwardly, clearly embarrassed. "Sir Macarius seems to think that everything is in order for our mission. We are set to leave two days from now, bright and early."

Rayla groaned. "Bright and early" was not her favorite time of day. Raiden ignored her and continued.

"Lord Hightower has already been informed, as have the twenty men that he will be sending with us. And Carrow and Luca, of course. The horses have been set aside and–"

Rayla drew a breath, but Raiden answered her question before she could ask it.

"Yes, you can take Dóchas," he said. "We are going to need a few battle horses. But Carrow and Sir Macarius wanted to lessen the bulk of the group, so we've arranged to borrow as many of the castle's other horses as can be spare."

Relief flushed through Rayla. She had spent as much time as she could with Dóchas, but it still wasn't enough. She longed to take a journey with the young mare.

"Can I have a real horse this time?" Sapphire asked, interrupting Rayla's thoughts. "Or do I have to ride a blasted pony again?"

Raiden laughed. Even Rayla chuckled at the humorous annoyance in Sapphire's voice.

"Considering you're officially a member of this journey and won't be sneaking around behind our backs, we'll have a real horse set aside just for you," Raiden promised.

Sapphire let out a sigh of relief, clearly trying to be funny. Still, Rayla wondered if part of the young girl's relief was real.

"And you're planning to continue training with Luca as we travel?" Rayla asked. Sapphire nodded.

"I am. And I can't wait. Throwing knives is so exciting. Of course, I love swordwork too, but knives are definitely my favorite."

Rayla wondered if what her friend was feeling with knives was what Rayla felt with her sword. It almost felt as if her sword wasn't a possession, but a part of her. She never parted with it. Rayla considered the fact that, with the right teacher, and the right amount of training, Sapphire could develop a very rare skill set with her knives.

Raiden suddenly let out a sigh so loud it made Rayla jump. She looked at her friend in shock. He was standing slowly to his feet.

"We'd better get home," he said. "Before it gets too dark."

"I swear if you do that one more time," Rayla muttered, standing as well. Beside her, Sapphire snickered.

"I suppose you're right." Rayla stretched again. She considered making a jab about having to work in the morning but decided against it. She didn't want to remind Raiden that he still didn't have a position yet. Or worse, rush him into something that may take him away from her. Suddenly, the thought of Raiden finding a position was no longer funny to her.

"We can walk together," Raiden said, pulling Rayla from her thoughts.

The three of them left the tavern, Rayla leaving a few copper coins on their table as payment for her meal, and began walking down the road. The walk was silent for a while before Sapphire spoke up.

"What happens if something goes wrong on this journey?" she asked quietly.

Rayla frowned. She shared a concerned glance with Raiden before answering.

"What do you mean?"

"Well, for instance, what would we do if Kuvira gets away? Or if Tenabris marches right up to us with an entire army?"

Again, Rayla glanced at Raiden. In the dim moonlight, she could see that he didn't have an answer for his sister. Unfortunately, neither did Rayla. It was a question they had all been asking themselves, and none of them had found a good answer.

The problem with this mission, Rayla had decided, was that they were placing a lot of trust in the assumption that Tenabris would value his father's life over the goal of overthrowing Maith. And the problem with such an assumption was that it was very possible that Tenabris would not choose his father.

The idea of Tenabris letting his father be killed sent a stab of anger through Rayla. If she had a family, she would do anything and everything to spare them. Just the thought of Tenabris willingly sacrificing his father's life made Rayla grit her teeth.

She hated Kuvira and Tenabris both.

Sooner than Rayla realized, they arrived at Sapphire's home.

"Goodnight," the fair-haired girl said cheerily.

"Goodnight, Saph," Raiden said, ruffling the girl's hair.

"See you in two days," Rayla called to Sapphire as the girl made her way to the door. She turned to wave as she entered the house. Rayla and Raiden waved back.

After making sure that Sapphire was safely in the house, the two friends walked a short distance before coming to a fork in the road. To the right was Rayla's small home.

"Does Sapphire even know where you live?" Rayla asked, amused.

"I don't think she does," Raiden chuckled. "Otherwise she would have insisted that I just go back home and not walk you both to your houses."

"You should have," Rayla replied sternly. "You and Macarius live on the other side of the town square."

"And leave you two to walk home in the dark, alone?"

"It's not any safer for you to walk home alone in the dark than it is for us."

"I'm a man," Raiden argued.

Rayla nodded. "A man with a bow. Which, might I add, would be completely useless if someone snuck up behind you. That thing is for long distances only."

"I can use a sword, too."

"Oh, I forgot." Rayla said sarcastically. "Although, I'm not sure tripping over your feet and cutting your own arm off would be any better than the bow."

Rayla stared at her friend, trying to choke down her amusement. Eventually, she couldn't help it. The look of indignance on Raiden's face forced a laugh out of Rayla's throat.

"I'm sorry," she said between breaths, "but you look so offended, it's funny."

"Hmph," Raiden huffed, rolling his eyes.

Finally, Rayla managed to stop laughing.

"At least I got a good laugh out of you," Raiden said, suddenly serious. He took Rayla's hand, sending a burst of tingles up her arm. Any trace of a smile left her face, and she looked into Raiden's eyes.

"Laughing is good," Raiden continued. "At least it's some form of emotion."

Rayla gulped, hoping it wasn't loud enough for Raiden to hear.

"I show emotion."

"'I don't care' isn't an emotion."

"It could be."

"It isn't."

Rayla took a deep breath, careful not to move her hand out of Raiden's.

"Shouldn't you get home?" she asked, her voice quieter than she'd expected it to come out. For some odd reason, she hated saying those words.

Raiden dropped her hand, and Rayla struggled to keep her disappointment from showing on her face.

"Yes," Raiden replied. "I need to help Sir Macarius wrap things up tomorrow. And you have to go back to guard duty bright and early."

"Right," Rayla sighed. "Bright and early."

Raiden chuckled. "Goodnight, Ray."

Rayla's heart seemed to skip a beat at the old childhood nickname.

"'Night."

Rayla stood in place until Raiden's form disappeared down the road. Then she turned and walked into her house, eagerly changing into her soft night clothes and flopping onto the bed.

Her mouth began to turn up at the corners, and she shook her head slowly. She and Raiden had been friends for years. Why was she suddenly so distracted by a lingering touch?

Rayla shook the thought away, sighing heavily. She had twelve hours to pack for their journey and get a good night's rest before she would have to head back to the wall once again.

chapter 11
Raiden

Raiden's nerves were on edge, and it was beginning to take a toll on his body.

The group was scheduled to leave early the next morning. Everything was packed safely in their saddle packs. Ten battle horses and sixteen of the castle's other steeds had been set aside. Kuvira, Sir Macarius had decided, would remain bound in a small wagon that would be pulled by one of the horses. He couldn't be trusted on a horse. If the man wanted to make a fast break, he would have to do so on foot.

Their food preserves were also accounted for. They had more than enough to get them to Castle Riraveth, which was only a few days away. The castles of Riraveth and Maith were within a short distance of each other. They had been placed strategically close to each other because of Riraveth's neighboring kingdom, Saodda. With the other castles so far away from the border province, the first king had wanted at least one source of quick aid in case of an attack from the Saoddans. Maith had been that source of aid.

Despite everything being ready for the journey, the stress still weighed on Raiden. He hadn't slept well for several nights. Not only that, but he hadn't been lying to Rayla when he told her that the weather was getting to him. He struggled to breathe through his nose, and he shivered and coughed on a regular basis now. Sir Macarius had insisted that he see the herbalist, but Raiden had refused. They simply didn't have the time. Eventually, Macarius had given up.

Now, the two men were studying the maps, looking for any possible campsites.

"If we stay together until we get through the gates of Riraveth, it will make Carrow's job of getting an audience with the lord much easier," Macarius thought aloud. "Of course, splitting up would make us less noticeable. But I think it's too dangerous to leave Kuvira with any fewer men that he's already with. Besides, this way, Carrow and a couple of the other guards can head to the castle while the rest of us look for an inn as soon as we enter the castle walls. We should stay in Riraveth for a few days at least. I'll have to send the signal to my informant in order to get him to meet me at the same spot. And we will need to restock on food and water before we head home."

Raiden nodded. "Makes sense," he said, his voice thick and husky from coughing.

"Raiden–" Sir Macarius began.

"No," Raiden cut in, knowing where his former master was going with the tone in his voice. "I don't need to waste time at the infirmary begging for herbs to fix a sore throat."

"Fine," Macarius growled. "But when you die, don't come crying to me."

"Wouldn't dream of it."

Macarius ignored the sarcasm in Raiden's voice and turned back to the map. As they studied the field between Maith and Riraveth's castles, a thought struck Raiden.

"How did you come across this man?" Raiden asked. "Or did he seek you out? Either way, doesn't it seem suspicious that he knew that you would be the right man to talk to?"

Sir Macarius looked up from the map, considering the question.

"Well, as I told you before, I was on a mission to Riraveth, looking for any clues to Rayla's history. I figured that if she was from here, her family would have found her by now. And since you say she arrived in Maith at a young age, I figured her home province would have to be close by. No child could wander very far on their own and survive. Riraveth is the closest province, so I started there."

"And this man just … found you?" Raiden asked in a monotone voice. Sir Macarius shot him a look, and Raiden took the hint, making a mental note to lose his sarcastic tone.

"I had stopped for the night at a tavern. He joined me in the corner of the tavern and immediately said, 'You look like a man on a mission.' Of course, I was very skeptical and tried to brush him off, but as it turns out, he had heard me asking about Rayla around the market square. He gradually shifted to more in-depth topics. It wasn't until he said something about the 'driving force of Riraveth's criminal activity' that I became truly interested and willing to trust him a bit more."

"And what did he mean by that?" Raiden asked.

"I asked him that very question. That was when he mentioned his knowledge of Kuvira and his troops, his own former status as commander, and Rayla's history. He wouldn't say any more, though. After some discussion we decided that it would be best for him to gather the information from other sources."

"Other sources?" Raiden asked.

"Men that he still trusts in Kuvira's ranks. Men that he claims wanted to follow him out, but he asked them to stay behind and be his spies. So that he could know when Kuvira began to search for him. He wanted to go back and make sure that the troops hadn't moved since he had last heard from his men, so he could give me the right information."

Raiden remembered the feeling of peace he had gotten when Macarius had assured him days earlier that they were not going to draw Tenabris out as soon as they reached Riraveth. That peace seemed to be long gone now.

"Forgive me, sir," Raiden began slowly. "But … "

Macarius smiled encouragingly. "You're a bowmaster now, Raiden," he reminded the boy. "You have every right to say whatever is on your mind."

Raiden nodded. "It just seems unwise to fully trust this man, or his spies."

"Oh, it is," Macarius said. "That's why I don't *fully* trust him. I trust him enough to see where this second meeting gets us, but not enough to remain unprepared in case he is lying to me. I told you I had an idea in case he double-crosses us. I think the troops we are bringing along could be used to arrest this man."

Raiden frowned. "But how can you just arrest him before–"

"He gives me a reason?" Macarius finished. "I couldn't. But fortunately, he has *already* given me a reason."

"How?"

"When he told me how to reach him again after our first meeting, I tried to do so for several days, but he never showed. That, to me, is reason enough to suspect foul play. I'm hoping that when I return, he will show himself so that I can see what information he gives and then arrest him for further questioning."

Raiden shook his head, confused.

"Why trust his word at all?"

Macarius watched him closely. "Because men who play two sides of the same war always weave truth into their lies, in case they ever get caught."

Raiden wasn't sure what to say to that, so the two men silently returned to their map. Raiden let his eyes wander over the area between the two provinces. There wasn't much to see. There were little to no trees; the woods remained mostly northeast. This area, Raiden knew from studying the map, was simply miles of tall, dying grass. It was completely open, with only one small village between the two provinces. The map showed a small river flowing from the northwest down to the Tacktan sea. The group would have to cross it, although hopefully it would be fairly shallow at this time of year.

Then another spot caught Raiden's eye. To the south and west of Castle Riraveth, in the farthest corner of the province, there were markings that Raiden recognized as Riraveth's hills.

"What's over here, in this corner?" he asked.

Sir Macarius grunted. "Hills, hills, and more hills," he said blankly.

Raiden glanced at him, a little agitated.

"I know that," he said. "I meant what's *in* the hills?"

Macarius hesitated before answering. "Nothing as far as I know. I've been there myself, once. There's a large valley near the edge. A couple of hills hide it from view. They are a few days' ride from Castle Riraveth."

Raiden frowned. It seemed strange for there to be such a large, uninhabited area. Villages were frequent throughout every province in the kingdom. Of course, each castle had a much larger town within its walls, such as the one Raiden lived in at Maith. But there were other established villages scattered over the kingdom. Places where farmers often lived and worked together. He decided to voice this to his former master.

Sir Macarius nodded in approval.

"You're correct," the bowmaster said. "There should be villages scattered nearby. And years ago, there were."

"What happened to them?" Raiden pressed.

Macarius considered him.

"There is a neighboring kingdom that borders Riraveth province."

"Saodda," Raiden stated. Macarius nodded again.

"For years, it posed a serious threat to Rathús. Eventually they were forced into a peace treaty with our kingdom. They needed our food, and we wanted to minimize the threat of an invasion."

"Okay," Raiden said slowly, struggling to connect the pieces of the story. "But the villages were attacked?"

"Before the treaty went into effect, yes. You won't remember this. It was at least thirty years ago."

Raiden was shocked to find that this event happened within Macarius's lifetime. To Raiden, the peace treaty with Saodda seemed like something that had been there since the beginning of time.

"Saodda never launched a full invasion into our lands," Macarius continued, "but they were responsible for countless villages being plundered. Eventually, the people decided it was too risky to live anywhere near the border, so they abandoned those villages and started new ones closer to the heart of the kingdom. I believe there are one or two that have resurfaced since then, but nowhere near as many as before."

Content with his master's explanation, Raiden dropped the matter. Sir Macarius stood, stretching his arms behind his head and yawning. He glanced around the room before turning to look back at Raiden.

"You've double-checked everything?" the bowmaster asked. Raiden stood as well.

"And triple-checked," he replied.

Macarius nodded to himself. "And the horses?"

"The stableboy said he'll have them saddled and ready to go in time," Raiden replied.

"I assume you'll want to ride one of the horses that has not been trained as a battle horse?"

"If it's alright with you."

Raiden had to admit that the battle horses made him nervous. He had been raised around farm horses, which were smaller and more gentle. The pent-up, nervous energy from the bulky battle horses made Raiden feel on edge.

"All the same to me," Macarius replied, jolting Raiden from his thoughts. "I assume Rayla will be riding her horse?"

"Yes."

"And Luca will want to ride his. Carrow will likely feel entitled to a battle horse as well."

Raiden raised an eyebrow at the comment, assuming it was a lasting joke between Sir Macarius and the scholar.

"That leaves seven more battle horses for the rest of the guards," Macarius continued. "We'll let Luca divide them up as he sees fit."

Slowly, the man made his way to the front door. He reached down and grabbed his bow and quiver, jerking his head in a motion for Raiden to do the same. The boy did so, knowing what Macarius was suggesting they do. The two exited the cabin and walked to the edge of the road where they turned around to face the trees.

In sync, both men raised their arms, Raiden using his right and Macarius his left, over their shoulders. They each drew an arrow and nocked it on the strings of their bows. In one fluid motion, they raised their weapons and drew back. Their muscles, specifically those in their backs, were tensed with power.

Raiden felt his body waver from the stress, and for just a moment, the boy thought that his mentor had been right. Maybe he did need to go to the healer. But stubbornness beat the idea down inside of him as quickly as it had arisen.

Both bowmasters released their shots almost as soon as they had drawn their bows, before their arms could tire or their minds could overthink their shots. Both arrows flew through the air and smacked into two different trees.

Raiden frowned. His arrow had landed slightly too far to the left. Unfortunately, Sir Macarius noticed.

"I'll get them," Macarius said.

The bowmaster sauntered to his own arrow, making a show of examining the shot. He placed his right hand on the tree trunk, with his thumb and index finger on either side of the arrow. Then, using his left hand, he gripped the shaft of the arrow from above and pulled back, straight and slow. Nodding in satisfaction at the centered mark, he moved to Raiden's arrow.

Raiden drew his eyebrows together in annoyance as Macarius shook his head and clicked his tongue in disappointment. He watched the older man remove the second arrow slowly. Raiden knew, of course, that Macarius was only making such a scene in order to agitate him. Sadly, he felt it working. Raiden was well aware that his shot wasn't perfect. He didn't need Sir Macarius to drag on about it.

Macarius turned to look at Raiden in confusion.

"You were aware that we were aiming for the *center* of the trees?" he asked innocently.

Raiden felt his irritation win out in his mind. He sighed loudly, march-ing over to Sir Macarius. He plucked the black-shafted arrow out of the bowmaster's hand and replaced it in his own quiver.

Shooting his mentor a withering look, he returned to the edge of the road.

chapter 12
Rayla

They left bright and early like Raiden had promised, in a solid formation.

Macarius, Raiden, and Carrow had taken the lead at the front of the group. An armed guard rode on the far left and right of them. Behind them, a row of four guards rode, then four rows of two guards. A second row of four guards closed in the box shape. Inside, Kuvira was bound by hands and feet and placed in a small wagon, pulled by one of the front horses. Finally, in the very back, two more guards rode on either side of Luca, Rayla, and Sapphire.

All were armed.

Rayla seriously wondered why they had not brought more battle horses after all. The sheer size of their group would inevitably draw attention, even if they were on foot. Still, Lord Hightower had insisted on having the guards, and Rayla didn't pretend to be dissapointed. She liked not having to worry about Kuvira trying to fight his way out. Horrible as the man might be, he was not stupid.

The sun's position told Rayla it was now about midmorning. Castle Maith was somewhere behind them. So far the ride had been fairly quiet. She and Luca had been making small talk most of the way, and now they were discussing her new position.

"How do you like being an official guard?" the swordmaster asked.

Rayla tried to force an air of excitement. She didn't want to let her former mentor know how disappointed she was.

"I love it," she lied. "I love every part of it. I look forward to it each day."

"I see," Luca said calmly. It was clear that he didn't believe Rayla. "And have you thought of any other options?"

Rayla sighed.

"This again?" she asked dismissively.

Luca laughed incredulously, and Rayla jumped at the loud noise. She looked at the man in surprise.

"Yes, this again," Luca pressed. "Please, Rayla, don't act so annoyed."

"With all due respect, I'm not acting," she commented. Sir Luca's nostrils flared.

"You know I'm only pushing you to be your best. You could travel to a different province, you could request to become one of Lord Hightower's personal guards, you could travel to Rathús Castle to seek knighthood—"

Rayla scoffed. "Knighthood? Luca, we've already talked about how ridiculous that idea is."

Luca frowned in her direction. "Why do you dismiss it so easily?"

"I would rather spend my time doing something that is at least achievable, thank you."

She glanced sidelong at Luca and saw that the man was looking back at her, completely serious.

"What?" she asked innocently.

"Don't underestimate yourself, Rayla," he said evenly.

They continued looking at each other for several long seconds before Rayla awkwardly broke eye contact. She stared straight ahead, ignoring the fact that even after she had looked away, Luca continued to watch her for several seconds. Her cheeks burned from embarrassment at her mentor's chastisement.

From atop her horse, Rayla could see Kuvira inside his wagon. With every bump that the wooden wheels hit, the man was thrown to one side or the other, unable to use his bound hands to steady himself.

As if feeling her eyes on him, Kuvira's gaze snapped up. His eyes met hers in an icy stare. He grinned, his thick eyebrows coming down as he looked up at her. Rayla swallowed, averting her gaze instantly.

She hated that Kuvira was out in the open, so close to freedom. No amount of guards or bondages would completely settle her nerves where he was concerned.

She mentally shook her worry aside, instead turning to her left, looking at Sapphire.

"How do you like riding on a full-sized horse?" Rayla asked in a forced, light tone.

Sapphire smiled. "I love it! It's a little bumpy, but it's still fun!"

Rayla could relate to that. The rhythmic sway of Dóchas's body was soothing to her. Of course, Rayla wasn't as good of a rider as Raiden, but she still felt comfortable atop her young mare.

Smiling softly to herself, Rayla leaned forward, affectionately patting Dóchas's neck. The horse snorted, shaking her mane in response to her master's touch.

As silence fell over the group, Rayla felt a small twinge of sadness. She would have liked for Raiden to ride in the back with her and Sapphire. Not that she didn't enjoy Luca's company. Rayla loved catching up with her mentor, when he wasn't pressuring her to consider a pointless goal. Still, she always felt the most at ease when Raiden was nearby. In fact, now that she thought about his absence, she felt rather shaky and nervous. She wondered what would cause such a sudden, intense need for Raiden's presence, but she dismissed the thought. Clearly she simply missed her friend's company. Unfortunately, Macarius had seen the long journey as a chance to go over anything that he might have forgotten to teach him, so the boy had been pulled to the front with the bowmaster and Carrow.

Annoyance shot through Rayla's mind. Such a thing wouldn't have been necessary if Macarius would have simply done his job and not skipped out on months of Raiden's training. Still, there wasn't much she could do. Even if she was an official guard now, Rayla still recognized her place. Macarius had a considerably greater amount of experience than Rayla, and she would always be his and Luca's inferior.

She sighed, already bored with the trip. Curiously, she looked on either side of her companions. She was sandwiched between Sapphire, who was to her left, and Luca to her right. Two of Maith's guards rode on the outside. Leaning forward to glance over Sapphire's body, Rayla could get a good look at the first guard. He was rather old and stone-faced. His gray hair reflected the morning sunlight. His expression clearly showed how unhappy he was with this assignment. Rayla rolled her eyes, turning to look at the guard on the other side of Luca.

A wave of shock went through her as she recognized the young man. It was the guard who had approached her only days ago about Finn.

"I know you," she announced, squinting at the man. He blinked, looking at her in surprise.

"Yes," he said slowly, as if surprised to be acknowledged.

"What's your name?"

"Nelgev," the man replied. "But my nonexistent friends call me Nel."

Rayla allowed a small smile to play on her lips. The first time she had met Nel, she hadn't been introduced to this sarcastic sense of humor. She decided that she might enjoy his company after all.

"Hi!" a young voice chirped from Rayla's left. She turned to see Sapphire now leaning forward, excited to meet a new friend. "I'm Sapphire. I'm Rayla's friend."

Nel smiled in return. "Hello, Sapphire," he replied smoothly.

"I'm also training with Sir Luca," she announced proudly. "I'm doing alright with a sword, but look at this!" Sapphire excitedly stood in her stirrups, gesturing to the knives strapped to her belt. "They're throwing knives!"

"Very impressive!" Nel replied politely. Sapphire smiled, returning to her saddle. In the split second that the younger girl wasn't looking their way, Nel shot Rayla an overwhelmed look. Rayla felt her abs constrict as she stifled a laugh. Between the two guards, she saw Luca attempt to do the same.

Across from Sapphire, Rayla heard the older guard groan in annoyance. She raised an eyebrow in his direction.

"Do you need a drink of water?" she asked, pretending to be concerned and polite.

"No," the man grunted, slightly confused by the question.

"Oh," Rayla replied. "I just thought you might have a bad taste in your mouth."

The guard looked at Rayla as if she was last week's dinner.

"And why would you think that?"

"Just because you've had such a sour look on your face all morning."

The man's face reddened in embarrassment and indignance, but Rayla was already looking away. Luca, she saw, was trying, and failing, to hide a look of amused approval. Nel openly gawked at her.

Rayla opened her mouth to ask Nel if every guard was so stuck up, but the words caught in her throat.

No, she remembered vividly, as the mental picture of a man with light brown hair and pale green eyes flashed through her mind. Not all guards. Most, perhaps, but not all.

The memory of her late friend somehow led Rayla to unconsciously slide her gaze back to Kurvira. He was looking elsewhere, much to Rayla's relief, but the fresh memory of Finn and the connection of that loss to Kuvira made Rayla tremble with a sudden onset of rage. She glared at Kuvira until she realized that another second of dwelling on her hatred would lead her to climb from her horse and kill him herself. She felt her throat close up as her anger threatened to overwhelm her.

In a desperate attempt to keep tears from her eyes, Rayla looked up at the sky, blinking wildly. When she was confident that no tears would come, she glanced at Sapphire. The young girl was looking back at her with a mischievous smile. She jerked her head to the older guard who had spoken so rudely moments ago.

"*Stick up his butt,*" she mouthed.

Rayla snorted in amusement.

"So, Nelgev," Luca was saying from Rayla's other side.

"Nel," the guard corrected politely.

"Okay. Nel," Luca said again, nodding. "How did you and Rayla meet?"

Rayla swallowed hard, praying silently that Nel wouldn't go into too much detail. She could already sense the awkward silence that would follow if the man mentioned Finn's name.

"We were positioned beside each other a few days ago," Nel replied. "She seemed likely to bite the head off anyone who approached her, so naturally I introduced myself."

Rayla struggled to hide a sigh of relief. Luckily, Luca was too busy laughing to notice.

"I like you," the swordmaster announced. "I am Sir Luca."

He offered a hand to Nel, who shook it firmly.

"I know," Nel said respectfully. "Captain of the guard."

Luca smiled. "Not much captaining to do at the moment," he admitted.

"That's a good thing," Rayla muttered under her breath. Unfortunately, Luca heard her.

"Indeed it is," he replied, turning to look at her with a challenge in his eyes. "Otherwise I would be forced to lead our guards into battle with inexperienced newcomers such as yourself behind our lines."

"I'm not inexperienced–"

"Ah ah ah," Luca warned, wagging his index finger. "I wouldn't disrespect the captain of the guard if I were you."

Rayla rolled her eyes. She allowed a small smile to play on her lips as both she and Luca turned to examine the baffled look on Nel's face.

"They're always like this," Sapphire explained, attempting to consol the guard.

"I see," Nel said slowly, clearly still uncomfortable.

"Nel," Luca said, turning to look forward in mock indignation.

"Sir?"

"Keep this one in check, will you?" Luca jerked a thumb in Rayla's direction.

"Yes, sir."

"I don't need anyone to keep me in check, thank you," Rayla spat.

"And keep a close eye on her," Luca warned, a hint of amusement in his voice. "She's quite feisty."

chapter 13
Rayla

They rode until the sun had begun to set, not bothering to stop for lunch. Of course they'd stopped a few times to give the horses breaks, but since they had been riding at a slow and steady pace, not many breaks were needed.

The ride itself had been uneventful and long. Rayla's legs were sore, as was her backside. Even Sapphire had grown quiet, which told Rayla that the girl was either uncomfortable or tired, or both. Sapphire, being stubborn, would never admit such a thing. She would always try to seem tough as long as everyone else around her was content with their situation. It was one of the things Rayla loved most about the young girl.

Nobody else in the group showed any signs of discomfort, either, and Rayla began to feel unprofessional. She was a Maith guard now. She should be able to endure all types of hardships. Instead, a single day's ride in the saddle of her own horse had her praying for rest.

As if on cue, the group stopped.

From the front of the line, Carrow came riding towards them.

"We'll stop here for the night," the scholar said before returning to the front.

Rayla fought hard to hide her relief. Sapphire, however, let out an involuntary sigh.

"Thank goodness," the young girl said dramatically. "I can't feel my legs."

Nearby, Nel let out a good-natured laugh.

Luca glanced at Sapphire, smiling. "Don't get too excited," he warned her.

Sapphire frowned. "Why?"

Luca raised his eyebrows. "You still have to make up for a day's worth of training," he reminded her. "Get your knives ready and meet me over there." He pointed to one side of the group.

Sapphire glanced at Rayla with a look that clearly said *"help."* Rayla laughed, and Sapphire obediently followed Luca.

Slowly, the group broke formation, although four guards kept Kuvira at bay at all times. Each guard stood at one corner of the small wagon, their gazes fixed carefully on the pale man they were charged with watching. They had left him bound in the wagon for the time being.

Rayla squinted skeptically at Kuvira. The man hadn't said a word the entire day. He hadn't questioned their mission or their destination, or even their motives. Although no one had offered him a bite of food at lunch, Kuvira hadn't asked. Rayla didn't like his silence. It made her feel like he was planning something.

Still, she tried to dismiss the idea. She wanted to be as far away from the man as she possibly could. Every movement he made reminded her of the whip he had wielded against her in the woods, and she couldn't help but flinch any time he looked in her direction.

But she comforted herself with the knowledge that he was being detained and watched constantly. He was surrounded by armed guards, and he himself was unarmed. Whatever he was planning, there was no possible way it could work.

Rayla spotted Raiden through the group. A quick glance to the side told her that Sapphire was preoccupied, practicing with her knives and sword under Luca's careful watch. Rayla smiled to herself as she casually led Dóchas toward Raiden. He was helping Macarius, Carrow, and six other guards discuss the proper setup for their campsite.

The group was still in the open field, which stretched as far as Rayla could see. Unfortunately, that meant that there wasn't much cover.

Rayla moved to Raiden's side, carefully listening as Carrow explained his idea.

"I'm thinking we set up in a circle," the scholar said. "Kuvira and his four guards can remain in the middle, but off to one side. We should have enough people for the guards to take two shifts detaining him through the night."

Macarius was nodding. "I was going to suggest the same," he agreed.

Carrow continued. "As for watching over the camp itself, I suggest three shifts with two guards on each shift. They can sit back to back in the center of the camp. That way, they can see every direction."

Macarius nodded. "Sounds excellent."

"Harrison and I will take the first watch," one of the six present guards offered.

"Thank you," Macarius replied. "Vic, would you and Gregory like to take the second shift?"

"Of course," the guard replied.

The remaining two guards offered to take the third watch. Everyone nodded consent.

"Wait," Macarius added, pausing briefly to consider his thoughts before voicing them to the group. "Three watches rounds out to roughly three hours for each shift. We could add a fourth watch. There are certainly enough people to spare."

"Raiden and I will take the last watch," Rayla offered immediately, wanting to establish her willingness to contribute. "We can wake the camp at sunrise."

Carrow nodded in satisfaction. "Sounds like a plan," he said. The group dispersed slowly.

"Raiden," Macarius called as he approached the boy. Raiden moved his attention to the man.

"Sir?" he asked.

"We've got twenty-five men, and eight of them are on guard duty to watch over the camp," Macarius explained. "That leaves the rest of us to take shifts watching Kuvira. Four at a time. I will be with the second group, and Luca will likely want to help as well."

"That makes sense, sir," Raiden agreed.

"Kuvira is dangerous," Macarius continued, pausing to consider his next words. "If he ... if something were to happen while we were on guard ... if he managed to bring harm to me–"

"Sir!" Raiden exclaimed, clearly shocked by the words.

"Let me finish," Macarius demanded gently. Rayla watched as Raiden closed his mouth, his eyes wide and his eyebrows drawn together. Clearly he didn't like listening to his mentor talk about the possibility of getting injured.

Satisfied that Raiden would interrupt no more, Macarius continued.

"If Kuvira gets the best of his guards while you and Rayla are on duty, you must ignore the group and retrieve Kuvira at all costs."

Raiden was silent, so Rayla spoke up.

"You mean if he harms you or anyone else ... " she began, but couldn't finish.

"Yes," Macarius agreed. "If he harms me or anyone else, you are to leave us and find him. Under no circumstances are you to check on anyone in the group until Kuvira is secured again."

For several seconds, no one said a word. It was a morbid thought to put in their minds, but Rayla could understand where Macarius was coming from. Kuvira was their leverage, after all. Losing him would completely upset their current plan.

"I am counting on you two to do what I ask," Macaruis said. His eyes bore into Raiden's. Rayla watched with tension in her shoulders as Raiden stared back at his former master, refusing to back down. Rayla could empathize with Raiden. She couldn't imagine leaving Luca or Raiden or Sapphire, knowing they were injured and in need of her help, to go after Kuvira.

Still, she understood more than most how important it was to keep Kuvira in their grasp.

"Raiden," Macarius warned. "This is not a request. It's an order."

With that he walked away.

Rayla glanced at Raiden awkwardly. The boy was standing stock still, staring into the distance and clenching his jaw.

Unsure of what to say to comfort her friend, Rayla decided to change the subject.

"Um," she began, clearing her throat. "Where are we supposed to tie our horses up? Considering we are in the middle of nowhere."

Raiden waited, finally taking a deep breath to clear his head before responding.

"There's a wooden peg in your saddle pack," he replied softly without making eye contact. Rayla frowned, giving Raiden a glance of concern before moving to check her pack. He was right. She pulled the peg out and examined it.

"The ground is soft enough that we should be able to drive them in with a little bit of work," Raiden explained. "But it's also hard enough that the horses won't be able to easily pull themselves free. Once they feel the resistance, they're usually pretty content to stay put."

Rayla kept her head down, but nodded in understanding.

"What is it?" Raiden asked. Rayla drew her eyebrows together as she looked up at Raiden. He was watching her closely now, apparently having recovered from the uncomfortable conversation with Macarius.

"What is what?" she asked.

"You're scowling. When you scowl, that means you're thinking about something."

Rayla sighed. Sometimes it was annoying how well her friend could read her expressions.

"I just feel so exposed out here," she admitted. "There are no walls or trees to provide any cover."

Raiden nodded.

"True," he said. "But that also means that if anyone wanted to attack us, they also wouldn't have any cover. They would be just as exposed as we are. Our scouts could easily see them coming."

Rayla cut her eyes to Raiden, keeping her face unamused.

"What?" he asked, clearly uncomfortable after several seconds of Rayla staring at him.

"Since when are you so smart?"

It was Raiden's turn to scowl now.

"I'm smart," he protested. Rayla raised her eyebrows.

"You only knew that because you asked Macarius on the way, didn't you?"

"I'm smart!" Raiden insisted once again.

Rayla snorted.

"I've always *been* smart," Raiden bragged, moving to loosen the girth strap on his horse's saddle. "You just don't listen to me."

"Why would I listen when all you ever say is nonsense?" Rayla retorted as she moved to loosen Dóchas's own strap.

"You just said–"

"Where are we putting our bedrolls?" an excited voice asked. Raiden and Rayla both turned to see Sapphire smiling up at them.

Rayla, glad that she had gotten the last word in their argument, was happy to answer Sapphire.

"I think this area is fine," she replied. "Don't you?"

Raiden gave her a look of annoyance before turning to look around him.

"I think it's just about the only option left," he admitted. "Everyone else has already set up camp."

Rayla felt her heart drop as she realized that Raiden was right. Once again, she had missed the chance to prove her worth. Every other member of the group had already laid out their bedrolls, tied up their horses, and were even starting a small fire for dinner.

"Oh," Rayla managed.

"So how was your ride?" Raiden asked, oblivious to Rayla's disappointment.

Rayla shook her head, forcing herself to recall the boring day.

"It could've been better," she admitted. "My tailbone is considerably bruised, I think."

Raiden smiled. "You'll get used to the constant riding."

"I hope so," Sapphire put in. "I feel like I'm waddling instead of walking around."

This time, Raiden let out a solid laugh.

"You'll get used to that, too."

"The waddling isn't as bad as the thoughts that kept running through my mind," Rayla pointed out. She glanced toward the wooden wagon, where guards were beginning to drag Kuvira out for the night. They didn't untie his hands and feet, but Rayla's stomach still twisted in fear and something else.

She mentally recoiled as she realized that she was pleased to see Kuvira in such a vulnerable position. For the first time, she *wanted* to approach him, to get a better look at him bound and held down. Not what he deserved, she thought, because he deserved to die. But this was better than him running free.

Perhaps it was because she was already diving so deep into her thoughts that Rayla said to Raiden without thinking, "I found myself wishing you had been with us."

As soon as the words left her mouth, she felt a blush creeping over her face. She managed a quick glance at Raiden and saw that his cheeks were tinged red as well.

Raiden cleared his throat awkwardly. "At least you didn't have to ride with Sir Macarius's constant humming and Carrow's neverending talk of scrolls," he said quickly.

"True," Rayla replied with a smile, grateful that Raiden had politely ignored her last comment. "Although grumple-butt wasn't much better."

"The old guard?" Raiden guessed.

"I think 'grumple-butt' describes him better, but yes."

"But Luca was there," Raiden reminded her.

"Yes, he was," Rayla admitted. "And Sapphire was good company, too."

"You're absolutely right, I was," Sapphire muttered as she laid out her bedroll.

Raiden and Rayla shared a smile.

"Don't forget about Nel," Sapphire added.

Rayla nodded, smiling.

"Oh, yes," she conceded. "And Nel was there, too."

Rayla noticed that Raiden was frowning in confusion.

"Who's Nel?"

Rayla considered the question. Explaining it would do no good, she realized. Raiden would likely have never met the guard before.

"Finish with your bedroll and come find me," she told her friend. "I'll introduce you."

chapter 14
Raiden

Late that night, or rather early the next morning, Raiden sat keeping watch over the sleeping camp. He had been introduced to Nel several hours earlier. Immediately, he felt the need to bristle up and keep Nel at arm's length. Raiden didn't like him.

He was justified in his feelings, he thought. Nel just seemed like an unpleasant person.

The way he flirted with Rayla, in particular, was so disgusting that it made Raiden sick to his stomach. And even worse, Rayla seemed to be playing along. Could they be any more obvious?

It didn't matter, of course. Rayla could make her own decisions. It just seemed immature to Raiden, for her to be spending so much time with this new guard. She should be focusing on their journey. It was incredibly important that this mission come out as a success. They didn't have time for distractions.

Besides, if Rayla didn't stay in the right mindset, she could end up getting hurt. Again.

Now Raiden and Rayla sat with their backs to each other in the center of the camp, keeping watch. Raiden was facing the direction from which they had come, while Rayla looked out over the field in front of them, where they had not yet traveled. Behind him, Raiden could feel Rayla stir uncomfortably for the third time in just a few short minutes.

"Did you have trouble sleeping?" he whispered, leaning back to get closer to Rayla's ear. Raiden waited patiently for a reply. Finally, Rayla leaned back toward him.

"No, that's not it," she said softly.

"Well, what is it? I've not seen you this squirmy since your first lessons at battle school."

For a minute or two, there was no answer. Rayla had gone still, and Raiden knew immediately that whatever it was would be no laughing matter. He frowned.

"It's not a big deal," she began, and Raiden quickly decided that it likely was. "Even though it was a few months ago, my back tends to get stiff and hurt when I sit or stand still for too long."

A deep scowl fell on Raiden's face as he recalled what had happened to his friend in the spring. Angrily, he shot a glare in Kuvira's direction. The man was sound asleep between his four guards. Raiden felt a sudden desire to march over and strangle the man in his sleep.

Unfortunately, Kuvira was vital to their mission. They needed him as leverage, in case Sir Macarius's informant double-crossed them and Tenabris's troops threatened their safety. Hopefully, holding a knife to Kuvira's neck would make Tenabris think twice before he engaged in combat. Without Kuvira, they were basically walking into a bear's den with meat strapped to their chests.

Frustrated, Raiden blinked several times and turned his head back in the direction of their home. Keeping watch, he was beginning to learn, was incredibly boring work – to stare off into the night, waiting for something that would most likely never come.

Suddenly, a thought struck him.

"Rayla?" he tried quietly.

"Yes?" came the girl's reply.

"What does guard duty feel like?"

"What do you mean?"

"I mean, is it anything like this?"

There was a pause. Eventually, Raiden heard his friend sigh softly.

"Unfortunately, yes it is," she admitted. "Although I do get the day shift, which isn't quite as bad as this."

Raiden nodded thoughtfully. "Do you regret taking the position?" he asked. He wondered if accepting Lord Hightower's offer of becoming a Maith archer and bowmaster would result in a job as boring as this. If so, he wondered if he might truly need to give more thought to a position elsewhere. But that would mean leaving his home. And Rayla.

"It's an honor and a privilege to be a Maith guard," Rayla replied, bringing Raiden out of his thoughts. He noticed the stiff edge in Rayla's voice. "I am happy to claim my new title."

Raiden brought his eyebrows together. Her words sounded mechanical, as if she had fiercely repeated them to herself on a regular basis. *Like she's trying to force herself to believe them,* Raiden thought.

"Do you remember," he whispered casually, "what we used to fantasize about as children? When we first started to play together. We were probably, what, about seven?"

Rayla laughed softly. "We thought we were going to be the best knights Rathús had ever seen," she replied.

"'The kingdom needs us!'" Raiden whispered passionately, repeating a phrase that they had often called out when they played. The two laughed softly.

Raiden let his mind wander back. They had played the game at least once a day as children. They would run through the streets with twigs or sticks as their mighty swords, whacking anything in sight. They were the warriors of the century, and at the beginning of whatever mission they had dreamt up that day, one of them would shout the familiar phrase at the top of their lungs before the two ran off to save the day. They had received several strange looks from passersby over the years, as well as a few whippings after accidentally whacking Mistress Collin, the blacksmith's wife, with their "swords". She had threatened to get one of her husband's fire-hot tools after them the next time it happened. Both of them had squealed and run away, avoiding that part of the town for at least a week.

Raiden could hear the smile in Rayla's voice when she broke through his thoughts again.

"We were certainly lost in our own world," she whispered.

Raiden couldn't help but wonder what had happened to his friend that had made her give up on her dream of becoming a knight. Until recently, she had been set on striving for the very best. Now, she was content to stay a simple Maith guard. Did she lose faith in herself?

Or worse, did she feel obligated to remain a guard as her way of honoring Finn? Was she worried that if she passed by the position to pursue knighthood, she would disappoint their dead friend?

Raiden felt a sudden ache in his heart as he considered the amount of pain his friend must still be in, despite the months that had gone by.

Before he could stop himself, he leaned back to whisper in her ear once more.

"Are you okay?"

"What do you mean?" Rayla replied. Her tone was light and obviously guarded.

Raiden wanted nothing more than to turn and look her in the eyes, but he couldn't. He had to keep a watchful eye on the horizon.

"I know you still hurt," he said gently. "From what happened in the spring. From losing Finn. But you bottle it up. I'm asking, as your closest friend and as your family, if you are going to be okay."

The silence that stretched on for seconds was painful. Raiden waited, his heart pounding. As close as they were, they rarely discussed such deep topics. Not because they didn't trust each other, but because Raiden didn't want to burden Rayla with any more problems than she already had, and she was so used to doing things on her own that she naturally kept her struggles hidden deep down inside.

When Rayla finally answered, the brokenness in her voice brought tears to Raiden's eyes.

"I ... I don't know," she choked. "I don't know if I'll ever be okay." Her voice was thick with emotion and pain.

Raiden's heart sank.

Desperate to show Rayla that she wasn't alone, Raiden reached his right hand behind him, grasping until he found Rayla's left hand. He squeezed tightly and then felt her body start shaking as she cried silently.

Comforted by each other's touch, they held that position until the sun rose.

chapter 15
Raiden

Walking in the front was beginning to test Raiden's patience.

Sir Macarius, having run out of songs to hum, was now repeating the tunes, only this time, he was singing. His voice was surprisingly good, Raiden had come to realize. Still, after a couple of hours, Raiden wished his former master would close his mouth.

Carrow didn't help matters. He would remain silent for an hour at most before turning to ask Raiden, who had been inconveniently stuck between the two older men, if he'd studied a certain historical scroll in his training with Macarius. Each time, Raiden calmly reminded the scholar that he was an archer, not a bookworm. This would send Carrow on a long explanation about how the scrolls of the past were something that everyone, not just scholars, should read.

"It increases knowledge and improves the mind," he would say two or three times within the day.

Aside from the constant noise, Raiden didn't feel like his usual self. He couldn't shake the stress of choosing an assignment now that his training had been completed. He would have to officially announce his decision shortly after they returned home, and Raiden still wasn't sure what he wanted for his future. On the one hand, he couldn't fathom choosing an assignment that would take him away from Rayla and his family. He had never talked about such a possibility with any of them, but surely they had to know it was an option. Raiden had certainly known that it was a possibility for Rayla to leave him behind and choose an assignment elsewhere.

He remembered the feeling of dread he had experienced before his friend and announced she would remain in Maith. Was Rayla feeling that same dread now, worrying if Raiden would leave?

But as difficult as it would be to leave his friends and family, there was a hesitation to choose to remain in Maith that was stuck in the back of Raiden's mind. He didn't want to make the wrong decision and be stuck in a place he didn't want to be.

To Raiden's right, Macarius suddenly stopped singing which improved Raiden's mood slightly.

"Not the best weather today, is it?" the bowmaster said casually as he glanced up at the sky. Raiden copied the action. Sir Macarius was right. There were dark clouds covering the sun, giving the day a dreary feel. Although it hadn't rained yet, it was obviously coming. Raiden reached back to check that his cloak was still securely covering his bow. He didn't want the weapon to get wet and warped.

The cold wind was blowing toward their faces, and Raiden became aware for the first time that day that he was cold again. He shivered. Up until now, he felt as if his health had been on the mend, but if it rained today, Raiden knew he would suffer another spell of fevers and coughing

"It might have been smart to pack a thicker cloak to keep the water out," Macarius admitted, looking at Raiden. "I told you I had forgotten something."

Raiden didn't feel like engaging in the conversation, but he decided to humor his mentor. The last thing he wanted was to have to answer Macarius's questions about what was going through his mind at the moment.

"You're the experienced one," Raiden retorted.

"Yes, well, I'm also the old one. We old men don't have the sharp minds we used to."

"Speak for yourself," Carrow piped in, returning from the other side of his horse. He was holding a thick cloak. In a show of pride, he draped the thick garment over his shoulders. "Some of us still have it together."

Macarius and Carrow shared a laugh.

Raiden kept his eyes forward, watching the stream that he and Macarius had pointed out on their map grow closer. There was no reason to laugh right now. They had a serious mission in front of them. It was nothing to take lightly. He found it easy to ignore everything around him, staring forward, when he kept those things in mind.

"How is life at the castle?" Macarius asked the guard to his right.

"Normal, sir," the guard replied. "But there is talk of something *mysterious* going on. It keeps Carrow and my Lord Hightower locked away all hours of the night," the man added in a whisper.

The guards, Raiden knew, had been briefed of the situation before the group had set out. They only knew what was necessary, of course; that Rayla had a unique gift and would need protection at all times, and that Kuvira had plans to harm her and overthrow Maith.

"You are correct," Raiden heard his master tell the guard. As silence fell over the group, Raiden became aware of a movement to his right. Macarius had inched his way closer to Raiden.

"What's on your mind?" he whispered to the boy. Raiden only shook his head.

When Macarius didn't move away, Raiden finally looked in the man's direction. Macarius's face was thick with confusion and a hint of concern.

"Raiden, if something–"

"I'm okay," Raiden lied smoothly. "I just think you were right about that doctor. I'm feeling a little out of it today."

The distraction was believable, and it would feed Macarius's ego to hear that he was right. It should cover the truth fairly well.

Macarius frowned.

"Are you still feverish?" As he spoke, he moved to raise a hand to Raiden's forehead. Raiden dodged the motion smoothly, gently pushing Macarius's arm away.

"No, my temperature is fine," Raiden told him bluntly. "I'm just exhausted, that's all."

Again, Macarius frowned. Raiden ignored the man's questioning looks, hoping he would take the subtle hint.

Eventually, the bowmaster moved back to his original position. Raiden kept his eyes on the distance. He squinted. There was something on the horizon. As they drew closer, he realized it was the hills that he'd noticed on the map.

Raiden took a moment to enjoy the new scene. He'd grown tired of the flat field after only a day of the sight.

From his peripheral vision, Raiden noticed that Sir Macarius had casually made his way closer to Raiden.

"Raiden," the man said under his breath so that only the two of them could hear. "I know you're distracted, and clearly you're agitated with me as well."

Sir Macarius paused as if seeking a response from Raiden. At first, Raiden planned to remain silent, but a small edge of guilt began to worm its way into his mind. Truly, there was no reason for him to be upset with Macarius.

"I'm sorry … " he whispered, lowering his head. "I'm not agitated with you. Not really. It's just this mission … It's so–"

"Dangerous," Sir Macarius finished. "I know. And I keep forgetting that while I might be used to this part of being a bowmaster – the planning and the risk – you are not. I'm sorry to have put all of this on your shoulders."

Raiden shook his head. "I'm glad you included me," he assured his master. "If I was still back home, I would be going crazy with worry."

Sir Macarius seemed to be relieved by his answer, and Raiden was glad he could reassure the man.

"How are you honestly feeling?" Macarius pressed gently. "If you feel that continuing on this journey would be detrimental to your health–"

"It won't," Raiden promised him. "I'm just having a particularly bad time with this weather. And I'm sure the oncoming rain won't help."

Sir Macarius seemed to consider this. Then, without speaking, he removed his cloak and handed it to Raiden. When Raiden protested, Macarius held up a hand.

"It won't do much, but wearing two cloaks will keep you a little warmer than just one will," he said. "And I'll be fine. I'm tough."

Sir Macarius winked before moving away from Raiden. Still feeling somewhat guilty, Raiden pulled the second cloak over his shoulders.

Soon they arrived at the river. It looked fairly shallow. Shallow enough for the horses to walk through easily and for Kuvira's wagon to be carried between four men on horseback while Kuvira rode behind a guard, still bound.

"We've been walking for over half the day," Macarius thought aloud. "I think it would be alright to ride for a couple of hours."

To Raiden's left, he heard a snorting sound. He turned to look at Carrow, who was rolling his eyes.

"Please," the scholar said, unamused. "You just don't want to have to walk across the stream and get your boots wet."

"Perhaps," Macarius admitted, mounting his horse as he spoke. "But if you'd like to do so, then by all means, be my guest."

Raiden glanced back and forth between the two men as they regarded each other, Macarius with amusement and Carrow with annoyance.

"Well if you get to be nice and dry, why shouldn't I?" Carrow finally conceded, mounting his own horse.

The rest of the group mounted their horses and continued across the stream, one row at a time. Once they'd reached the other side, Raiden looked to Macarius, making sure the man had made no move to dismount before Raiden relaxed in his own saddle.

They rode in silence before the first drizzle of the day began to fall. Raiden shivered deeply. Between the rain and the wind, it was set to be a miserable rest of the day. Suddenly his previous guilt for having taken Sir Macarius's cloak turned to deep gratitude for the extra warmth.

The silence caused Raiden's mind to wander. It occurred to him that his life was about to change in a major way. For years, he had done the same thing. He'd followed Macarius in his footsteps, learning everything he could from the man. He'd practiced his skills with a bow as much as possible. He had been a student. Now, he was no longer training to be an archer. He was an archer. And not just any archer. A bowmaster.

The idea of being sent out on his own with no guidance from Macarius seemed both terrifying and unreal. In just a short time, he wouldn't be able to ask Macarius a question when he was stuck or confused. He would have to figure things out for himself.

It was as if, for eighteen years, he'd been told to follow his dreams and shoot for the highest possible goals, ignoring any obstacles that got in his way. And now, his world was beginning to come crashing down under the crushing blow of reality. He had lost a friend. He had experienced true fear. He'd been heartbroken.

If this was what all of life was like, Raiden thought sourly, it was ugly and disgusting. And he didn't like it.

chapter 16
Rayla

Rayla felt much better with the distant hills of Riraveth well in sight. It had now been a full day since they had crossed the stream and endured the misery of the rain. It had only taken half an hour for the rain to go from a drizzle to a drenching downpour. There had been thunder and lightning as well, which had spooked the horses enough that the group had stopped early the night before to tie the beasts down and settle them as best they could. Then they had waited the storm out before deciding that there would be no dry spots for sleep. They had been forced to lay their bedrolls in the mud, then use the cleanest puddles available the next morning to clean their equipment.

Today, they had ridden at the usual pace. At one point, Rayla had taken to watching Kuvira as he was jostled around in the bumpy wagon. The sight gave her more pleasure than she cared to admit, and this time, when Kuvira met her gaze, she gave him a nasty sneer, ignoring the pounding of her heart.

As the day had slowly dragged on, the hills had grown larger and larger. Now, even a small hint of Riraveth's castle walls could be seen.

Despite the cold weather, Rayla had wanted to ride through the night. She was desperate to reach Castle Riraveth as soon as possible. When she'd voiced this to Luca, he simply replied that both the men and the horses needed rest, especially after so much labor in the cold wind. It didn't help, the swordmaster had pointed out, that some of their cloaks were still soaked from the previous night's rain.

Rayla had to admit, she was tired. After nearly a full day of walking, followed by today's even pace of walking and riding, her feet and back ached. Dóchas, too, kept her head drooped as the group began to set up camp.

"I'm sorry, girl," Rayla whispered to the mare. "Let's find a good spot for the night."

Rayla pulled on Dóchas's lead, taking them to one side of the already-forming circular camp. She considered using the wooden peg to tie Dóchas up for the night, but decided to let the horse graze for a while.

Rayla reached into her saddle pack, retrieving one of the two canteens of water that she had refilled at the stream the previous day.

"Here," Rayla said, pooling some of the water into her palm before holding it up to Dóchas. The young horse drank gratefully until Rayla eventually stopped refilling her hand.

Satisfied that Dóchas had gotten a decent amount, she took a single swig of the liquid herself before stoppering the top and repacking the canteen. Sighing, she retrieved her bedroll and began to lay it along the ground beside Dóchas.

"I thought Sapphire might be over here with you," a voice said from behind Rayla. She turned to see Nel looking down at her. She stood, brushing the dirt from her knees.

"I think she went to find her brother before she and Luca started her training for the night," Rayla replied. It occurred to Rayla that Nel was quite tall. Taller than Raiden. She had to crane her neck up slightly to look him in the eyes.

"She asked me earlier if I had ever thrown knives," Nel explained, bending to tie his horse up beside Dóchas. It seemed that he had picked his spot for the night.

"Have you?" Rayla asked curiously.

"Yes," Nel replied. "I have a very special throwing knife that I keep on me at all times. I've never used it, though."

"I thought you said you had thrown knives?"

Nel laughed softly.

"I have. I don't use this one because my father gave it to me the day before I started my guard duty. He told me to try not to use it if I could help it. He didn't want any damage brought to it. Apparently it's been in the family for a long time."

Rayla dropped her eyes, hesitating.

"That must be nice," she said slowly.

"What?"

"Having something of your father's to remind you of him when he's gone."

Nel considered the statement.

"It is," he said. "I've never really thought of it that way, though. I just assumed it was his way of congratulating me on my position. You know, like, 'You're a man now, have this really old and special knife.'"

Rayla didn't bother to force a smile. It would just look fake.

"That's because he's still alive."

She looked up to see confusion in Nel's eyes.

"You don't think of the knife as something to remember your father by because you don't need to. He's still alive. When he's gone, though, you'll see the knife and think of him. Then you'll understand."

Nel stared deeply at Rayla until she dropped her gaze again, afraid that she had shared too much.

"You sound like you know how that feels," Nel said. His tone was questioning, and to Rayla's surprise, full of compassion.

She turned to look at Dóchas, who had remained rooted to her spot with the company of Nel's horse.

"I never knew my parents," she explained quietly. "Or even where I'm from. So for the longest time, I didn't understand the idea of having a prized possession like a family heirloom. The closest thing I had to that was my sword, and it wasn't from my father. Luca gave it to me. But it was mine. It was something."

Rayla paused, squeezing her eyes shut.

"But now I get it," she continued. Her voice was wavering. "Every time I look at Dóchas, I'm reminded of Finn. And I love Dóchas. But part of why she is so special to me is because she belonged to Finn first. It's like … " Rayla's voice trailed off.

"You're still connected to him," Nel finished, and Rayla looked up in surprise.

"Yes," she said. "Exactly like that."

Nel pursed his lips.

"I'm sorry that you had to go through all that," he said. "They wouldn't let me go as part of the scout party because I was one of the younger and less experienced members of the guard. But you're younger and even less experienced than I am, and you had to go through all that pain. It made you grow up too much too fast."

Rayla let a small huff of breath out, shaking her head.

"Believe me, I was grown up way before that," she said matter-of-factly.

Nel didn't respond for some time. Finally he cleared his throat.

"So, I guess I'll have to wait until tomorrow to show Sapphire my knife," he said.

Rayla gave Nel a small smile.

"That or you'll have to find Raiden."

As she said the words, it occurred to Rayla that she hadn't spoken to Raiden since the day before, when they'd had the last watch together. And that hadn't been the most pleasant of conversations. Rayla hated to talk about her feelings, and Raiden knew that.

But something about the next morning had been different. Rather than feeling awkward and closed-up like she usually did, Rayla felt for once in her life she was getting the help she needed. Raiden didn't care about the excuses she used to justify that she bottled things inside her, she realized. He only wanted to help. And after over ten years of friendship, Rayla felt he deserved for her to trust and confide in him.

Quickly, she looked around, making sure there was no work to be done. Apparently there would be no fire tonight. Rayla sighed. That meant cold rations. Still, it also meant fewer chores.

Satisfied that there was nothing that needed to be done in terms of setting up the camp, she decided to face her discomfort and talk to Raiden.

She glanced around, spotting the dark-haired boy across the camp. To Rayla's disgust, she saw that she would have to walk past Kuvira to reach Raiden. Her eyes lingered on Kuvira, bound in his wagon and somehow still holding his head pridefully high. She grit her teeth together.

"I'll be back," she told Nel.

Squaring her shoulders, she walked across the camp. The closer she drew to Kuvira, the more her heart raced. But this time it wasn't just out of fear. She felt angry at him. Angry for his control over her in the spring, and even still now. Angry for his role in everything, and the way he had unsettled her entire life. Angry at the gaping hole that Finn's death had left in her heart. She felt a cord of tension in her chest, tightening to the point of becoming unbearable.

When she reached Kuvira, she paused directly in front of the man, keeping her body straight. She glanced down at him, her limbs trembling in rage.

Four guards were holding each of Kuvira's ropes. Kuvira himself was kneeling, calmly making his own bedroll. Why Lord Hightower had allowed Kuvira to have such comfort, Rayla didn't know. He could sleep on the wet ground and fall ill for all she cared.

"Can I help you?" Kuvira's gravelly voice said calmly. He was still concentrating on his bedroll, but it was clear that he had been talking to Rayla.

The girl drew her eyebrows together, balling her fists at her side in an attempt to stay calm.

"What game are you playing?" she asked before her voice could fail her.

Kuvira stopped messing with his blanket and looked up at her. His face was masked with innocence and surprise. It made Rayla's blood boil. Kuvira was anything but innocent.

"Whatever do you mean?" he asked.

A pulse of anger coursed through Rayla's body.

"You're too calm and cooperative. You're plotting something."

Kuvira smiled wickedly, and the hairs on Rayla's arms pricked up.

"What else can I do but cooperate?" The man asked with a menacing edge to his voice. Still, he had evaded Rayla's unspoken question.

Rayla kept a straight face, wanting to appear as though she didn't care about what he said. Inside, though, she felt her curiosity peak, refusing to let her leave the man without some form of answer. She carefully considered his dark hair and obsidian eyes. His muscular, scarred body seemed both relaxed and ready to attack when needed.

Suddenly, Rayla felt uncomfortable. As if she might be walking into a trap.

Still, she shrugged.

"I suppose you won't tell me what your plan is?" she asked. "I know you have one, *Kuvira*."

She watched as Kuvira's lips turned up at the corners. He shook his head.

As Rayla moved to walk away, resigning to get her answers later, Kuvira spoke again.

"I could tell you my long-term plan," he offered. "If you'd like?"

Rayla froze. Everything inside of her screamed "It's a TRAP!" She should keep walking and ignore his taunts, but she was curious as to what Kuvira would say if she accepted his invitation.

Plastering a look of boredom on her face, she turned and approached Kuvira, who was still kneeling beside his bedroll. She glanced once at the four guards, who didn't seem to care what she was doing. Their job was to make sure Kuvira didn't escape, and nothing else.

Despite being allowed to approach Kuvira, Rayla was careful to keep plenty of distance between the two of them in case Kuvira tried to attack her.

Kuvira, however, simply smiled. "I knew you couldn't resist," he said coolly.

Unsure of what to say, she motioned for him to continue.

"It's simple, really," the man said, shrugging. "I want to see you hurt, Rayla. Because of what you did to my men in the forest."

Rayla felt her jaw drop in indignation. What *she* had done in the forest? Everything in those woods had been *Kuvira's* fault! But Kuvira was still speaking.

"Because of how you tried to make me question myself in the cellar," he spat. "Nice try, by the way, but I'm much too experienced to let little girls get in my head. And because you have refused my generous offer to become one of the most valuable members amongst my ranks. And finally, because you were *most* uncooperative when I asked you for your help in the spring. I want to see you hurt."

Rayla swallowed thickly, her body tensing more than it already was at his words. *See me hurt?* She thought in disbelief. *You've already hurt me plenty.*

"You want to know my goal?" Kurvira sneered. "It is this; to kill everyone you love, until you are the only one left. I will kill them slowly, one by one. And I will give you a front row seat to watch. I will take the young, blonde one first and skin her alive."

Rayla took a step back in shock, feeling her blood roar in her ears. Bile rose in her throat.

"I will finally get to see Hightower come crashing down. And I will drive my sword through his heart."

Her vision went red.

"I will take that inadequate man with the sword, Luca, and I will put a bag over his head and hold him underwater until he stops thrashing, coughing, or breathing."

She shook her head, squeezing her eyes shut. Her breath came in vicious gasps as she tried to contemplate how so much hate could manifest itself in a single man. How much hate was manifesting itself in her *now*.

"And finally, that boy with the bow. I will tie him up, just like I tied you up. And I will give him a new, deep cut every minute. I will make it deep enough so that his screams fill the air. And I will let you watch as his blood pools around him and his eyes slowly glass over as he dies, in pain and wanting you to help him. But you won't."

Whether intentional or not, whether he knew what he was saying or it was pure coincidence, Kuvira spoke the one phrase, the one fear, that had been taunting her since the moment Finn had died in the woods.

"You won't help because you can't."

Inside of Rayla, somewhere deep down, she felt a snap. Before a reasonable thought could even cross her mind, her hands were gripping Kuvira's forearms with a force so strong she felt his bones snap beneath her fingers. Dimly, she was aware of the guards reaching to pull her off, but the world around her seemed to grow darker, and the men stumbled away in fear.

Rayla didn't pull Kuvira closer. She didn't move her hands to his neck to snap it like she wanted to. She didn't even unsheathe her sword. Instead, she looked into his eyes, recalling every little thing she hated the man for.

He had nearly killed Raiden. Rayla remembered the fear in her heart when she had found her friend, bloody and unconscious, on the floor of his burning cabin. Kuvira had done that.

A strange, sickening pulse coursed through her body.

He had whipped her, leaving unhealing scars on her back and even in her mind.

Another pulse.

He had been the cause of Finn's death. Rayla saw Finn's smile, his laughing face as he made a joke. As she stared into Kuvira's black eyes, Rayla recalled the still form of Finn, lying on the ground in the forest, with an arrow sticking out of his chest. She remembered the way Kuvira had laughed at her pain. Rayla felt her body tremble with uncontrollable rage as she finally leaned forward, growling through her clenched teeth.

"I hate you," she hissed.

Rayla didn't think. She simply opened her mouth as a bloodchilling cry escaped her lips. The pulses that had been going through her quickened until they became one, sheer force of power flowing out of her. Hatred seemed to seep out from within her. Kuvira's dark eyes slowly changed from arrogance, to shock, to fear, and finally, to nothing.

It was as if a switch had been flipped inside Rayla. In an instant, the power she had been feeling disappeared. Every rational thought that had been unreachable a moment earlier suddenly returned to her. She stumbled away, terrified and confused. She looked at her hands.

A strange, black glow was slowly fading away.

She cautiously approached the limp form of Kuvira. His four guards had turned and ran at some point. They were now standing at a distance, eyeing her with wide, fear-filled eyes. Kuvira lay unmoving. Rayla took one cautious step at a time, peering at the man. She waited several seconds, staring at his unmoving chest, before she allowed herself to believe it.

He was dead.

She glanced around her slowly. Every guard had their weapons drawn, pointing them at her. Macarius and Luca hadn't drawn their weapons, but they were staring at her in horror.

Finally, Rayla's eyes found Raiden and Sapphire. The young girl was clinging to her brother's arm in fear.

As Rayla looked at them, Raiden moved an arm out to shield Sapphire. To protect the girl. From her.

chapter 17
Rayla

She'd been given the night off from watch duty. Luca had said she needed rest, but Rayla knew the action wasn't out of generosity. They simply didn't trust her.

Nobody had approached her, aside from Luca and Raiden. They had been the only two who had even looked at her, asking if she was alright, although they kept an obvious distance. Carrow had moved to approach her as well, but as she watched him, several guards had come to ask him for help in deciding what to do with Kuvira's body. Rayla could see in the scholar's eyes that he was glad to have a distraction.

Luca had placed his bedroll to Rayla's right. Raiden had lain to her left. He had quietly and strategically placed Sapphire between himself and Macarius. The boy hadn't made a fuss about the issue, but Rayla had noticed. Even Raiden, her closest friend and the only family she had, didn't trust her. After all that had happened in the last several months between her, Raiden, and Sapphire, the boy thought Rayla might hurt his younger sister. It made Rayla want to cry, but she fought to hide how much it hurt her.

Rayla had chosen to focus on the reactions of her friends in an attempt to ignore the growing horror in her own mind. She had killed him. And it hadn't been like the battle in the woods. No, in that instance she had been defending herself. This time she had killed an unarmed man out of pure hatred. It didn't matter that the man had been Kuvira. She had still used her own two hands to …

She wasn't even exactly sure what she had done to him.

Rayla had said nothing since the incident, not even when Luca and Raiden had asked if she was alright. She had simply walked away, trembling.

She'd gone outside of the camp to throw up. Nobody had come to check on her.

Nobody except, to Rayla's surprise, Dóchas. While the other horses had become extremely skittish after Rayla's loss of control, her display of dark, deadly power, Dóchas had done nothing more than flick her tail. The young mare had followed her to the edge of the camp, bumping the girl with her muzzle when Rayla had sat still for too long.

Now, it was several hours into the night. Dóchas stood a short distance away, tied to her peg. Several men snored throughout the camp. There were still two guards kept watch in the middle of the circle, only this time, Rayla noticed, one of the men had been carefully placed to face directly toward her.

Despite the late hour and the silence of the field, Rayla wasn't asleep. There would be no sleep for her tonight, she knew. All she could do was lie still and focus on her breathing.

She wanted to ask Carrow about what had happened. He was the only one who had known what to do when she'd accidentally discovered her gift months ago. He had even been able to train her on how to use and control them. Surely he would have heard something about this dark glow, or the terrible cry that had escaped from within her. But the look of terror that had been on the scholar's face after the awful moment returned to Rayla's mind and made her dismiss her curiosity. If Carrow had known what it was that Rayla had done, he would have tried to help her calm down. It was clear that Carrow was just as confused and terrified as she was.

It was strange, Rayla thought. She could remember what she had done, but she couldn't remember deciding to do it. It was as if she had been watching herself from afar. And yet, as she had felt the power course through her, she had known exactly what she was doing.

Even more strange was the fact that the thought of killing Kuvira at that moment had never crossed her mind. She had never consciously thought about killing him for what he had said. It was as if something had pushed her into action. And from there, she had somehow known what to do.

Despite whatever had happened, there was one thing that Rayla knew for sure. Nobody would be able to help her with this. Not Carrow and all of his books. Not Luca and all of his experience. Not Sapphire and her comfort. Not even Raiden and his capacity to understand how Rayla was feeling in most situations.

She herself had no idea how to stop it from happening again. The thought of hurting someone she cared for by accident crossed her mind for the first time, and that was enough to jolt her into action.

With a nauseating feeling in the bottom of her stomach, Rayla rose quietly. At the center of the camp, she could hear the two watch guards muttering to each other while watching her. Still, they had done nothing to stop her yet. Rayla calmly gathered her bedroll and blanket and moved toward Dóchas. She bent down, freeing the mare from her peg, which Rayla stored in her saddle pack.

Rayla leaned in toward Dóchas's ear. Behind her, she could hear the guards stirring, undoubtedly coming to stop her.

"I know you're tired, girl," Rayla whispered quickly. "But I need just one more burst of energy from you. Can you do that for me?"

As Rayla tightened Dóchas's girth strap, she caught a twinkle in the mare's eye. Before she could second-guess herself, Rayla mounted.

"Stop!" Several men had begun to call out to her. Rayla ignored them. One man, broader than the rest, pushed forward.

"Rayla, stop!" Luca called. She could tell by his voice that the man had never been asleep. He hadn't trusted her enough to sleep. The thought only added to Rayla's pain.

"Rayla," Luca tried again. There was a hint of desperation in his voice. "Dismount. Now."

As Luca approached, Rayla tapped her right foot to Dóchas's side and the mare pranced a few paces away from Luca. Rayla felt tears sting her eyes. She didn't bother to hide them. It would be too hard. At this point, she had too much pain to bury.

In Luca's face, Rayla could see pain as well. She could hear the fear and concern in his voice as he attempted once more to get her to dismount.

"Rayla, please," he begged. "Don't do something you will regret. Just stop."

She wanted to stop. She wanted to dismount. But she knew that if she stayed she would only cause more hardships. They couldn't trust her. She was a hazard. A danger. A threat to their safety.

"I-I'm sorry," she said quietly, hearing her own voice break. "I ruined the mission. We have no leverage to protect ourselves with. You should all go home, where it's safe."

"Rayla," Luca said in a louder voice, his desperation clear now.

Rayla felt hot tears flowing freely down her face now. She had ruined any and all relationships she had ever had. Nobody would ever trust her again. How could they?

"Rayla!" A painfully familiar voice cried in horror. Raiden burst from the back of the group, his eyes wide in shock. "What are you doing? Get down, now!"

Rayla's breaths were coming in rapid, shaky gasps now.

"I'm so sorry," she whispered. Before Luca, Raiden, or anybody else could stop her, she kicked Dóchas's sides. The mare bolted into action, sending up a cloud of dust behind them. The cold air whipped at her face, stinging her eyes. Her long hair flew behind her as she dropped her head to Dóchas's neck, sobbing. She turned one last time to look at the camp behind her, where her friends all stood, watching.

Nobody was following her.

chapter 18
Raiden

Fury clouded both his face and his mind, diminishing any proper thughts that might have helped to filter his tone of voice. Raiden didn't care.

"Let her go?" he and Luca roared at the same time. Raiden had never been so furious in his life. Carrow stood in front of both men with his arms crossed, unyielding.

"Yes," the scholar said calmly, although it was obvious that he was struggling to keep his own temper in check. "Let. Her. Go."

"You listen well, Carrow," Luca demanded in a dangerously low voice. Carrow looked small next to Luca's muscular fame, but Raiden had no doubt that the scholar could likely hold his own in a fight if it came to that.

"If you think," Luca continued, "for one *second* that I am going to let my best student ride off, alone, into Riraveth province because she is scared and confused, then you are *sorely* mistaken."

Carrow stared back at Luca, unfazed. For a moment, Raiden thought he could see a glimpse of sympathy in the scholar's face. Carrow may not have trained Rayla for as long as Luca had, but the man had certainly spent a great deal of time and care on Rayla and her safety.

"And if you think," Carrow replied evenly, "that I don't care about Rayla's well being just as much as you do, then *you* are mistaken. But she is dangerous. She doesn't know how to control this new power. And until I can figure out what it is that she has done, and find a way to help her, she needs to be away from people. She could hurt–"

"This is not one of your fairy tales, Carrow!" Luca exclaimed. "This is real life! We do not have time for you to run back to your precious library and stick your nose in a dusty book!"

"And you think you will be able to offer her any answers?" Carrow retorted, clearly too angry to keep his temper in check now. "If she thought any of us could actually help her right now, she would have stopped when you had asked her too, rather than riding off into the night!"

"At least I moved to stop her!" Luca bellowed.

"Luca, I understand your worry–"

"I don't think you do!"

"But we need to discuss what to do next! Now that we no longer have Kuvira as proof to Lord Dunmann or protection against Tenabris, we need to return home–"

Raiden was fed up with the useless talk. Angrily, he grabbed Sapphire's hand and marched over to a dark corner, away from the crowd. He made his way to the two horses that he and Sapphire had been given. Glancing at his sister, he drew a breath to give her orders to pack her things, but the girl was already moving to do so. They quietly packed their bedrolls and blankets onto their horses. As they bent to tighten the animals' girth straps, Raiden heard his sister whisper in a low voice.

"Are we doing what I think we're doing?" she asked.

Raiden nodded. "We're going after her."

"Good," was all the girl said in reply.

Together, the two mounted their horses. Raiden glanced to his left, toward the camp. The crowd hadn't seemed to notice his and Sapphire's absence. Luca and Carrow's angry voices could still be heard, bantering back and forth. Several other voices were also joining in the argument. Raiden set his jaw, taking the lead as he moved his horse forward a few paces.

"Are you ready?" he asked Sapphire, turning to look at the girl. She nodded, determination strong on her face.

Raiden felt a surge of pride toward her. She was always ready to do the right thing. Anytime he needed her help, she never asked questions. She simply followed him in trust and loyalty.

Raiden kicked at his horse's sides as he turned back around, ready to take off in a full gallop. Instead, he gasped, bringing his horse to a sudden stop. Behind him, Sapphire did the same.

"And just where do you think you are sneaking off to?"

Raiden felt both shame and anger battling inside of him. He wanted nothing more than to get out of the political circle and take action. But the idea of disappointing the man before him was disheartening enough to make Raiden think twice.

"Let us go," Raiden tried in a reasonable tone. "We can bring her back."

Macarius shook his head. The bowmaster crossed his arms and set his stance in a way that told Raiden they would not be getting past him, even on horseback.

"She trusts us the most," Raiden tried again. Sir Macarius didn't budge.

"You are acting on impulse, Raiden," the bowmaster warned. "That's a very dangerous thing and you know it."

"She's alone!" Raiden retorted in desperation. "She is alone and she's scared, sir! She could get hurt!"

"Yes, she is alone," Macarius said sadly, conceding the point. "But we are going to find her."

"How? By standing in a circle and saying unkind things to each other?" Raiden demanded, gesturing angrily to the crowd now directly to their left. Macarius, however, shook his head slowly, frowning.

"You can't go running off to save her. Not right now."

"Why not?" Raiden demanded angrily.

"Because she is dangerous. Right now, if any of us caught her when she didn't want to be caught, there's no telling what she may accidentally do in her panic."

Raiden felt his pulse quicken. His mind inevitably went back to months ago, when Rayla had been kidnapped in the woods. He hadn't known if she was dead or alive. And now, with this new power she seemed to have unleashed, there was no telling what could go wrong. She needed him.

Raiden let his eyes wander behind Macarius, to the open field where Rayla had disappeared. He looked back to his master, seeing the warning in the man's eyes. Then, Raiden considered the girl behind him.

If it were not for Sapphire, Raiden might try to make a run for it. He might have ignored his master and gone after Rayla. But to do so with his sister following his every move would mean putting her in danger, if what Macarius said was right. Raiden could handle risking his own life, but not Sapphire's.

Defeated, Raiden dismounted. He retrieved the peg from his saddle pack once more and tied his horse up. Behind him, he could hear Sapphire do the same.

"Saph," he said in a low voice. "Go lay your bedroll back out."

"But I–" the girl argued, but Raiden cut her off.

"Sapphire," he begged, turning to give his sister a rare, pained expression. "Please."

Sapphire looked to her brother for several seconds before finally nodding and leaving the small group. Satisfied that she was out of earshot, Raiden turned back to Macarius, who was still standing with his arms crossed.

There was silence between the two archers for several minutes. Raiden studied his former master's face. There was determination there, he saw. There had been no way that Macarius was going to let them ride off. But there was also, Raiden noticed, a hint of pain and concern.

Shame finally beat down the anger inside of Raiden. Of course, Macarius had only been trying to make Raiden see the reality of the situation. Riding after Rayla when she was in such a chaotic state could have cost him his life. Macarius had only been trying to protect him.

Raiden lowered his gaze to the ground.

A comforting hand fell on Raiden's shoulder, drawing the boy's eyes back up. This time, Macarius's expression was completely gentle.

"I *promise*, Raiden," the bowmaster said softly. "We *will* look for her until we find her. Just not right now. Not when she is still dangerous. She needs time to calm herself down."

"The last time she disappeared, Kuvira and his men kidnapped her," Raiden said, allowing his fear and worry to show. He wanted Macarius to understand why he had acted so impulsively.

"I know," Macarius said calmly.

"They whipped her and beat her," Raiden continued, his voice shaking. "And now, if it's true that Riraveth has a horrible crime record and she's out there alone–"

"We will find her, Raiden," Macarius promised.

Raiden believed his master. Still, he glanced back in the direction of Luca and Carrow.

"But, Carrow–" the boy began.

Macarius squeezed his shoulder, cutting him off.

"Don't underestimate Carrow's care for the girl," Macarius said softly. "He does want to protect Rayla. But you have to remember that Carrow's mind works differently than most. He thinks in practical terms rather than with his emotions. Yes, he is worried for Rayla. But at the moment, he is also worried about the danger she could cause if she cannot control … whatever it is that she has done."

Raiden nodded. Sir Macarius was right, he knew. Still, the response didn't make him feel much better.

"Besides," Macarius added in a stronger tone. "This is my mission, not Carrow's."

Raiden looked into the eyes of his mentor and saw resolution there.

"And I say we will not return until we've found her."

chapter 19
Raiden

It wasn't like the last time they had lost Rayla. That was for sure.

Raiden could vividly remember that day in the woods when Sapphire had asked in a shaky voice where Rayla had gone, and Lord Hightower called for an immediate search. Their simple scouting party had quickly transformed into a search and rescue where top priority had been retrieving Rayla from the clutches of Kuvira and his men.

This had been before they had known what, or rather whom, they were up against. At that time, Lord Hightower and the others had thought of Rayla's enemies as nothing more than a cult. In fact, that had been what they had all thought. But when Rayla had escaped and returned to their camp, she'd been able to reveal Kuvira's identity.

Still, the fact remained that Lord Hightower had gone after Rayla in a heartbeat.

This time was different by all accounts. Rather than being captured, Rayla had willingly run off. And instead of scrambling to rescue her from danger, the group seemed rather careless about what happened to the girl.

Part of Raiden wondered if things would be different if Lord Hightower had accompanied them. The lord had called for the men to join him in rescuing Rayla the first time. Perhaps he would have done so now as well. But the thought was a pointless one, Raiden knew. Lord Hightower was not here. He would have to trust Macarius's promise.

But no matter how much he tried to ignore it, the atmosphere of the group made Raiden feel as if finding Rayla was the last thing on their agenda.

As soon as Rayla had ridden off, the group had been thrown into chaos as every man felt a need to voice his own opinion. The numerous conversations were so loud that Raiden could barely hear his own thoughts. Luca, Raiden, Sapphire, and even a few guards were the leading voices that demanded an immediate search for Rayla. When some of the other guards had disagreed, there had been a series of curse words that had flown around the group, and Raiden had been forced to cover his younger sister's ears, and then later her mouth as she'd begun to repeat the words she had heard.

Eventually, Macarius stepped up. Careful to explain his reasoning for every decision, the bowmaster presented the plan.

They would continue to Castle Riraveth as they had originally discussed. Even without Kuvira as leverage, Macarius still wanted to see what his informant could provide him with, and still had plans to arrest the man. They would also be bringing Kuvira's body with them. Perhaps they could still use it to convince Lord Dunnman to take action. Also, there was nowhere in sight to lay the body, nor did any of the men have the proper tools to dig a grave. And, Macarius had pointed out, they could hardly leave Kuvira's body lying in the open field. At that, Raiden had scoffed. For all he cared, they could do exactly that.

After arriving at the castle, Carrow could request a meeting with Lord Dunnman. They would bring Kuvira's body as proof that they were telling the truth, hoping that Lord Dunnman would recognize a former captain of the guard for his neighboring province now that Kuvira couldn't speak to identify himself. Meanwhile, Macarius would attempt to contact his informant. The rest of the group could spend their time searching for an inn that they could stay in until it was time to return to Maith. They had planned to remain in Riraveth for a week. Now, Macarius had said plainly, they would remain until they found Rayla. In that time, they would send out search parties and request aid from Riraveth's lord.

Under no circumstances, Macarius had said strongly, would they return until they found Rayla.

Despite everything that Macarius had done to help Rayla and ease Raiden's concern, the boy still found himself itching to go after his friend now. Luca, being a seasoned soldier, had seen the logic in Macarius's plan after taking some time to calm himself down. Sapphire, unaware of how to react, had been quiet.

Nel, Rayla's new guard friend, had seemed unhappy with the decision. It was clear that he did not want to wait before searching for Rayla, which had slightly annoyed Raiden. Nel barely knew Rayla, after all. While his support was touching, Raiden saw no reason for the guard to be quite as upset as he pretended to be.

All of this, combined with Raiden's running nose from the previous rain and ongoing cold, led Raiden to expect this day to be long from the start. It didn't help that he hadn't gone back to sleep after the night's events. He'd laid in his bedroll, staring at the stars above and trying to keep himself from shivering.

Now, with his concern about Rayla, exhaustion, and poor health, the morning had been miserable. And the day was only half over.

Walking alongside his horse as the rest of the group was doing, Raiden stared ahead. The silhouette of Castle Riraveth lay in the distance, much closer than the hills to their right. The group would reach the castle within the day, just as Macarius had said.

Raiden glanced to his left. Carrow was walking alongside his horse, staring straight ahead. The expression on the scholar's face was so unconcerned that it caused Raiden's anger to resurface. Since the day he had met Carrow, Raiden had always respected the man. He had clearly seen battles in his time, and the scars proved that he had participated in his share of fighting. And he had been very kind and helpful in teaching Rayla to control her gift.

Now, however, that respect was tainted by Raiden's disappointment. It was difficult to believe that the same scholar who had eagerly taken Rayla in as his personal student had just watched the terrified girl ride away and done nothing about it.

Before he could stop himself, Raiden opened his mouth to speak.

"Rayla deeply trusts you," he said matter-of-factly. Carrow started, turning to the boy in surprise. To Raiden's right, Macarius cleared his throat. Raiden ignored the warning.

"She's never said it," he continued. "But I can tell. She was terrified when she first healed me, after the fire. In fact, she had completely pushed the incident out of her mind because she thought she had been imagining things. But when we finally came to you, and she discovered her gift, all that fear and confusion came back."

Raiden turned to look ahead of him. Tears had begun to fill his eyes, and he didn't want Carrow to see them.

"Rayla never talks about her family because she doesn't remember them. She never wants to discuss her past. But the role that both have played in her life have been *so* important. It makes her who she is. It makes her tough. It makes her emotionally closed off to the world. And it gives her *serious* trust issues."

As the tears gradually went away, Raiden turned to face Carrow again. The scholar was listening intently, his eyes fixed on Raiden's face.

"When you so quickly offered to help her," Raiden explained, "she finally began to trust again. She trusted you to give her all the answers you could. To help her work through her fear. She hates her gift. She doesn't want it. It only reminds her of a family she never knew. And the idea that she is so different, the responsibility she feels like she has with this gift, it is something she still can't work through. But she always trusts you to help her. Even if you don't have the immediate answer. She knows that she can go to you."

There was silence for several minutes. Raiden cleared his throat, his voice suddenly soft. Tears shone in his eyes again, but this time he didn't hide them.

"My point is, Rayla doesn't open up to people easily," Raiden said in a clipped tone. "And after last night, I don't know if she'll ever trust any of us again."

Nobody spoke. Carrow had lowered his gaze to the ground, unsure of what to say. Even Macarius had been silent as Raiden spoke.

Raiden sighed, looking ahead once more. He set his jaw in defiance, wanting Carrow to see his anger.

Raiden thought of his friend, alone. Judging from the direction she had ridden off in, she was somewhere in the province. A province that, from what Raiden had been told, was renowned for high levels of criminal activities. Not that he didn't think Rayla could protect herself. She was undoubtedly very capable of doing that. But if she was ambushed, she may not be stable enough to hold her own. And there was always the chance that she would be outnumbered and would inevitably lose. Especially if she still wasn't thinking straight after what had happened last night.

"I can't even imagine what went through her mind," he said bitterly. "She must have been terrified. She didn't do it on purpose, anyone could see that. You *knew* that. She has no idea what she did or how she did it. And not a single one of us tried to comfort her. Instead, we avoided her. She must have felt more alone than she has in a long time."

Raiden took a shaky breath.

"I … I should have gone to her. I never should have left her alone."

Finally, Raiden turned to Carrow one last time, condemnation clear in his eyes.

"And you never should have let her ride away, alone, thinking that nobody wanted her to stay."

chapter 20

Raiden

They had reached Castle Riraveth two days ago. It was a dirty, grimy place. The smell had hit Raiden almost as soon as the group had ridden through the gates.

He had quickly moved to find Sapphire as they passed through, and rarely left the girl's side now, unless he knew someone of their group was with her. He didn't trust the people here. They all seemed to be studying them, seeing what they could get out of them. It set Raiden's nerves on edge.

On the first day, Carrow had requested a meeting with Lord Dunnman, the lord of Riraveth. Raiden had never seen the man in person, but anyone who let their province become such a horrid place deserved no respect. Lord Hightower would never stand for such a thing, Raiden reasoned. Nevertheless, Carrow had been polite each time he had asked the guards outside the castle to meet with the lord. Each time, he had been denied.

Earlier that morning, the scholar had set out again with a couple Maith guards. They hadn't returned in the last few hours, so Raiden assumed they had finally been successful. It was about time, the boy thought. Somebody needed to get something done.

So far, the only thing the group had accomplished was getting rid of Kuvira's heavy, stinking body. The guards at the gate had immediately took the corpse off their hands, claiming that they would not permit such vulgar sights in their streets. Raiden had been tempted to ask the men if they had looked around lately, but Carrow had spoken before he'd gotten the chance. The scholar had tried his best to explain how important it was that the men let Lord Dunnman see Kuvira's body and tell him that "Carrow of Maith" had brought it. The guards had shrugged Carrow's concern aside.

In the last two days, the rest of the group had been split up between an inn that stood close to the marketplace, and a tavern that was relatively close to the castle and held several spare rooms. Carrow and several other guards had taken the tavern rooms, seeing as how they would be at the castle more than the others. The rest of the group had taken over most of the rooms in the inn. Macarius, Raiden, and Luca had all ended up sharing a room, being the only three to suffer such discomfort. The rest of the guards were split evenly, two to a room. Sapphire was given her own room, across from Raiden's, for privacy reasons.

Macarius had also been absent most of the time since they had arrived. Each day he would sneak off, bringing two guards with him but refusing to tell anybody else where they were going. At night, he would return, clearly disappointed. Raiden hadn't asked if he had been successful in finding his informant. It was obvious that Macarius had not seen the man yet.

Luca and Sapphire spent most of their time practicing in the grassy area just outside of the market square. They had found a good place for Sapphire to practice throwing her knives on the wall of a small, abandoned house. Luca had returned each night to brag on the girl and her improvement. Raiden had been glad, both that Sapphire was getting better and that Luca was distracting the girl from the stress of Rayla's absence.

The guards who weren't sent out to look for Rayla spent their days either accompanying Carrow to the castle or mingling about the town. Some spent too much time in the tavern, drinking and disturbing the quiet bystanders. There had been no complaints, however. Apparently the people of Riraveth were accustomed to such things.

That left Raiden. He hadn't wanted to bother Sapphire while she was practicing, nor Luca while he taught. He had no right to follow Carrow to the castle, and frankly, he wanted nothing to do with the scholar right now. Macarius had insisted that he be alone, aside from the guards he brought with him. He had also refused when Raiden had requested to assist in looking for Rayla, claiming that he didn't trust the boy not to run off on his own. And none of the guards seemed to feel the need to have Raiden tag along. None, Raiden thought drearily, except Nel.

The young guard had found Raiden one day sitting alone in a dark corner of one of the roads with his back up against a building. At once, he noticed the bruise on Raiden's left cheek. In his state of anger, Raiden had snapped at one of the men in the market square who had bumped into him. Unfortunately, one well-placed swing from the man had sent Raiden reeling to the ground, holding his cheek gingerly.

Without pressing Raiden for details, without asking if Raiden wanted any company, Nel plopped down beside him. At first, Raiden had been blunt about his feelings toward the man, even when Nel had been kind enough to offer to buy Raiden a drink.

"I don't drink," Raiden had replied coldly.

Then, Nel offered to introduce him to some of the other guards. The "nicer" ones, as the man had put it. Raiden had shaken his head, claiming that he didn't care to know anyone that didn't want to speak to him on their own terms. Nel had frowned at that, but had dropped the subject.

Finally, at the end of their second day, Nel had made Raiden an offer that the boy couldn't refuse.

"I noticed you carry a sword and a bow," the guard had said. Raiden grunted.

"Did you?" he had replied carelessly.

"Are you any good?" Nel had prompted. "With the sword, I mean? I figure you spend most of your time practicing archery."

Raiden had frowned. How dare Nel question his skills.

"I'm alright," he had lied.

"Do you want to be better than alright?"

"Excuse me?"

"I used to be the worst swordsman in my class," Nel explained. "I tripped over my own feet. I couldn't hit a thing. I was horrible. An embarrassment, really."

Despite the dislike Raiden had for Nel, he could relate to that.

He had motioned for the guard to continue.

"I learned a few tricks that helped with footwork. If you are interested, I could show you."

And so, for the rest of that day, and most of the current morning, Raiden had allowed Nel to teach him his tricks. As the sessions progressed, Raiden felt his mental guard against Nel slipping. Nel's tricks were working, to Raiden's amazement. Not only that, but Raiden began to wonder if he had judged Nel too quickly. Yes, his interest in Rayla was annoying. Compared to Raiden's relationship with the girl, Nel was nothing more than an acquaintance. But the man was constantly making an effort to help, and despite how much Raiden wanted to hate the guard, he couldn't help but see a hint of someone else in Nel. A friend. Nel's care and concern for others reminded Raiden of Finn.

Now the two men were in a secluded corner of the town. Raiden felt sweat dripping from his hair and into his eyes. His muscles were sore, but he didn't care. The pain distracted him from his constant fear for Rayla.

"No, not so tensely," Nel advised him. Raiden rolled his eyes.

"What the devil is that supposed to mean?" he demanded. Nel only laughed.

"Relax your muscles, Raiden. You're never going to be able to jump into action if you're so tense. You can't move quickly enough. That's why you keep tripping."

Raiden shot him a glare, which Nel ignored.

"Your mind is working faster than your feet can," the guard continued patiently. "If you relax your muscles up until the point that you are going to move, everything will be one fluid motion."

"Oh, yes, goodness," Raiden replied sarcastically. "Why didn't I think of that? Relaxing your muscles in order to move? That makes so much sense."

Still, Raiden did as Nel said. To his surprise, and slight annoyance, it worked. Raiden was able to spin and leap into the air, cutting his sword across the sky, without tripping himself.

Nel smiled approvingly.

"See?"

"Don't be so cocky," Raiden replied evenly.

Nel, who had been tolerant of Raiden's poor attitude so far, threw his hands into the air.

"Okay, what is it?" the guard demanded.

"What?"

"What is your problem with me? Because as far as I know, I've treated you with nothing but respect and kindness. And the same goes for your friends. So what is it that makes you hate me so much? Why are you *constantly* trying to pick a fight with me?"

Raiden frowned.

"Have you ever considered that not everybody in life is going to like you?" he asked dismissively. "That's just the way that it is. Maybe you just need to learn how to get over it."

"No," Nel pressed. "Because from how Rayla talks about you, you're very kind and level-headed. But that's not how you seem toward me. And I don't think Rayla is a liar, so that means that you must have some reason for treating me like–"

"You want to know why I don't like you?" Raiden cut in, raising his voice. "It's because of that right there! You talk about Rayla and act like you know her so well. Like you can understand how she thinks. Like you have a right to care about her. But you don't. I have grown up with Rayla. I've been in her life longer than anyone else ever has. I know her. I can read her like a book. You have no *idea* what kind of pain she's seen. But you act like you are the closest of friends. And it drives me *insane*!"

Raiden stared at the guard in front of him, letting his anger show clearly on his face. Nel seemed calm, which surprised Raiden. He had just been disrespected, and by someone younger and much less experienced than him at that. And yet, Nel didn't retaliate. And when he finally replied, he didn't raise his voice.

"I know that," he said softly. "I know that I barely know her. And that you are everything to her and for her. I'm not pretending like I care about her. I will admit, I don't care enough to cry myself to sleep at night because she is missing. But I do know that she is a great warrior."

Raiden squinted at Nel. "How could you know that? You've never seen her in battle."

"Rumors of her talent with the sword aren't just battle school gossip," Nel commented dryly. "And I've seen her in action *now*, with this gift that she has. And I know that she is honorable. That she held a service for Finn … That she honored him in a way that he deserved. And for those reasons, I admire your friend."

Raiden watched silently as Nel paused, gathering his thoughts.

"She is new to guard duty," he continued. "She has no friends there. She is alone. And yes, she would probably be fine to stay that way. But I was like her once, in the sense that I was new and confused and alone on duty. That was when a young, tall guard with a big smile on his face had taken me under his wing. He taught me all the tricks to guard duty. He gave me confidence. Finnegan is the reason that I survived to become the guard … no, the man that I am today."

At the mention of Finn's name, Raiden gave an involuntary gasp. Nel, however, continued without stopping.

"Without Finn's help, I would have turned tail and ran within the first week. I know that I have no right to pretend to be a part of Rayla's life. But Finn is gone. And somebody needs to keep his legacy going. When I saw Rayla that day on the wall, she was alone, confused, and obviously hurting.

I'm not trying to play the role of a perfect friend, Raiden. I'm just trying to fill Finn's shoes."

Raiden stood completely dumbfounded. He'd had no idea that Nel had ever known Finn, much less shared such a deep connection with the man. That alone would have changed Raiden's mind. But the fact that Nel had tried to carry on the man's legacy by attempting to help Rayla only added to Raiden's surprise and guilt. He had severely misjudged Nel.

"I-I'm sorry," Raiden said slowly. "I just … Rayla doesn't let people in easily, if ever. I just assumed you were trying to force your way in, and I got annoyed."

"It's alright," Nel said. "But Raiden, you need to consider the fact that Rayla has opened a new chapter in her life. Guard duty is not something that the two of you share. Not yet, anyway."

The words hurt Raiden's heart, and he made a face as if he had a bitter taste in his mouth.

"Perhaps you will soon be given a similar position alongside her," Nel said quickly, trying to smooth the moment over. "Or perhaps your advanced talents will take you elsewhere. Either way, she's in a new place. And you might not be the only person that she can rely on anymore. Despite whatever pain she has endured in her past, she is going to have to rely on others for support and for help. Not just herself. Not just you. She's going to have to learn to open up to the world."

Raiden nodded, lowering his gaze.

"I highly doubt that will happen," the boy said slowly. "She's extremely stubborn."

At that, Nel laughed.

"She's a woman," the guard said. "Aren't they all?"

chapter 21
Rayla

Had it been three days since she'd run? Four? A week?

Rayla wasn't sure. She had ridden straight past Castle Riraveth and onward until she had found the hills. The first few nights in the field had been terrifying. She'd gotten no sleep, afraid that she would be attacked when she wasn't watching. She had passed a village several days ago, but had decided against stopping to sleep in the inn. She didn't want to come into contact with anyone. Not now, when she felt so unstable. The most she could bring herself to risk was to sneak some food from a garden, and then oats from the nearby barn, when the owner hadn't been present. She'd left a hearty amount of copper coins on the doorstep and tried not to feel guilty about it.

Eventually, after a miserable night in the open field, Rayla had reached her target. The hills had been the only other place she could think of. There wasn't much else around, besides the castle. But that was where her group was supposed to be heading, unless they'd gone home as she'd told them to. She didn't want to risk running into them.

There also weren't any forests in Riraveth to comfort her, either. Even if there had been, Rayla wasn't sure if she could have entered them. The woods only made her think of Finn now, and she wanted nothing more than to cut off any memories that brought her pain.

The hills were a welcome relief. They were secluded and quiet. Making a mental note of the direction she was coming from, she had led Dóchas to a narrow valley between the hills, and a river that ran south. The water was much needed, and Rayla let Dóchas drink from the river while she had refilled her canteens before she led Dóchas along the stream.

Eventually they came across a cave. It wasn't very big. She and Dóchas could fit comfortably, though, with enough room to spare. Rayla had noticed with a jolt of shock that if there had been a tree beside the cave, it would have nearly resembled Finn's tomb.

Good, Rayla had thought to herself. *I deserve to be swallowed up by a grave.*

The memory of Kuvira's dying eyes flooded her mind for the millionth time already. She hadn't meant to destroy their only means of leverage, of course. It had just happened.

And yet, part of Rayla knew that she *had* meant to kill Kuvira. She'd let her hatred spill out of her. Part of Rayla had known exactly what she was doing. And that part, tiny as it was, terrified her. Because not only had it killed a man on purpose, but that part of her had *liked* it.

Dóchas's warm breath on Rayla's face pulled the girl from her thoughts. She'd been sitting at the entrance of the cave, hugging her knees to her chest and staring out into the hills. Dóchas continued to brush her muzzle against Rayla's cheek until the girl sat up straight. Rayla managed a small smile. She reached up and scratched the mare under her jaw.

"Thanks for being so loyal," Rayla said softly.

As if in reply, Dóchas nickered and shook her mane.

Rayla sighed, standing to stretch her legs. While the cave wasn't very deep, it was plenty tall enough for both she and Dóchas to stand at full height. Rayla was grateful for that, if nothing else.

She could see the back wall easily from the mouth of the cave. It provided enough protection from the cold wind to keep them from freezing to death, but it was still chilly enough to be uncomfortable.

Still, Rayla liked knowing that nobody could surprise her from behind. This way, she only had to guard one direction. It was easier.

Not that anyone would be in these hills, Rayla reasoned. The wind made an eerie noise as it whistled through the valley. Rayla imagined that the hills would be beautiful in the spring, with green grass covering every surface. But now, in the midst of autumn, everything looked dead. The rare patches of grass that had yet to turn brown were higher up, where there was more sunlight. Here in the valley, everything was cold and dull.

Worst of all, Rayla knew that she and Dóchas were severely lacking in food. They'd only packed enough to get them to Castle Riraveth, and Rayla had overshot by a good amount. Even accounting for what she had taken from the small village, she had decided to cut their portions in half in order to last several extra days. But she would have to leave for the castle, with its abundant options for food, within the day unless she and Dóchas wanted to starve.

Rayla sighed again. Dóchas clopped over to the girl, tossing her head. Rayla glanced at the young battle horse and stuck her bottom lip out in sympathy.

"I'm sorry," she said. "But you've already eaten today. You won't have enough to make it back to the castle to restock if you eat again."

Dóchas whinnied, and Rayla rolled her eyes, frowning.

"Well I'm hungry too, but you don't see me complaining, do you?"

The realization that she was arguing with a horse hit Rayla, and she plopped herself down again, this time against the cave wall. She let her head fall back so that she was looking up at the ceiling.

"I'm losing my mind," she mumbled.

Outside, a sudden gust of wind caught Rayla's attention. She rolled her head to the side to look out the cave entrance. It was cold. Rayla was hungry. She herself had only eaten once that day, and she knew she would have to wait until tomorrow to eat again. The stream provided them with enough water to drink, but that water was cold, and Rayla wanted nothing more than to be warm. She had tried to start a fire, but the wind seemed to be blowing directly into the mouth of the cave, and her flames wouldn't stay lit for more than a few seconds before being whisked out.

Around the whistling of the wind, Rayla thought she heard a noise. Her body tensed, and she glanced at Dóchas. The mare's ears were perked – a sign that there had definitely been a sound. Slowly, Rayla stood to her feet.

The sound came again, and Rayla's breath caught in her throat as she recognized it. Voices. Frantically, she grabbed Dóchas's reins and pulled the mare farther into the cave.

"Shh," Rayla soothed as the animal made a low rumbling sound. She pet Dóchas's muzzle gently, and the mare quieted.

Rayla's heart pounded. The voices seemed to be getting quieter already, but she was frozen in fear and couldn't make herself move to examine the mouth of the cave. For several minutes, Rayla barely dared to breathe.

Finally, once there had been a long enough stretch of silence that Rayla had managed to stop quivering, she inched closer to the exit. Cautiously, she poked her head out. In every direction, she could see nothing more than the hills.

Still, Rayla had no intentions of staying here for a moment longer. She knew from experience that when her gut told her there was danger nearby, she should always listen.

Rayla clicked her tongue quietly and Dóchas walked over to her. She tightened the girth strap on her horse before grabbing the mare's reins to lead her outside. Before mounting, Rayla grabbed the thinner of her two blankets from her saddle pack and draped it around her shoulders. Rayla had placed the thicker blanket between Dóchas's body and her saddle blanket, hoping to give the horse as much warmth as possible. It wasn't her fault that Rayla had dragged her out here.

Mounting Dóchas, Rayla kicked the horse's sides gently, sending her off toward the castle. As she rode, she pulled her blanket tighter around her shoulders. It did no good. Not only because it was thin, but because Rayla was cold on the inside.

chapter 22
Raiden

Raiden was convinced that his stress was going to be the death of him.

They had been at Castle Riraveth for just over a week. Carrow had gotten nowhere with Lord Dunnman. Judging by the way Carrow described him, Dunnman was just as foul as Raiden had imagined him. The lord had accepted the group for who they were, acknowledging that they obviously had authority and were from Maith. But Dunnman had refused to do anything to help them search for or stop Kuvira's troops. He seemed to think that Kuvira was completely Lord Hightower's problem.

The only aid he had given them was sending a few men a day out to help search for Rayla. At first, Raiden had been grateful for the extra eyes. Macarius had forbidden him and Sapphire from going to look for Rayla, clearly not trusting the two to ride off.

However, after a few days, Raiden learned that Dunmann's guards would not be much help. Raiden bitterly recalled their faces as they returned each day, clearly unaffected by their failure to find Rayla. They didn't care, Raiden thought. Even if they had found her, they probably would have been too lazy to bring her back.

He'd said as much to one of the Riraveth guards one day. It had earned him a bloodied nose, which Raiden had cleaned before anyone else could see.

As for Macarius, his mood had declined a little each day as he came back with no results. His informant, it seemed, was either dead, missing, or not planning to show himself to Macarius a second time. The bowmaster had slowly gone from hopeful to miserable in the past week. He wouldn't say it, but the man was also extremely concerned about finding Rayla.

And that was where Raiden's stress lay. There had been absolutely no sign of the girl or even what direction she might have gone. Macarius had sent several guards out of the castle walls each day to scout around, but they had come back each time with no success. The rest of the guards were getting impatient, obviously eager to return home where a more "worthwhile" task would be given to them.

The only relief that Raiden experienced was hearing Luca's stories of how Sapphire was improving, and knowing his own skills were improving with Nel. Raiden could now combat the young guard and hold his own for several minutes. It wasn't ideal, Raiden had to admit, but it was progress. Besides, he would spend most of his time in battles from afar, with his bow.

All in all, his time at Castle Riraveth had been a sour experience. The Riraveth high court, the guards, and even the citizens were rude, dirty, and mischievous. It made Raiden want to stay in his room at the inn at all times.

But, in an attempt to rid himself of his bad mood, Raiden had agreed to take a walk around the town with Sapphire and Nel.

"What should we do tonight?" Sapphire, who was walking to his right, asked. The sudden sound made Raiden flinch. He had been so lost in his thoughts, he'd forgotten he wasn't alone.

"I was thinking we could take a nice ride in the field," Nel, to Raiden's left, replied.

Raiden frowned.

"I don't know," he said slowly. "This place is crawling with danger. Riding alone with the sun setting seems like we could be just asking for someone to take advantage of us."

Sapphire grinned, unsheathing one of her knives and twirling it around.

"I'd like to see them try."

Raiden and Nel both laughed. Sometimes, Raiden wondered if Sapphire might give Rayla a run for her money when it came to spunky attitudes.

"Alright," Raiden said, sighing. "I guess if Sapphire promises to protect me, we can go. But we might want to head out pretty soon. There's not a lot of daylight left."

"Wait," Sapphire said, reseathing her weapon. "Should you be out much longer, with how you have been feeling lately?"

Raiden smiled at his sister.

"I'm feeling much better than I was a few days ago," he assured her. "I promise."

"Great!" Sapphire exclaimed. "Then let's go saddle the horses!" Despite his stress, Raiden couldn't help but smile. His sister had clearly attached herself to the horses. He had found her in the stables on multiple occasions, brushing and talking to the animals. It was sweet, he thought.

The three of them made their way to the castle stables, where their horses had been stalled for them. Raiden had made many trips on his own to check on his horse. He didn't trust the Riraveth stablemen to properly care for the animal, and rightfully so.

Unlike Maith's relatively clean stables, where every stall was mucked frequently and every horse was groomed often, Riraveth's stables were a reflection of the rest of the province. Several of the stalls had obviously not been cleaned in weeks. Most horses, apart from those that had been brought by the Maith group, were covered in mud or dirt. Fortunately, the animals had at least been provided with blankets as the colder weather had blown in, although the majority of the blankets were thin and had holes in them.

The sight disgusted Raiden. He wanted nothing more than to bring the horses back to his father, where they would be better off than they were here, living in such poor conditions and with so little care.

Raiden shoved his anger aside. As he approached his horse's stall, the animal stuck it's head out and nickered in greeting. Raiden rubbed the horse's muzzle before entering the stall to saddle the animal. Once he had finished, he moved to help Sapphire. The saddles were surprisingly heavy, and he doubted his sister could carry it on her own, much less lift it over her head to place on her horse's back. However, when Raiden arrived at Sapphire's stall, he saw that Nel had already helped the young girl. Raiden nodded his thanks.

Together the three of them set off toward the gates. It would be relatively easy for them to reenter, with Nel by their side in his Maith armor. The Riraveth guards had grown accustomed to seeing the Maith guards. The former rather despised the latter, based on their expressions as Lord Hightower's men walked around the town. Nevertheless, the men of Riraveth knew that Maith's guards held just as much authority as they did themselves, and there had been no interaction between the two groups, violent or otherwise.

Unless Raiden counted the brawls he'd seemed to find himself in recently. Which he chose not to consider.

"–not sure why we have to keep doing it," Raiden heard a nearby Riraveth guard say. He slowed his horse to barely a walk, curiously listening in on the conversation. Sapphire and Nel did the same, shooting a confused glance at Raiden, who had leaned to his right to listen closer.

"I doubt she's even still alive," the second guard replied carelessly.

"Wonder why she's so special," the first guard asked. "I mean, the whole Maith force seems to be looking for one little girl. That's just plain pointless, if you ask me."

"Some bandits have probably gotten ahold of her," the second man decided.

"Bet they're having more fun than we are."

In seconds, Raiden had dismounted his horse and drawn his bow, nocking an arrow to the string. He lifted the weapon.

Only to be jerked backward by a strong hand.

"No, Raiden," Nel's voice hissed in his ear. Raiden could hear the anger in the other man's voice.

"Let me go," Raiden demanded, trembling in fury.

"Raiden," Sapphire begged from atop her horse.

Raiden glanced behind him to his sister. She grabbed the reins of both his and Nel's horses to keep them still. Raiden guessed his eyes must have reflected the pure rage he felt, because Sapphire recoiled at his look.

"You'll start something that we can't finish," Nel whispered to him.

Raiden looked back at the two guards. They were laughing together, oblivious to him or his bow. He didn't move.

"Sapphire could get hurt," Nel prompted.

Raiden remained still for several minutes, battling his anger.

"Raiden," Nel said quietly, so that only the two of them could hear. "You've been getting into fights ever since–"

"I have not," Raiden immediately responded, defensive.

Nel clenched his jaws. "The bruises, the foul mood, the angry glares to certain Riravethian guards," Nel rattled off. "I'm not stupid. I know the signs of someone who has been picking fights."

"How could you possibly know I've been the one picking the fights?" Raiden spat. Nel just glared at him.

"Because you've been trying to do the same thing with me. I know you're worried about Rayla, and you're frustrated that you aren't being allowed to help find her. But if you don't stop taking that frustration and anger out in constant fights, you're going to get hurt."

Raiden stood, clenching his own jaw in anger. He knew Nel was right, but that didn't make his anger subside. He swallowed, his throat bobbing once. Twice.

Finally, he took a deep breath and turned again, remounting his horse. Avoiding eye contact with Nel, he sent his horse walking toward the Riraveth gate again. Judging by the sound of hooves behind him, Nel and Sapphire chose to follow closely.

As they rode, Nel tried to lighten the mood by telling Sapphire several jokes that he claimed to have come up with himself. Raiden doubted it.

As they emerged from the gates, Raiden immediately sucked in a deep breath. He turned to the left.

He wanted to ride toward the hills in order to give himself something to look at. It was amazing how big the hills looked compared to how far away they truly were. Upon his asking, a citizen in the castle walls had told Raiden that the hills were roughly two days' ride from the castle. And yet, Raiden felt as though he could reach them by tomorrow if he took off in a gallop.

"It's the flat field," Luca had told Raiden when the boy had voiced his thoughts. "It makes them look closer because they're the only thing you can see. There's nothing else to compare them to, so they look big."

That had made sense to Raiden. If they hadn't been so far away, he might have used his free time to ride to them. They were quite beautiful, he had to admit. Especially with the autumn colors, Raiden felt drawn to the hills for some reason.

"Raiden?" Nel asked from beside him.

"Hmm?" he said, pulling himself out of his thoughts.

"Nothing," Nel replied, a weird look on his face. "Just that you looked as if you wanted to court those hills."

Raiden frowned. "What?"

"You were getting all googly eyed at the hills," Sapphire explained patiently.

"It was kind of disturbing," Nel added.

"I'm sorry that I'm enjoying the autumn scene," Raiden replied sarcastically. Nel shook his head.

"Not me," he said. "I prefer the spring, when everything is warm and active. You honestly prefer when things are cold?"

"Yes," Raiden replied evenly.

Nel watched him for a few seconds, as if expecting something more.

"Actually," Raiden added thoughtfully, "I love autumn. I don't really see it as a time for things to start dying. I see it as a break before a new beginning."

Nel considered the words.

"A break …" he repeated.

Raiden nodded. "I mean, think about it. The same trees regrow their leaves in the spring. The same weeds and flowers and grasses sprout again in the same places. The same birds return. The same rain falls to water the earth. Nature brings us beauty for several months. It just needs a break."

After several long seconds of silence, Raiden glanced awkwardly to his left. Both Sapphire and Nel were staring at him with wide eyes.

"What?" the boy asked in shock.

"Nothing," Nel said, shaking his head. "Just that I didn't realize you were such a poet."

Raiden drew his eyebrows together, but before he could reply, Sapphire laid a hand on his arm.

"I think you're right," she said softly. "I hadn't ever thought of it that way, but it makes sense. I mean, not just for nature, but for us too. Life is hard; I think we can all agree. After a while, everybody needs a break."

The words hit Raiden in an uncomfortable way. It was how he had been feeling about himself for some time, but he hadn't realized it until his sister had connected the dots. He and Rayla had been through so much already, and there was no end in sight. The worry about what would happen to Rayla, to himself, to Sapphire, and to their home had weighed on him for too long now, and he needed a break.

"Everybody needs a break," he repeated slowly.

chapter 23
Rayla

She had been riding for a full day and would reach the castle soon.

Or so she hoped. Dóchas had what Rayla considered to be a day's amount of food left. The mare had been eating more than usual because they'd been traveling so much. Rayla had forced their pace to the maximum, hoping to reach the castle faster. It hadn't occurred to her that she had been riding at a gallop when she had run from her group a few days ago, so the time would be about the same.

As for herself, she had eaten the last of her food that morning. With the castle in sight, she was confident that she could make it before she became too famished to move, even if her calculations were off and she had to ride an extra day. Of course, she could have stopped at the village she had passed on her way to the hills, but when she had considered doing so, she remembered those voices that had come so close to her in the cave and she decided to press forward. She wanted to get to the castle as soon as possible. In addition to wanting some protection from the men she'd come across, she was curious to see if the party from Maith had continued to Riraveth or turned back.

Either way, if she arrived soon, she should make it before she starved. She'd learned at a young age how to survive on little to no food. It would be difficult, as she had grown accustomed to a full stomach over the past few years, but she could do it.

"It's not too bad today, huh, girl?" Rayla asked. After she had attempted to strike up a conversation with Dóchas for the fifth time since they had left their cave, Rayla had decided to give up on her sanity. She was on her own now, with Dóchas being the only company she had. So what if she talked to a horse? Who would know?

Dóchas, as she often did upon hearing her master's voice, whinnied and tossed her head. Rayla patted her neck.

"I know, but it could be worse. The wind isn't awful today."

Indeed, the cold autumn wind seemed to have paused, if only for that day. There was a slight chill in the air, but it was bearable without strong gusts whisking away any warmth their bodies might have conjured. Rayla was almost enjoying her ride. Even the rhythmic bump of Dóchas's gallop was peaceful.

But she couldn't let herself completely fall into ease. She'd had a dream last night, and to her horror, it was one she'd had many times before.

She had thought that after the incident in the woods, it had gone away. When she was younger, the dream was almost a guarantee each time Rayla would close her eyes. As she had aged, it had occurred less often, but there was still the occasional night that it would appear in her subconscious.

After the scouting party ride, her dreams had shifted to Finn and his death. She had rarely gotten a break from that horrible memory, so the less frightening childhood nightmare had not come to her in several months. Now, however, it seemed to be back.

It was always the same. It started with Rayla looking up at a pair of light brown eyes. So light, they were almost yellow. Then, as her vision cleared a bit, she could see the jet black hair of the boy standing over her. Occasionally, the eyes belonged to a blonde haired woman, but more often than not, they were the boy's. Slowly, the piercing eyes became full of fear. There was something bright behind the boy. It was red and yellow, and it almost seemed to be glowing. Then, the face disappeared, and Rayla woke up in a cold sweat.

She wished she could know where the dream came from and why it was the same every time. It seemed as though it was more than a dream. It seemed important somehow. It felt too real to be something her mind had simply come up with on its own.

Rayla couldn't help but wonder if the dream was connected to her past. But that was impossible, wasn't it? Rayla had been too young when she had lost her family to remember anything.

A raspy snort drew Rayla from her thoughts. She glanced down to see Dóchas frothing at the mouth. Sweat was pouring off the mare's body. Rayla quickly checked the horse and dismounted. Hoping to cool Dóchas off faster, she chose to unsaddle the mare.

"I'm sorry, girl," she said, dropping the saddle to the ground to let the mare rest for a few minutes.

"Here," Rayla said, grabbing her canteen and pooling water in her palm. She allowed Dóchas to drink nearly half of the canteen. Rayla could always refill it when they reached the castle. Still, the fact that she only had half a canteen of water left set Rayla's nerves on edge.

As Dóchas moved to graze nearby, Rayla stared at the castle in the distance. Her group should have already gone home, she wagered. If, that is, they had continued on to the castle after she had ruined their original plan. Either way, there should be no risk of her running into them.

Still, part of Rayla hoped that she did. She had thought that she wanted to be left alone. She didn't want anyone to beg her to come back home with them. It was too risky. She could hurt someone.

Since she and Dóchas had run, Rayla hadn't had another spell like she had that night, but she also didn't feel in control of her gift anymore. She was afraid that if someone made her angry, she would explode and hurt them. Or worse.

And yet, the fact that nobody had come after her had hurt Rayla. Not even Raiden, who had remained by her side for over ten years, had tried to stop her after she had ridden away. She didn't want to hurt anyone else, but she also felt alone.

Being alone was something she thought she loved. She liked being in control of her own life. She liked that she only had herself to rely on. It made her strong. And yet, over the past few years, she had grown close to Raiden, and even Luca. In just a few short months, Carrow and Sapphire had become her friends as well. She hadn't realized how much she had been missing in her life until she had found it in these people. And now, she realized just how hard being alone truly was.

Of course, she had Dóchas. Rayla glanced over to the mare, who seemed to be recovering from their hard morning ride quite nicely. The young horse was rolling in the grass with her legs in the air. Rayla allowed a small smile to play on her lips.

Dóchas was good company. At times, Rayla even felt like the mare had a human personality. More times than Rayla could count, Dóchas had seemed to detect Rayla's mood and had stuck her muzzle in Rayla's face until the girl had smiled or laughed. The horse had even given her several looks that reminded Rayla of her own sarcasm and wit. In short, without Dóchas, Rayla was sure she would have gone mad by now.

"Hey, goofball," Rayla said, approaching the rolling horse. Dóchas stopped rolling just long enough to cut her eyes at Rayla before resuming the task. Rayla rolled her own eyes.

"Come on," she said. "We have to go if we are going to reach the castle in time for your food."

Almost as if she was disappointed, the mare slowly stood, allowing Rayla to resaddle her and grab her reins.

"I'll walk for a little while, if it helps," Rayla offered, turning to look at the remaining distance the two had to cover. She stood still, taking in the sight. It was so close.

From behind Rayla, Dóchas nickered, nudging Rayla's shoulder with her forehead and causing Rayla to stumble forward a few paces.

"Alright, alright, I'm going," Rayla said.

They began walking toward the castle, Rayla leading Dóchas alongside her.

"You know, you're kind of rude."

Dóchas tossed her head, and Rayla could have sworn it looked like the horse was nodding.

"Alright," she said, shrugging. "As long as you're aware of it."

chapter 24
Rayla

She'd been close in her guess. A day later, Rayla and Dóchas reached Castle Riraveth.

The castle's walls were a dreary brown color with spires and points along the top. Rayla thought the place was quite unappealing. Then again, the rest of the province seemed to be bland and boring as well. Perhaps the castle fit rather well.

By the size of the wall, Rayla knew instantly that Castle Riraveth mirrored Maith in the sense that both were home to a village inside. She had never traveled to a different province before, so Rayla was unfamiliar with how each division of the kingdom was set up. She knew from looking at several different maps that Castle Riraveth was positioned on the innermost border of the province, near Maith Castle. Luca had told her that this was for protective reasons. It allowed for the troops of each province to travel quickly to the other's aid in times of war, which had proven important in the past. She could just barely recall the threat of the bordering kingdom that lay just to the left of Riraveth; Saodda, the kingdom was called.

Also, each province had a specific characteristic. Maith was the province known for its battle school, as well as its forest. Riraveth had the hills, of course, and was known for its criminal activity. Seol, to the south, was Rathús's peaceful, coastal province. Tiri marked the kingdom's eastern border and was known for its dryness, due to the nearby Marfoch Desert. Finally, there was Rathús Province, which lay in the center of the kingdom. The capital province was known for its market and the bustling town that lay inside the castle walls.

So far, Riraveth had lived up to what she had imagined it would be. The hills were as big as she had pictured. The castle looked as horrid. She could only hope the people weren't as bad as she was expecting.

As she approached the wall, Rayla dismounted and tied Dóchas up to her peg. Her stomach growled as she worked. Rayla frowned. Years ago, she would just be beginning to get hungry. After having to go three or four days without food, two days had been easy. Now, however, she felt a familiar pain in her stomach that told her if she didn't eat something soon, things could get bad quickly.

"I'll be back," Rayla promised. As she turned to walk away, Dóchas whinnied.

Rayla paused. It suddenly occurred to her that it might be dangerous to leave Dóchas tied up outside the walls. In Maith, she could do something like that without thinking twice, but with the rumors of Riraveth's crime, she decided she had better leave Dóchas in the castle stables. She untied the mare and led her by the reins.

As she approached the gates, she noticed two guards standing watch. Both had the symbol of Riraveth on their shields. The silver boar seemed to stare into Rayla's mind. She shivered.

As she took a step toward the gates, the two guards crossed swords in front of Rayla, causing her to flinch. Dóchas whinnied in surprise. The guards had been none too careful about where they swung the swords, and the guard on the left had nearly taken Rayla's arm off.

"State your business, girl," one of the guards demanded. Rayla frowned.

Of course, she had been expecting the question. It was protocol at Maith as well to question strangers that entered the castle walls. Still, even the unpleasant guards from her home were not as rude as the men in front of her.

"I come on behalf of Maith province," she stated plainly. To prove her point, she gestured to the dragon emblazoned chestplate she wore.

This was the fragile part of her plan. No guard would believe that she had any authority. She was a woman. Female warriors were not common in

Rathús, much less in Riraveth. At best, the men might believe that she truly was from Maith, and would let her pass through.

There was, of course, a second part of the plan that could potentially cause Rayla issues, but that fear was disbanded with the guard's next question.

"I assume you're with the other Maith rats that have crowded our streets for the past two weeks?"

So Rayla's friends were still here. She would have to be careful.

Despite the sudden shock she felt at the news, she crossed her arms. This man was incredibly ill-mannered, and Rayla didn't like it.

"Well I suppose that would make sense, don't you think?" she spat.

The guard's face reddened in anger.

"Then why aren't you with your fancy men?" he taunted. "Shouldn't a little girl like you stay where the men can protect her?"

"I can take care of myself, thank you."

"I don't know," the second guard joined in. "Keep that mouth of yours running, and you may want to find your friends pretty fast."

"I've stated my business," Rayla said sourly. "Now let me through."

"I don't think so," the first guard said, grinning. "I would much rather–"

Before he could finish, Rayla had unsheathed her sword. Knocking the two men's crossed weapons up and out of the way, she ducked under them and slipped through the gate. The surprised men were only knocked further off balance when they turned to watch her, only to feel themselves shoved aside by Dóchas's bulky body.

Rayla considered her options as she turned to face the men again. She could run, but the men would likely pursue her. Not that they had a reason. But men like these didn't take well to being disrespected. Or rather, they didn't take to anyone questioning their authority. Sighing, Rayla held her sword out to keep the men at bay.

"What in heaven's name–"

"I have every right to pass into the castle walls," Rayla said confidently.

"Not until we give you permission!" one guard exclaimed.

"Actually," Rayla calmly replied, "no guard in the kingdom has any right to withhold entry of a person without rightful cause. And seeing as how you have no cause, I have every right to pass through. So thank you, sirs, but I will be on my way."

With that, Rayla turned and marched away. Shaking her head, she continued into the castle's village.

The first thing she noticed was the horrid smell. It reminded Rayla of the manure piles in the back of the stables at home. She fought the urge to pinch her nose and continued to walk through the crowd. Thankfully, the people seemed to part for her once they saw Dóchas behind her.

Rayla reached the stables, the scent now threatening to cut her air off completely.

"I need to keep my horse here," she told the stableboy. He wrinkled his nose at her, his white-blonde hair stained with mud and dirt.

"No room," he said curtly.

Rayla clenched her teeth. "Just for an hour," she pressed. "Maybe less than that."

The boy, Rayla could now see as he approached her, was close to Rayla's age. His blue eyes were pale and half-lidded, like he could fall asleep at any second. He grinned at her, and she noticed several missing teeth.

"It's going to cost you," he said, holding a hand out and wiggling his fingers at her. Rayla eyed his dirty hand carefully. Finally, she sighed, reaching into her coin purse and dropping a few copper pieces into the boy's hand.

He dropped his eyes to the coins before looking back up at her.

"Not enough there," he said. Rayla's nostrils flared.

"Forget the hour," she said. "I'll be back in half that time. And I'll place her in the stall myself. *You* don't have to touch her. Just give her a little feed and some water. I think my coins will buy that much."

The man considered her carefully before closing his fingers around the coins.

"Last stall on the left."

Rayla quickly moved to place Dóchas in the allotted stall, not bothering to unsaddle the mare.

"I'll be back soon," she promised. Then she jogged back out into the street.

Without Dóchas to clear the way, Rayla was pushed and shoved around like everyone else in the crowded road.

"Out of the way, imbecile," one man spat as Rayla accidentally bumped the man's shoulder. She wrinkled her nose in disgust.

"Lucky I don't unsheathe my sword," she said under her breath.

As she walked, Rayla kept her eyes peeled for any familiar faces or armor. As none of her group members showed themselves, she let herself relax slightly. Over the top of the crowd, Rayla spotted several market stands. She fought her way to one about halfway through the market, where she purchased several shiny red apples. Dóchas deserved a treat, she thought. The mare had given Rayla more than enough help and company in the past two weeks.

"Do you have a bag?" Rayla asked politely.

"Cost ya," the man in charge of the stand grunted. Rayla pursed her lips, drawing out a few more coins.

The man handed Rayla a woven bag, and she dropped the apples inside.

Next, she searched for some food for herself. A small baker's stand held several decent looking loaves of bread. Rayla bought enough to last herself a couple of weeks.

Unfortunately, her money supply wouldn't last very long. She'd brought the coins she had earned for her few days' work as a guard, plus what Carrow had distributed to each person from Lord Hightower's supplies. Still, without a proper income, the pouch would quickly dwindle down to nothing.

After buying plenty of jerky for herself and oats for Dóchas, Rayla decided that she probably had enough food to last the two of them for at least three weeks. She'd had to purchase a second, and then a third, bag to carry all the food, tying one bag to her belt and throwing the other two over her shoulders. She turned to leave, but another stand caught her eye. She bit her bottom lip as her mind fought between desire and reason. Bright colors of thick, squared blankets were draped over one of the stands.

The weaver continued to pull her yarn from the basket as the blanket grew bigger and bigger. Rayla desperately wanted to buy another blanket. The thin one she had been using was barely sufficient at best, but she refused to take the better blanket from Dóchas.

Rayla glanced into her money pouch. She had plenty of money to purchase a blanket, especially with how cheap everything seemed to go in Riraveth. But she knew she would regret spending the money when she and Dóchas were starving within a month. She would have to find work somewhere. Perhaps she could find work in the village outside the castle.

"Forget it," she muttered to herself, her eyes still lingering on the blankets.

She turned, forcing herself to walk away. The crowd had seemed to thicken in the past hour. She sighed, standing on her toes. The stables were about a stone's throw away, but she could see no clear path to them.

She began pushing her way through people. Not because she wanted to, but because it was the only way to get through.

Suddenly, Rayla ducked under the shoulders of the masses. She had spotted a very familiar pair of broad shoulders amongst the citizens of riraveth and had panicked. It was Sir Luca. As Rayla crouched her way through the last of the people, she couldn't help but whisper aloud.

"Please don't see me," she prayed. "Please, *please* don't follow me."

She fought to keep her breathing steady. If she lost control again, with all these people in the crowd …

If Luca found her, and she couldn't control this other side of her gift, she might hurt him. She had to get away, to protect him.

As she reached the stables, she didn't even wait for the stableboy to speak. She bolted to the last stall and grabbed Dóchas's reins, leading the mare to the gates. Her heart pounded as she glanced behind her, but Luca was nowhere in sight. Quickly, she placed as much of the food as she could in her saddle packs. The rest, she left in the bag tied around her belt.

As Rayla looked behind her once again, she decided that her mentor hadn't seen her. She took enough time to pull one of the apples out of the bag, leaning forward to feed the treat to Dóchas.

"I'm not sure if that's your reward for what you've done or your fuel for what I'm about to ask you to do," she admitted. "Either way, you deserve it."

Dóchas munched happily on the treat. Rayla let her horse enjoy the moment before she sent them galloping through the gates toward the village she had stopped at days before.

chapter 25
Raiden

They had not seen any sign of Rayla in over a week. He was sick with worry, unable to sleep at night or enjoy any moment of the day without wondering where Rayla could possibly be. The moment someone saw her, or as soon as Carrow decided they should head back to Maith without Rayla, Raiden would lose control. He already felt as if his mind was on the edge as it was.

The guards had managed to settle into a routine. Nobody suggested that they leave. Nobody saw Rayla. Each day, Carrow took a few of the guards to the castle to meet with Lord Dunnman, making plans to search the province for Kuvira's forces. The problem was, the lord didn't seem fully convinced that Kuvira's forces were in his province. Sir Macarius still had not heard from his informant, and with Kuvira dead, Lord Dunnman said they had no real proof to convince him to risk his men's lives.

The rest of the guards were sent out of the castle walls every morning and returned every evening. Some were looking for signs of Rayla, though Raiden questioned how hard they were actually trying to find the girl. Others scouted the field for any sign of Tenabris or one of his men.

Raiden had watched some of the more disagreeable aspects of living in Riraveth slowly become more bearable. After the first week of sharing a room with Sir Macarius and Sir Luca, he had finally been able to tune the sound of Luca's snores out, for which he was grateful.

Nel, to Raiden's surprise, had turned out to be a rather kind and friendly person. Once Raiden put his judgment aside, he grew to like the young guard. The previous night, Nel had taken him and Sapphire out for drinks. Water, of course, had been their beverage of choice. Raiden had noticed that once they had ordered, Nel seemed to take note of the awkwardness around the table, and he too had ordered water.

Raiden was appreciative. He didn't like the idea of Sapphire being around alcohol at such a young age. Nel had seemed to take note of Raiden's discomfort and quickly adjusted his actions to ease the younger boy's nerves.

Now the three were walking around the more secluded parts of the town. They needed something to do, and this seemed as good as any other option. The day was decent, not too cold or windy, but they had decided not to go for a ride. Instead they had spent the afternoon exploring Riraveth's town.

"How did you and Rayla meet?" Nel asked casually. A few weeks ago, the question might have irked Raiden. Now, however, the memory simply made the boy smile slightly.

"She ran into me," he said, and then laughed. "Literally. We were seven at the time. She'd stolen an apple from one of the food stands back home, and she was running away, before the guards or the owner of the fruit stand could see her."

"She thought she could outrun a guard?" Nel chuckled, but Raiden shook his head.

"She was faster than you would believe. I truly think she could have outrun a guard, if one had been chasing her."

Nel pursed his lips, apparently impressed.

Raiden smiled, his mind returning to the memory of meeting Rayla. "She was looking behind her and I was watching her run right at me, thinking she might see me and stop. She knocked me over, and we ended up with scrapes everywhere."

Nel snickered. "What did you do?"

"I asked what she was doing. She was very standoffish, which I for some reason found interesting. I kept asking her what was wrong until she finally gave in and spoke to me. All she would say was that I wouldn't understand, but that she had to eat something that day. I was so confused until she finally told me that she'd stolen the apple because she hadn't eaten in three days."

"Wow," Nel said, suddenly more somber than a moment before. Raiden was surprised to find that the guard sounded genuinely upset. "Three days? She really has been through it all, hasn't she?"

"Yes," Raiden said, looking at the dirt. "She has. Anyway, after that, I would bring her meals once a day. At first, she didn't trust me, and it was obvious that she didn't want my help. But over time, she became more friendly. We would play together in the roads, running around with sticks and pretending to be knights. And as we got older, we just naturally grew closer. She learned to open up and trust me more. Especially after Luca found her and enrolled her in the battle school."

"Luca seems to really care about her," Nel pointed out. "I noticed how he watches her, kind of protectively. Like he wants her to do well, and wants to keep her from getting hurt."

Raiden nodded. "I've noticed that too. I think she looks at him as a father. If she lost Luca, I would hate to see what would happen to her. Especially after what happened to Finn … "

An awkward silence stretched over the group.

Nel cleared his throat, turning to Sapphire. "What about you? How did you meet Raiden and Rayla?"

"Mother and Father found me. I was on my own," Sapphire explained after some hesitation.

Raiden smiled as his sister referred to his parents as "Mother and Father." She had so easily accepted them as her new family. Raiden was happy about that.

"But I'm not as brave as Rayla," Sapphire continued. "And my past isn't as sad as hers. I knew my family. And I can remember what happened to me. It may not be the happiest memory, but at least I'm not stuck guessing and wondering about my past. I don't understand how Rayla deals with that."

"And what *did* happen?" Nel asked. "In your past, I mean?"

Raiden felt his body tense. Sapphire didn't talk about her past. Of course, Raiden had never asked. It was a habit. He didn't ask Rayla about hers because it was too painful for the girl. He assumed the same was true for Sapphire.

To his surprise, though, his sister answered.

"It's a long story," she began calmly. "But I lived in a small village outside of Maith's walls. I could go back, if I wanted. But I won't. Ever."

The firmness in her voice concerned Raiden. Something horrible must have happened to make Sapphire hate her own home as much as she clearly did.

"I look just like my mother," Sapphire continued. "And nothing like my father. I had two younger sisters and an older one."

"You had sisters?" Raiden asked before he could stop himself. "You've never mentioned that before."

Sapphire looked at him calmly.

"You never asked," she said plainly.

Raiden blinked, realizing she was right.

"Anyway," Sapphire continued, turning back to Nel. "We had pretty good money. My father was a blacksmith. Mother sold woven goods to travelers. Both of my parents always paid good money for the luxuries. Mother liked perfumes, and my father wanted the best liquor in the town."

Raiden tensed at the thought of Sapphire living in a house where so much money was spent on alcohol.

"But a few years ago," Sapphire was saying, "my older sister Eva started spending all her time with a boy from our town. My father didn't like him. They went off on their own too often, and she became really secretive about what they did. I guess Father found out one night, and he didn't like it. He threw my sister out of our house and told her to never come back. That she had disgraced our family name. I was six at the time. My other two sisters and I watched the whole thing."

Raiden and Nel shared a look.

Sapphire drew a deep breath. "Then Lenice, my youngest sister, ran off into the field one day when she was about three." Sapphire's voice began to waver for the first time. "It was a few years after Eva … left. Lenice was running from my father. He had been getting more violent toward us and our mother."

Raiden grit his teeth. He had to turn away from the others to regain his composure.

Sapphire continued in a voice that was now shaking. "We hated it, but Mother didn't seem to care. Business wasn't going well, she said. Everyone in the town had apparently found out about Eva, and they stopped coming to Father for his work. We had to give up our horses, our cow, and one of our pigs. The day that Lenice ran, Father had hit Renee, our middle sister, in the face. She had a bruise on her left eye. I guess Lenice thought she was next, so she took off. Mother found her body that night. She'd been attacked, they said. By an animal. Renee and I weren't allowed to see the body."

Raiden felt his heart hammering. Of course he had been curious about his sister's past. But now, he wasn't so sure he wanted to know. Still, he couldn't help but watch Sapphire with wide eyes as she continued her story. Tears were falling from her eyes now.

"Lenice died when I was nine. When I was ten, Father broke my wrist trying to keep me in the house one night."

"What?" Raiden growled.

"He thought I was sneaking off to follow in Eva's footsteps," Sapphire pressed forward, "but really, I was trying to find some extra food for Renee. After he broke my wrist, I felt different. More angry, I guess. I felt older, too. It was like, all of a sudden, I understood that I was the oldest sister now. I was the one that was supposed to be brave."

A lump formed in Raiden's throat.

"I'd had enough of him abusing us. Mother kept making excuses, saying he was just stressed because of work. But I knew better. He'd gotten two of us already. Renee and I were the only two left. So, after my wrist healed enough for me to use it again, I snuck Renee out of the house. We stole what little food was left. Father didn't deserve it, and Mother didn't care about anything anyway."

Sapphire paused, sniffling and wiping at her tears. Nel leaned forward, watching her closely.

"Sapphire," he said gently. "You don't have to continue if you don't want to."

Sapphire sighed shakily, shaking her head. "Then we ran," she pressed on. "That first night, we made it part-way to Maith. But one night soon after that, it was raining, and Renee asked if we could go into the woods for shelter. The trees had been to our right the whole time. I had been using them to help with my sense of direction. At first I thought the woods seemed a little scary, but eventually I decided it would be a smart idea to get out of the rain. So we slept at the edge of the woods, where the first of the trees could keep the rain off our heads, but we didn't travel too far into the woods. The next morning, Renee was coughing and sniffling."

Dread began to pool in Raiden's stomach.

"She was shivering, too. I knew what was wrong. She'd gotten ill."

Her voice broke off with a single, heavy sob. She choked back the next one.

"Saph, you don't have to–" Raiden began softly.

"We had left home in the winter, you know," she interrupted, tears sliding down her face. "It had rained, and she was cold. We didn't have extra clothes, and we didn't have any food left. We only had one canteen of water. After one look at her, I gave it all to her."

Raiden felt his heart drop. He knew what was coming.

"We stayed there for a few days. I *tried* to find berries for her, and fresh water, but there just wasn't enough," she cried. "I woke up one morning–"

Sapphire let out a low sob, sniffing once again.

"I woke up, and Renee was … She was cold and stiff. She wasn't breathing. She wouldn't answer me, no matter how hard I cried or how loud I screamed her name."

Raiden felt his own tears falling freely down his face now. Sapphire was leaning forward, hugging her arms around herself.

"She … d-died in her sleep. Holding my hand. She trusted me to take care of her."

Sapphire hiccuped around her sobs. She wrung her hands together helplessly. "I didn't know what to do," she choked out. "I had to d-d-drag her to the wood's edge and then I … I laid her against a tree. And I braided her hair, just like she always liked. And I kissed her forehead. And then I left her."

When Sapphire paused, the silence seemed to smother Raiden.

Sapphire turned a tear streaked face to him. "Sometime at the end of winter, I arrived at Castle Maith," she finished softly. "A few months later, Raiden's parents took me in."

Sapphire began wiping at her face again, brushing her tears away. Raiden swallowed hard. He felt so powerless watching her suffer like this.

Her story was far worse than he had imagined. It made Raiden furious to know that Sapphire's father had beaten her. That she'd been forced to watch all three of her sisters die or be shunned. He wanted to comfort Sapphire, but he had no idea how to do that. He had no idea what she was feeling, having spoken about her past for what was probably the first time since she had arrived at Maith. He didn't understand how she was feeling right now.

Sapphire had said she wasn't as brave as Rayla, but Raiden was beginning to believe that she was just as brave. Only, she was brave in a different way.

"Wow," Nel said quietly. "Sapphire, I'm so sorry … "

"It's okay," she said. Her voice was slowly becoming steady again.

"No it's not," Nel pressed. "If I had known you'd been through that much, I never would have asked you about it."

Sapphire sniffed once. "I … I have to learn to deal with it. I can't change it. It's part of who I am now. And talking about it … actually helped."

The group was fairly quiet for several minutes. Nobody knew what to say. They simply followed the random twists and turns of the roads, each mulling over his or her own thoughts about what Sapphire had said.

"Well," Sapphire said, clearly eager to change the subject. She cleared her throat, forcing her back to straighten. "That was a happy topic. Next question, Nel."

Nel perked up, happy to oblige. "Right. Um, okay. Here's one. Is it just me, or have you guys noticed that Rayla wrinkles her nose when she gets quiet?"

Raiden felt his mouth twitch into a small smile. "It's not when she gets quiet, it's when she's thinking. You can tell because she looks up at the roof or the sky, too."

Raiden noticed that nobody else was adding to the conversation. Awkwardly, he looked back toward his friends. Both were looking at him in amusement.

"What?" he asked indignantly.

"Nothing," Nel said, shrugging. "Nothing at all."

Raiden frowned.

"So I was thinking we could go for a ride again, after all," Nel said. "I know we decided not to, but we've got nothing else to do, and I feel like our horses need a break from those disgusting stables."

"Sounds fun!" Sapphire agreed.

"I don't feel up for it," Raiden admitted. "But you guys can go."

"Let's do it," Sapphire said, excited to spend time with her horse.

"You sure?" Nel asked. Raiden nodded.

"Just take care of my sister," he warned. "Or else."

"Please, with those knives, she's the one that needs to take care of me."

After finding their way back to the inn, the three said their goodbyes. Nel and Sapphire left for the stables, and Raiden turned to head inside.

As he climbed the stairs, he sighed. He had known ever since he met Rayla that his life had been a fortunate one. Now, after hearing about Sapphire's equally difficult childhood, he felt like his happy lifestyle wasn't just fortunate. It was also rare.

He entered the room that he, Luca, and Macarius shared. It was empty.

"Good," Raiden said to himself. "Maybe Sir Macarius will finally meet that informant of his and lose his attitude."

As he sat on his bedroll on the floor, he muttered once more.

"And maybe Luca will get some more food."

He rolled onto his stomach, stretching his muscles out and groaning as he did so.

After a few minutes of silence, Raiden found himself dozing off. He sat up, shaking his head. It was too early to be going to sleep.

He let his mind focus on Rayla. They had all been given only enough food to last until they had gotten to the castle. There was a chance that Rayla hadn't found anywhere to replenish her supply. Which would mean that the girl had been without food for weeks. Which would mean …

"Please be okay," He prayed softly.

After several minutes of silence, Raiden sighed.

There was still plenty of daylight left. Glancing over, he saw his bow and quiver propped against the wall by the door. He could get some practice shots in, if for no other reason than to pass time.

He walked to the doorway and grabbed the weapon. As he moved to place the leather strap of his quiver around his shoulder, a small piece of parchment fell to the ground. Frowning, he bent to pick it up and unfolded it.

His eyes scanned over the words. He blinked several times, reading them again. He read the note three, then four times.

His heart leapt into his throat, and he laughed. In fact, he suddenly couldn't stop laughing. And then he was crying. Chest-rattling sobs escaped his mouth, which was still pulled into a wide smile. Unable to stop his crying, he simply leaned against the wall and held the note to his chest.

chapter 26
Raiden

"Gone?" Sir Macarius repeated the word for a second time. Raiden nodded slowly, feeling his face pull into a grin. He hadn't told anyone else about Sir Luca's note yet. He had wanted Macarius to read it first.

He handed his former master the note and watched as the archer's eyes scanned the parchment several times. Slowly, the man's face went slack, as if he was in shock.

The two bowmasters were sitting in their room in the inn. It was late. Macarius had only just returned from a day which, Raiden guessed, had been successful. The man had been in somewhat better spirits since his departure that morning, though he was still obviously bothered by something.

Raiden had finally managed to calm himself down earlier, and had spent the afternoon practicing with his bow in the corner of the castle walls. His mind had hardly been on the task, however. Instead, he had been thinking of the note, and what Macarius would say when he read it. Raiden had been anticipating this moment. Macarius, he knew, would understand the relief that Raiden himself felt.

As if reading Raiden's thoughts, Sir Macarius huffed out a short laugh and shook his head. A small smile of disbelief was playing on the man's face. Raiden's own grin grew wider.

"That bone-headed swordsman actually *can* use his brain," Macarius muttered.

Raiden chuckled at his master's words. The taunt had been a running joke between Macarius and Luca for several years. Everyone within Maith's walls knew about it. Both men were always trying to prove who was smarter.

Raiden reached out and accepted the note that Macarius had moved to hand back to him. Eagerly, he shoved the parchment back into his pocket.

"I just can't believe she was *here*," Raiden said, shaking his head. He began pacing the room. "And Luca saw her! He said they had all been assuming she would be looking for villages around the castle, and that's where they had been looking. But she must have been somewhere else this whole time!"

Macarius was following Raiden with his eyes.

"Yes, I know," he said calmly. "I read the note, too."

"So what do we do next?" Raiden asked, almost giddily. He stopped pacing and whipped around to face Macarius. The older man looked at him in understanding, but there was a warning in his eyes.

"Wait," he said.

Raiden frowned.

"Why shouldn't we go help him? Surely he could use a hand?"

Macarius stood, stretching his arms high into the air. Then, he walked over to his saddle pack and began rummaging through it.

"No," he said plainly. "He doesn't need any help."

"But–"

"Luca looks to be all brute, but he is a seasoned soldier. He is a decent tracker, and he even has a dash of common sense in that big head of his," Macarius added with a wink. "He does not need our help."

"I'm sure he's very capable, but it's–"

"I know, Raiden," Macarius said, having returned from his pack. He laid a comforting hand on Raiden's shoulder. "I know. You want to act. You want to help save your friend. But sometimes, getting involved in things can make them worse. There are times when your part is to sit back and just wait."

Raiden said nothing. Macarius sat across from the boy, holding out a piece of jerky to him. Raiden accepted and bit into the savory treat.

"Luca is not exactly vital to our cause right now. We don't need his authority or his sword. We have twenty other guards, and the official adviser from Maith is here already. Luca knew that. It's why he knew that he would be clear to leave. We need to let him do his work while we stay here to do ours."

"I have no job to do here," Raiden said, letting his tone show his exasperation. "I would be better off going with Sir Luca."

"Raiden," Sir Macarius said, not in a stern voice but in a compassionate one. Raiden lifted his eyes to his master's. "I've known Luca for nearly fifteen years. If there is anything I've learned in that time, it is that you should *never* underestimate what Luca will do to find the one man that has been left behind. Luca will not return until he has found Rayla. He is going to bring her back. It's what he does."

Raiden chewed his lip. He respected Luca greatly, but to trust him enough to bring Rayla back …

"How can you be so sure that he won't lose her trail and give up?" Raiden found himself asking.

Macarius hesitating, evidently questioning if he should share his next words with Raiden. Finally, he said, "He won't give up. I know that much."

"How?" Raiden pressed.

"Because," Macarius responded quietly. "He has done something like this for me before."

Raiden felt himself stiffen, caught off guard. Macarius looked at him with a pained expression.

"My sister was once taken by a group of bandits," Macarius explained. "I was frantic and could not think straight enough on my own to find her. So Luca found her for me. He searched for weeks, but he found her."

Raiden swallowed.

"But … " he said slowly. "You've never mentioned a sister before."

Macarius didn't answer, but instead looked away. Raiden suddenly got the feeling that, though Luca had found Macarius's sister, there was more to the story. Macarius clearly wasn't interested in sharing the rest, however, so Raiden chose to return the conversation to their current problem.

"Why couldn't Sir Luca track Rayla before," he asked softly, "instead of waiting for a week to go after her?"

Macarius forced an understanding smile onto his face.

"Because," he reminded Raiden gently. "Until now, he wasn't sure which direction she had gone. Now that he has seen her, he probably has a good estimate of where her tracks are. And he saw which direction she rode away in."

Raiden nodded, accepting the wisdom of a man who had seen much more than Raiden himself had. Macarius was right. Luca wouldn't give up until he had succeeded in finding and returning Rayla safely to their group.

As the two finished their jerky, Raiden cleared his throat, eager to change the subject.

"How was the meeting today?" he asked. Macarius's head snapped up.

"How did you know that I finally got to meet with him?"

"I just assumed," Raiden explained. "Seeing as how you finally came through the door *without* kicking or swearing."

Macarius laughed nervously.

"Ah, yes," he admitted. "I suppose I could have handled my stress in a better way. In any case, you were right in your assumption. I finally met with my informant, although it wasn't quite what I thought it would be."

"What do you mean?"

"Well I told you that I had plans to arrest him after he gave me all the information he had."

Raiden nodded, and Macarius seemed to hesitate.

"What happened?" Raiden asked, leaning forward. "Did he not have the information? Did he get away?"

Sir Macarius held up a hand. "Let me start from the beginning. It will make more sense."

Raiden settled his nerves, and Macarius leaned against the wall, sighing.

"I arrived in the tavern just like I have every other day," he began. "I was honestly expecting to sit there for several hours to no avail, just like every other day has turned out. But within a few minutes, he slid into a chair beside me. He told me everything he had learned from his spies."

"Which was?" Raiden couldn't help but rush his former mentor. Macarius gave him a wary look, but answered his question nonetheless.

"Our assumptions of Kuvira's motives aren't quite correct, it would seem," he said slowly. "It is much worse than we imagined, if what this man says is true. Ever since Lord Hightower discovered that Kuvira was on the move again, and he began meeting with Luca, Carrow and I, we have assumed that his goal was to destroy both Maith, because of his hatred for Lord Hightower, and Riraveth."

"Why Riraveth?" Raiden asked.

"We assumed that Kuvira had hated the Riravethians since the attack on his family years ago," Macarius explained. "Aside from Lord Hightower, these are the people that Kuvira likely blames for his wife's death. But rather than seeking immediate revenge after his family's murder, Kuvira simply went missing. We knew he was still out there, but from that moment on, he became strictly Maith's problem."

Raiden frowned. "Why would Riraveth just dismiss Kuvira so easily?"

Macarius shrugged. "Several reasons. For one thing, one man wouldn't be able to do any harm to all of Riraveth. He had lost his position of captain of Maith's guard, so Kuvira had no forces. For another, the king had just ordered the death of Riraveth's lord at that time for his treasonous act of marching against Maith. After that, Lord Dunnman was given the position, and he didn't seem too concerned with Kuvira."

Raiden wrinkled his nose at the thought of Lord Dunnman being given his position.

"Why would the king give the position of Riraveth's lord to a man like Lord Dunnman?"

Macarius nodded his understanding. "I wonder about that myself, sometimes. But we have to consider that people can appear however they please. It's possible that Lord Dunnman either *was* a decent man before his power went to his head, or he played the role well enough to win the position."

Macarius sighed. "Anyway, after the battle between Maith and Riraveth eighteen years ago, Maith found itself without a captain of the guard. And Lord Hightower has always dreaded the day that his brother-in-law returned. After what my informant told me today, though, I think a lot of what we thought we knew is irrelevant."

"How could it be irrelevant?" Raiden wanted to know.

"Apparently," Macarius continued, "Kuvira's forces are indeed here in Riraveth. And not only that, but Kuvira has seemingly made peace with his hatred for these people. Many of his men were originally from Riraveth's own guard."

"What?" Raiden exclaimed.

"It explains why this province is so crime-stricken. I hadn't noticed it until this afternoon, but the number of Riravethian guards is unbelievably low. According to my source, Kuvira had united a massive army under one, single goal."

Raiden sat still, unsure of which question to ask first.

"And that goal is … ?"

Macarius looked at him with tired eyes.

"To conquer the entire kingdom."

Raiden balked.

"But … how could he have gathered so many men? His army can't be numbered any more than Maith's guard, especially with our battle school students accounted for."

"You're right," Macarius said, nodding solemnly. "And that is where the main problem lies. Riraveth isn't his only aid."

"You mean he's gotten the other four provinces to agree to attack us?" Raiden asked in shock.

"No," Macarius replied. "Not the other provinces."

"Then … " Raiden let his voice trail off. A faint memory flashed through his mind. An old peace treaty between Rathús and a nearby kingdom.

"Yes indeed. You remember what kingdom lies to the west of this very province. You have seen its name on maps. You have heard of its conquests in nearby lands."

"Saodda?" Raiden breathed.

"It seems that our late friend reached out to the kingdom for aid. Saodda desperately wants the land of Rathús, but the ancient treaty and the undeniable force of the united kingdom stands in its way. But with Riraveth on Saodda's side, they will certainly stand a chance at conquering our land. And Kuvira had managed to unite the two forces under that very goal."

The men sat quietly for several minutes. Raiden was grateful for the silence. He needed time to digest what his master had just told him. This was no light discussion. They were talking about the possible doom of Rathús. What had originally started as a threat to Maith had turned into what could be a war for their entire kingdom. The other four provinces had to be warned. And Lord Dunnman should be questioned. It was certainly suspicious that so many of Riraveth's men had joined Kuvira. At the very least, the lord could be an accomplice receiving money to turn a blind eye. At worst … Raiden shuddered to think what it would mean if Lord Dunnman was completely joined with Kuvira.

As Raiden thought, another question occurred to him.

"And you said your informant knew where Kuvira's forces were located?"

Macarius nodded grimly.

"Where?" Raiden asked, almost afraid of the answer.

"Here," Macarius replied. "In the hills to the south. Directly on the border between Riraveth and Saodda."

"Can we trust that information?"

Macarius rubbed at his chest, drawing a deep breath.

"Raiden," he said in a way that made the boy's stomach drop. "I'm going to be honest with you. This doesn't look good for us. In order to confirm what my informant told me, we're going to have to scout the hills ourselves. And that's going to be dangerous because … "

Macarius seemed to struggle with his next words.

"Because of what?" Raiden demanded, unable to take the suspense any longer.

Macarius released a breath he must have been holding. "Because as I moved to have two of our guards arrest my informant, another man took off from the tavern."

Raiden swallowed hard.

"He had someone with him?"

Macarius nodded. "Likely one of his spies. I should have known to observe the people in the tavern more closely, but I was tricked into laziness after so many days of the man not showing up. Likely, that is what he had planned all along. The spy got away, and we can only assume the worst."

"Which is?"

"He's probably gone to inform Tenabris about us."

Raiden began to shake. If Lord Dunnman *was* working with Kuvira's troops, then they wouldn't be safe in the castle walls. They couldn't rely on Riraveth's troops to attack Tenabris's army.

But they couldn't leave until Sir Luca returned with Rayla.

"What do we do?" Raiden asked, his voice shaking.

"Several things," Macarius said. He must have noticed Raiden's panic, because he moved to lay a hand on his shoulder. The action helped steady Raiden. "First, we inform Carrow of the situation immediately. He will need to question Lord Dunnman. Then, I suggest you and I ride into the hills and look for Tenabris and the rest of Kuvira's men. We need an estimate of what we are up against to take back to Lord Hightower. The king, of course, will also have to be informed."

"Okay," Raiden said. "But Sapphire is not coming with us. Not if we are riding toward Tenabris and his men, and especially not if they might know we are coming."

The thought made Raiden feel sick, but he pushed his nausea aside. This had to be done, and he would not fail his kingdom.

"I should say not," Macarius agreed about Sapphire. "It's much too dangerous, and the smaller the number of people who go, the better. We can remain undetected and, if worse comes to worse, outrun any pursuers."

Raiden nodded, his hands trembling. Again, Macarius noticed. He drew his eyes from Raiden's hands to his face.

"If I thought that you would actually obey if I asked you to stay back, you wouldn't be going either," he told the boy. "But I have a feeling that you are stubborn and would follow me anyway."

"You can blame the man who trained me for that," Raiden told him, trying for a smile. He couldn't seem to muster the expression. "He once told me to follow my instinct, especially when it told me that someone was in danger."

Macarius shot Raiden a look, but Raiden was surprised to find true relief and gratitude in his mentor's eyes.

"So it's settled," Macarius said after a moment. "I will inform Carrow now. I'll also send two of our guards back to Maith at once to inform Lord Hightower of the danger. They can take my informant with them."

Raiden nodded. "And our part?"

"We will allot four days to ride to the hills and back and take note of Tenabris's location and numbers. Once we return, and Luca has arrived with Rayla, we can set out for Maith immediately."

"Sounds like a plan," Raiden agreed.

"Good."

Macarius had moved to smooth out his bedroll when another thought struck Raiden.

"What about Rayla?"

Macarius turned to look at Raiden, clearly confused.

"I mean, what did your informant say about her," Raiden elaborated. "You said he had mentioned that he knew about her past?"

"Oh," Macarius replied, nodding. "Yes. It would seem that Kuvira knew about her gift because he knew her mother."

"He *what*?" Raiden exclaimed.

"Shh," Macarius urged. "Do you want to wake everyone in this place?"

Raiden shook his head in shock.

"He knew Rayla's mother? How is that possible?"

"I don't know," Macarius admitted. "The man wouldn't say. Only that Rayla's mother apparently carried the same gift that Rayla does, and that Kuvira knew her."

Raiden tried to digest the information.

"We'd better get to sleep early," Macarius said, pulling Raiden from his thoughts. "This might be the last decent night's rest we will get in a while."

"Sure," Raiden said distractedly. "Of course."

They both made themselves comfortable on their bedrolls. In a matter of minutes, Macarius's breathing became deep, and Raiden knew the man was asleep. Raiden, however, remained very much awake.

As he lay in the dark, thoughts of what could happen next wandered into Raiden's mind. With Saodda on his side, Tenabris could quite possibly finish what his father had started. Before, they had been counting on the fact that Tenabris was inexperienced and possibly not yet trusted by his father's troops. Now, however, there was a far more sinister threat. The military forces of Saodda were significantly superior to Tenabris and his men, and would provide a strong ally. With Saodda's aid, Tenabris stood a much better chance at success. Maith was facing not only a more dangerous, but also a possibly more immediate threat.

There was another concern that Raiden couldn't shake. It hadn't occurred to him until just now, but the idea seemed so obvious that he wanted to kick himself for not thinking of it sooner. If he knew Rayla at all, then he knew that she would have been smart enough to find shelter. And there was only one place nearby that could provide protection for her and Dóchas. The hills were a few days' ride away, which could explain why nobody had seen her in the surrounding villages.

If Rayla was in those hills, she was alone and dangerously close to Tenabris and his army. Not only that, but she was completely unaware of the dangerous threat nearby.

Please don't go scouting around those hills, Raiden prayed silently. *I swear on my life, Rayla, if you get caught again …*

The thought of how he would rescue her was so exhausting, Raiden finally fell asleep. And in his dreams, he saw the many scenarios in which things could go wrong for him and Rayla.

chapter 27
Rayla

It was definitely one of the coldest nights yet. The wind was unusually rough and bone-chilling. It was sure to be the first of many cold spells, marking the approach of winter.

Still, Rayla had a semi-full stomach for the first time in days, so there was at least one thing to be content with. She had arrived at the village earlier that day and had immediately found herself knocking on the door of the home she had taken food from on her first time passing through. She had explained herself to the owners, asking if they had found the money she'd left them. The polite farmer and his wife had offered Rayla a meal and allowed her to bed down in their barn with Dóchas. Rayla was grateful.

The wind outside of the barn doors had begun to blow at alarming speeds as the night had fallen. Rayla glanced around her at the hay and dirt on the barn floor. One of the stalls had become Dóchas's temporary home, while the few other stalls held dairy cows and a single mule. Rayla hoped to find another place to stay, or continue staying here, until she knew the group from Maith left the province.

Rayla sighed. Not only was the wind blowing harder, but the direction seemed to be pushing the chill directly into the barn, through the cracks in the door and the walls. Rayla had been shivering viciously for hours now, and a large part of herself wanted to go back in time and buy the blanket she had seen in the market square. After all, money for food would do her no good if she froze to death.

Once again, she had given Dóchas the best blanket for the night. Still, the mare was shaking almost as badly as Rayla, and Rayla wanted desperately to give Dóchas more warmth. But they had no means of starting a fire, and even if they had, she couldn't very well do so inside a barn.

Rayla's heart ached knowing that her horse was just as miserable as she was. She regretted taking Dóchas with her. She wished the animal could be back in the Maith stables, warm and well fed. Instead, Rayla had ruined that chance for either of them. The cold, hard reality was beginning to sink in. Neither of them would survive the winter if Rayla couldn't find a more suitable place to stay. In fact, Rayla felt as if she may not survive the night.

It didn't help that both Rayla and Dóchas were still damp from that afternoon. The small rain shower had only lasted for an hour, stopping shortly after they had reached the village. But it had been enough to dampen Rayla's clothes and Dóchas's dirty coat, and the sun had not been out to dry or warm them up. The cold air mixed with the dampness around them doubled the chill they were forced to endure.

The thought of going out in the morning to search for work was slowly becoming less and less desirable.

"If I can even m-move by tom-m-morrow," Rayla muttered to herself. It was a valid concern. The cold air had practically frozen her limbs, rendering them useless. Her fingers wouldn't bend, her toes wouldn't flex, and the only movement that her limbs would make was to shiver.

Rayla heaved a deep, shaky sigh. She was pushed to the very back of the barn, but it hadn't made much of a difference. She was seated on a stack of hay with her back pressed against the wooden wall. Dóchas paced in her stall, as if sensing Rayla's discomfort.

A large gust of wind came rushing through the cracks in the walls, and Rayla was sent into another fit of uncontrollable shaking.

Rayla sniffled and closed her eyes. She let her mind wander back to the summer days. She imagined the warmth of the sun shining down on her face. She remembered the sweat that would pour down her neck when she sat outside for too long.

Dóchas whinnied softly.

"I know, girl," Rayla said through chattering teeth. "I'm s-s-sorry."

Dóchas nickered. Something about the sound seemed off. It had been considerably louder than the horse's first noise. Rayla opened her eyes and shot Dóchas a concerned glance.

"D-Dóchas?"

The mare turned her miserable eyes on her master. Rayla watched as the sound of a whinnying horse cried through the loud wind. To Rayla's shock, the sound hadn't come from Dóchas at all. Rather, Dóchas's ears had perked up, as if she too was confused about the other sound.

Before Rayla could stop her, Dóchas nickered in return.

"No!" Rayla whispered harshly. "Shh, D-D-Dóchas! Quiet!"

With difficulty, Rayla stood on shaky feet. In her stall, Dóchas had begun to prance around. Rayla leaned against the wall behind her for support.

"Dóchas, b-be *quiet*! We d-don't know who's out th-th-there!"

Rayla's mind raced. She considered mounting Dóchas and making a run for it. She had left Dóchas's saddle on for warmth, only loosening the girth strap. She could tighten the strap and be gone in seconds.

But the doorway of the barn wasn't tall enough for her height and Dóchas's combined. She could try to physically run, but she knew that she would get nowhere. Besides, she couldn't leave Dóchas behind.

Rayla backed into the barn wall. The cold wood behind her sent multiple chills down her spine. She shook miserably, partly because she was so cold and partly out of fear. With stiff hands, she fumbled at her waist until she managed to unsheath her sword. She held it out before her, knowing it would do her no good in a fight. She could barely keep the pommel in her hand, much less hold the weapon steady enough to take an accurate swing.

The doors of the barn creaked open, and Rayla flinched in fear. The moonlight shone in the doorway. Another gust of freezing wind blew into the barn, sending Rayla into more shivers. Outside, the horse whinnied again, much closer this time. Dóchas pranced nervously.

Rayla felt her body tense more than it already was. In the doorway of the barn was the silhouette of a large man, holding the reins of a horse. The man inched his way into the barn. Rayla whimpered slightly, attempting to raise her sword in warning. She knew, however, that the man would not be intimidated. Rayla was forced to hold the sword with both hands to keep it from falling as she shook.

The man led his horse into the barn and dropped the reins. Rayla breathed heavily. She couldn't see the man's face. The moonlight behind him was playing tricks on her eyes. Nearby, Dóchas inched forward, sticking her head out of her stall. The new horse walked over to her, and Dóchas bumped its muzzle with her own in a friendly manner. The sight confused Rayla.

She looked back toward the man. Something about him seemed familiar. He was fit, large, and obviously prepared for action. But he hadn't drawn his weapon yet. With a jolt of shock, Rayla let her blade clatter to the barn floor, not believing her eyes.

The man took one step forward, his shoulders tense.

"Rayla?" he tested. His voice was thick with concern.

Rayla shook uncontrollably. Her voice wavered as she replied.

"L-l-luca?"

chapter 28
Rayla

Relief.

That's what Rayla felt coursing through her body. From the familiar sight of her mentor, to the physical relief of the warmth of his sudden embrace as his body blocked the wind rushing into the barn.

At first, Rayla didn't move. She didn't fight the hug, but she also didn't move to embrace Luca in return. Rather, she simply stood, arms limp at her side, shivering into Luca's arms.

The longer they stood there, the more Rayla's mind began to work. She began to remember why he was there, why she was hiding, and eventually the painful memory of why she had run in the first place.

The heart-stopping realization that she was in an enclosed barn with someone she cared deeply for, after having lost control of her gift and killing a man, crashed into her mind. Frantically, she pushed away from Luca.

Clearly startled by her reaction, Luca allowed himself to be forced back. Meanwhile, Rayla retreated as much as she could until her back struck the wall of the barn again. With nowhere else to go, she began inching along the side of the wall, toward the opening.

"Rayla," Luca said quickly, holding his palms out to her in a gesture of calmness.

Rayla felt tears spring to her eyes. She shook her head viciously, feeling her body begin to shake again. This time, however, she had a feeling that it was more than the wind that was sending shivers through her.

Until this moment, with Luca here, Rayla hadn't realized how much she had truly wanted to be found. And yet, she also hadn't realized how much she wanted to stay hidden. She was still so unsure of what she had done, how she had accessed and controlled the dark magic that seemed to emit from somewhere deep within her. She didn't want to hurt anyone, especially someone that she cared for. What if she lost control again, and hurt her mentor? Luca had given her so much. He had taken her off the streets. He had poured countless years into training her, giving her a future. He had ignored the scrutinizing looks that others gave him for apprenticing a lady, and had encouraged her to write her own destiny.

Killing Kuvira had made her feel bad enough. If she ever hurt Luca, she wouldn't be able to live with herself.

These feelings welled up inside of Rayla as she looked at the man before her. A familiar stir tugged at her gut. She gasped.

"No," she mumbled, her voice wavering in panic. "Luca, get away. Right now."

Luca moved toward her slowly. Rayla felt herself shrink into the wall behind her. She looked into her mentor's eyes. He was looking back at her with determination and desperation. His eyes seemed to be silently begging her to stay put, to let him come to her. To let him help her.

"Luca, get out!"

He was the reason she was anything more than an orphaned girl. She owed him everything.

"Get away!" The feeling grew stronger. "Luca—!"

Desperate to force her mentor away, she lifted a hand to shove him. Something snapped, and power shot out of her hand. Not like it had every time before, seeping from her core to her palms, but stronger. More sudden, like a blast.

A terrified sob escaped Rayla's throat as she heard Luca's grunt of pain and surprise. She dropped to her knees, trembling and sobbing, lowering her head to the floor and grabbing fists full of her hair.

"I'm sorry," she choked out. "I didn't mean to … I can't … Luca … "

Rayla rocked back and forth, gasping between sobs for breath. What had she done?

A hand gently rubbed her back. Just like Raiden always did when they were kids and Rayla would get upset. Despite the situation, she felt soothed, if only slightly so.

"Rayla."

Rayla sobbed harder at the sound of Luca's voice. Unharmed. Unphased.

"Luca …" she choked out, turning to look at him and scooting away from his hand at the same time. "I didn't … are you … ?"

"The light was golden, Rayla," Luca explained calmly. "You hit me with your healing gift. Not the … other kind."

Rayla sobbed once more. Luca finally accepted that she wasn't going to let him touch her again. He squatted a short distance away, watching her closely.

"Are you alright?" Luca asked softly. Rayla shook her head again, squeezing her eyes shut.

"P-please," she begged, her voice almost a whisper. "Don't. I d-d-don't wanna h-hurt you."

"You won't," Luca replied firmly.

"You don't know that!" Rayla exclaimed. Her fear was evident in her face, she knew. Still, she couldn't help but hope that the force behind her reply would scare Luca away. That he would stop trusting her, before it cost him his life.

"Rayla, let me help you."

"You can't help me! No one can help me!"

"If you would just let us try–"

"Do you have this g-gift?" Rayla demanded, tears now pouring from her eyes. "Did you k-k-kill a man without even r-realizing how you were doing it?"

"Rayla, that was an accident."

"No, it wasn't!" she cried. "I knew what I was d-d-doing! I can remember what I did, why I did it, and even w-what I thought as it did it! None of it was a-an accident."

"But you didn't know–"

"I *did* know!"

"Rayla, stop."

"Get away! G-get away before I h-hurt you!"

"You're not going to hurt me!"

"I can't control it, don't you g-get th-that? You don't know that I won't hurt you, because *I* don't even k-know!"

Suddenly struck with an intense burst of fear, Rayla tried to bolt past Luca.

Instead, the man reached out, grabbing hold of Rayla's forearm. The girl's breath caught in her throat as she tried to jerk away. Luca held fast. Eventually accepting that she wasn't going to break free, Rayla stared in fear at his hands, where they met her skin.

"I do know," Luca said strongly. "Take hold of my arms."

"No," Rayla fought, but Luca only tightened his grip. Not in an unkind way, but in a way that told Rayla she wasn't going to be able to run off again.

"Do it," he insisted.

Rayla looked into the man's eyes for the first time, uncertainty evident in her face.

Slowly, Rayla allowed her hands to move, trembling, until she was gripping Luca's forearms as well. Nothing was happening, she realized. She didn't feel anything like what she had felt with Kuvira. There was no black glow around her.

Finally convinced that she would not hurt Luca at this moment, Rayla sighed deeply.

"See?" Luca pressed.

The stress of the past several weeks seemed to crash down on Rayla within seconds. She had been on her own, not only trying to keep herself alive but also trying to keep her beloved Dóchas comfortable and cared for. It brought back so many memories of her past.

The feeling of being alone had been weighing on her since she had run away. Like before, she would have had to fend for herself, with no family or friends. Only this time, it would have been harder. Before, she didn't realize what life could be like with people alongside her. Now, she would have to start all over, knowing all the while what she was missing out on. What she was leaving behind.

Knowing that she had left the only family she had ever known had been too much for her to process. Only now, in the comfortable presence of her mentor, could she admit to herself how afraid she had been.

Again, tears pressed their way to the surface. But she would not cry. Not in front of Luca. Not again.

"W-what are you d-d-doing here?" she said, beginning to shiver and chatter worse, now that Luca was no longer blocking the wind.

"You know what I am doing here," Luca replied meaningfully.

"How did you f-find me?"

"I saw you in the market. Then I tracked you here. Rayla, what were you *thinking* running off like that? It's dangerous for you to be on your own out here."

"B-but it rained," Rayla pointed out, deciding to ignore her master's rebuke. "How d-did you see the t-t-tracks?"

"I followed the direction I saw you ride off in until I found this village. I figured you would at least be smart enough to stay near shelter and food. I was about to give up and find a place to stay for the night when I heard your horse call out. Are you sure you're alright?"

He added the last question as another wave of violent shivers went through Rayla's body. She nodded, waving away his concern. Still, Luca was too smart to believe her.

"No, you're not," he decided. He moved to his horse's saddle pack, where he retrieved a thick blanket. Bringing it back over to Rayla, he draped it across the girl's shoulders.

"Th-thanks," she muttered. Luca nodded, still frowning.

"You should have had a blanket similar to this," he pointed out. Rayla's eyes darted momentarily to Dóchas, standing in close quarters with Luca's horse. Noticing the action, Luca followed her gaze.

"You gave your blanket to the horse?" He asked incredulously. Rayla shrugged.

"She was sh-shivering, too," the girl admitted. "And she d-didn't ask to be dragged out h-here."

Luca stared at her, mouth agape, for several seconds. Finally, he shook his head. Rayla thought she could see a small smile on the man's face, but she lost sight of it as Luca put a comforting arm around Rayla. He led her to the stack of hay again, where she slid down the wall until she was seated on the scratchy straw, exactly where she had been before Luca had arrived. With shaky fingers, she covered herself up with Luca's blanket from her toes to her chin.

The wind had died down a bit, she realized. It was still bitter and cold, but no longer was it coming through the cracks in the barn in unbearable gusts. Still, she was shivering. Her damp clothes, she had decided, were likely frozen stiff by now. Soon, she thought, she would be too. Rayla sighed.

Luca had gone to tie his horse's reins to the post of Dóchas's stall. Rayla had watched with approval and thankfulness as Luca had moved his own horse to block Dóchas from the wind.

The small barn was definitely cramped now. It had comfortably fit Rayla and Dóchas in with the other animals, but with two more members added, there was barely enough room for a rabbit left. Still, the close quarters provided a source of heat, for which Rayla was thankful. Even if the smell wasn't the best.

For the first time in weeks, Rayla felt comfortable enough to sleep. Her eyes began to drift shut.

Luca knelt down beside her, and she blinked several times, forcing her eyes to refocus. However, the man only lifted the blanket back up and over her shoulder where it had fallen. Then, he moved to sit beside her. Instinctively, Rayla curled inward, toward the warmth of her master's body. She needed it desperately, she realized. Otherwise, she would fall ill.

"Why are your clothes wet?" Luca asked softly. "I would have thought that you would know better than to sleep in cold, wet clothes."

"This *is* my extra set of clothes. The others are still wadded up from the rain on our way into Riraveth," Rayla muttered between sniffles and a cough. "I haven't had time to lay them out to dry off."

Rayla glanced over to see Luca frowning. After several minutes of silence, she dropped her head on the man's shoulder.

"You were wrong to ride off," he said quietly. Rayla felt her heart drop. She hated knowing that she had disappointed him.

She shivered again, pulling the blanket closer around her.

"N-nobody trusted me," she whispered. "Everyone was afraid of me."

Rayla felt Luca shake his head.

"No, Rayla," he said firmly but gently. "We were all shocked, but we were not afraid of you. You have to stop using that as an excuse to cover up your own fear and pain."

The brutally honest truth struck a chord inside Rayla. That was exactly what she had been doing. She said nothing, knowing that Luca was right.

"And I know that you remember the first lesson I taught you. A soldier–"

"Never runs," Rayla finished. She looked up at Luca, who smiled in approval.

"Get some rest," the man said. "Heaven knows you need it."

Too tired to argue, she said nothing. Instead, she shrank into her blanket, allowing its warmth to console her, and Luca's presence lull her to sleep.

chapter 29
Rayla

Rayla woke to a loud grunting noise. She opened her eyes slowly, knowing the bright sunlight would be blinding if she opened them too fast. She sat up, confused as to what the noise could possibly be.

As her eyes adjusted, she saw Luca bent over, tightening the girth on the saddle of his horse. At some point in the night, Rayla reasoned, she must have gone from sitting up with her head on Luca's shoulder to laying down on the floor. Luca's blanket was also still wrapped around Rayla's shoulders, which meant that the swordmaster had gone without any means of warmth last night. Suddenly feeling guilty, she untangled the blanket from around her and stood, stretching.

Her nose was still running from the night before, she noticed. She sniffed several times until the action eventually sent her into a cough. Luca, hearing the noise, stood up straight and turned her way. Rayla smiled sheepishly in greeting.

"Sleep well?" he asked, approaching and taking back his blanket.

"Yes," she replied. To her disappointment, her voice sounded just as nasally as she thought it might.

"Mhm," Luca replied, clearly not believing her. "And do you feel much better now that you've rested?"

"I do."

Luca turned nonchalauntly back to his horse and replaced his blanket beside the bedroll, behind his saddle. When he turned to look at Rayla again, she avoided his eyes, looking instead toward the doors of the barn or down at her feet.

"I see," Luca dragged out. "And this is just my observation, but it sounds to me like sleeping in cold, wet clothes has given you a head cold."

Rayla said nothing. Sighing, Luca returned to his previous task of preparing his horse. Rayla decided to do the same, if for no other reason than to escape any further scrutiny.

"Hello," she muttered to Dóchas as she reached into the food bag. Rayla produced several handfuls of oats, letting her horse munch out of her palm until she was satisfied that Dóchas had eaten enough. Then, she rummaged through her supplies until she found an apple.

Dóchas reached her neck out in an attempt to bite the treat.

"No," Rayla said, pulling away. "This one isn't for you."

The mare snorted.

"You've had your breakfast," Rayla retorted. "If you eat any more, your saddle strap won't fit around your belly."

Rayla turned as she bit into the apple to see Luca staring at her with an amused expression on his face.

"What?" she demanded around her breakfast. Luca fought a grin, which broke through anyway. Still, the swordmaster said nothing, only shaking his head. Rayla decided to ignore the man.

"We should head back to Castle Riraveth today," Luca told her. "We need to get back to Maith as soon as we can."

Rayla's breakfast suddenly felt like lead in her stomach.

"Because it's too dangerous for us here, now that Kuvira is dead?"

Luca didn't answer, and Rayla lowered her gaze.

"Because I killed him," she managed. Luca laid a hand on her shoulder.

"We can't change that now," he reminded her gently. "But we can't stay here, either. We've been staying inside the castle walls while we looked for you. With you back, we can go home."

Rayla hesitated. Luca seemed to notice the look of discomfort on her face.

"What is it?" He pressed.

Rayla swallowed. "What if … " she began slowly, "I get back, and I hurt someone else?"

Luca held her stare for several seconds, his eyes softening.

"You won't," he promised her. "But we will find a way to make you more comfortable. We'll tell everyone to give you space, if that's what you need."

Rayla thought about it, finally nodding.

Together, the two packed their things and tied their bedrolls behind their saddles. Of course, they kept their swords out, strapping them to their sides almost in sync. It was a familiar action that both Rayla and Luca did each day, routinely.

They led their horses outside of the barn and mounted.

The young farmer that had allowed Rayla to bed down in his barn was standing just outside his house.

"'Mornin'!" He called. Rayla noticed the nervous glance that the man gave Luca. She gave him her best encouraging smile, which she doubted did much good to comfort him.

"This is my mentor," she said. "I'll be traveling home with him now. Thank you for letting me use your barn."

The farmer nodded once, clearly relieved to have soldiers off of his property. Rayla turned Dóchas's head to leave. Luca followed.

Once they were a good distance away from the village, Rayla glanced at her mentor.

"I'm sorry," she said softly. "I've been meaning to say it, but I just … "

Luca seemed content to let Rayla find her words. Rayla opened and closed her mouth several times, finally sighing.

"I was … scared," she admitted with difficulty.

Luca turned to look at her. "I know," he said gently. "But there was no reason to run off."

"I just ... I thought that if I could get far enough away, nobody else would have to worry about getting hurt."

"And you wouldn't have to worry about hurting anyone else?" Luca guessed.

Rayla nodded.

"Not knowing how I healed Raiden all those months ago was stressful enough. But not knowing how I killed someone? It's terrifying. I could accidentally heal someone and it wouldn't be a big deal. But what if I accidently ... hurt ... you? Or Raiden? Or Sapphire? I didn't want to risk it."

Luca glanced her way, giving her a look of compassion.

"That's why you have to share the burden with us," he replied firmly. "You could have explained that to us, and we would have kept as much distance as you needed while still being there for you. That's what a family does."

Rayla balked. "Family?"

"Surely by now you've come to realize that's what we are?" Luca replied with a smile. "You and Raiden have been inseparable for years now. Sapphire follows you both around like she's your apprentice, and she clearly looks up to you both."

Rayla blinked, surprised by the words.

"You know I would do anything to protect and teach you," Luca continued, and Rayla felt a strange, warm feeling in her chest. "And even Carrow and Macarius care deeply for you."

Rayla bit her bottom lip, unsure if she wanted to say what was on her mind. After several seconds of consideration, she decided it was worth saying. She couldn't keep her emotions hidden inside of her forever, after all.

"You're right," she admitted. "I have come to recognize you all as my family. I just didn't realize that you thought of me as your family."

Luca smiled. "Of course we do."

"I rely on you all, but I've never considered that any of you would value me as much as family," Rayla continued. She felt awkward sharing such a vulnerable part of her emotions, but she couldn't seem to stop. She didn't *want* to stop. "If anyone would think of me like that, I would have guessed Sapphire or Raiden. But I've always considered myself to be just any other student to you, and maybe a simple girl to Macarius. Even Carrow, I thought, just saw me as a new item to study."

Luca blinked, clearly taken aback.

"Well, I suppose I can't officially speak for Macarius or Carrow," the man said. "But I can certainly speak for myself. Believe me, Rayla, you are not just any other student to me."

"Really?" She asked, surprised at how hopeful she sounded.

Luca nodded. "Aside from the fact that I know your background, aside from the fact that I have gone out of my way to provide you extra protection, and aside from the fact that you have more skill that anyone I've ever seen your age, including myself, I have come to think of you as my own daughter."

Rayla felt her head snap toward Luca as he had undoubtedly said the word. Yet she couldn't help but ask her next question anyway.

"Daughter?"

Luca looked her in the eyes, unwavering.

"Yes," he said. It was obvious that he was unashamed to admit his feelings, a virtue that Rayla now understood had always set Luca apart from many others she had seen in authority.

Rayla also sensed an odd mixture of emotions in herself as well. It was as if she could finally admit to herself that she had always longed to view Sir Luca as a father, but hadn't felt she was allowed to. Or maybe she had just been afraid to.

But now that she could admit it to herself, she felt true, rare joy inside. Followed by a sudden need to express her gratitude to Luca. She didn't want to lose the chance to do so, as she had with Finn.

"I–" she choked. "I've always looked up to you."

Luca smiled softly to show that he understood what she was trying to say. Rayla wasn't sure why the words were so hard to get out. She could easily leave the conversation there. But she also knew that this was something that needed to be said. She had learned once before how it felt to lose the opportunity to say something important. To wait until it was too late. She didn't want to make the same mistake again.

"I can't say that I know exactly how to picture a father, since I never had one," she pressed on. "But I know that I want your approval when I do things. I look to see if you are nodding or shaking your head. And … Last night, I felt safer when you were there. I guess, even though I have nothing to compare you to, you are my father figure."

Luca smiled, and Rayla couldn't help but smile as well.

"I'm glad we've finally gotten that out in the open," Luca said, clearing his throat. "Now when I tell you to do something, maybe you'll have a little more respect for your old man."

Rayla rolled her eyes, but she couldn't hide the tears of joy lining them.

They continued to ride in comfortable silence for several minutes before Rayla spotted something in the distance.

"What is that?" she asked.

Luca turned to look where she was pointing. Clearly just as confused as she was, he frowned.

"Riders," he said slowly. "Though I'm not sure who."

They squinted at the oncoming pair of riders until Rayla felt her heart skip a beat. She recognized the men.

"That's–"

"Sir Macarius," Luca finished in the same surprised tone that Rayla had used. "And Raiden is with him."

chapter 30
Raiden

Raiden and Macarius had left a day ago. They had explained to Carrow what they were doing, and why they had to go alone. Then they'd left the scholar to find out what he could about Lord Dunnman's involvement in Kuvira's plans.

Raiden had disliked the idea of leaving Sapphire, especially with Macarius and Luca being gone as well. He hardly trusted Carrow with his sister, after how the man had let Rayla go so easily. But Nel was there.

The thought almost made Raiden laugh. A few weeks prior, the thought of completely entrusting the guard with his sister's protection would have sent Raiden into a fit of stress and anger. Now, however, the thought of Nel watching over Sapphire was a comforting one.

Just before setting out from Castle Riraveth, Macarius had suggested that they stock up on food and purchase extra blankets from Riraveth's market square. Raiden hadn't argued. The hills were several days' ride away, and the weather was only going to get colder. So, after buying what they needed, they set out.

Now they were riding toward the hills, and Raiden could feel his nerves making his skin crawl. He felt paranoid.

Suddenly, Raiden sat up straight, his eyes squinting to see farther ahead of him. He wasn't paranoid at all; there were two riders coming directly for them!

"Macarius!" Raiden warned, drawing his bow. Startled, his master jumped to attention and did the same.

The two men stood up in their stirrups, nocking arrows to their bowstrings. They held the weapons low, ready for use.

"What is it?" Macarius asked. It occurred to Raiden that his master didn't question *if* Raiden had seen anything, only *what* he had seen. The thought that his master had such faith in him was comforting.

"Riders," Raiden replied quietly. He pointed and Macarius followed his finger, nodding. He saw them too now. As Raiden stared into the distance, the two figures came into better view, galloping toward them.

Raiden recognized them immediately. The familiar dark brown of the smaller horse, and the brown-red hair of its rider pulled a gasp from Raiden's lips. Quickly, the boy replaced his arrow in his quiver, slung his bow back around his shoulder, and sent his horse speeding toward the two riders.

In seconds, the three of them met, slowing their horses until they stood still. Raiden didn't even bother to dismount, and neither did Rayla. He rode straight up to the side of her and Dóchas, leaning over to cup Rayla's face in his hands. To his surprise, she flinched, but Raiden didn't release her.

"What in the name of the king himself were you *thinking?*" he demanded, his voice wavering. "Rayla, you could have died or been hurt or lost and – do you even know what's going on in the hills, not a *day's* ride from here? You could have been found by the wrong people and then–"

"Raiden," Rayla interrupted, daring to laugh. "I'm fine."

"It isn't funny!" Raiden exclaimed, not removing his hands from his friend's face.

"It kind of is, if you think about it."

It occurred to Raiden that Luca had been intuitive enough to ride forward until he reached Macarius, leaving Raiden and Rayla as alone as they could be in the open field.

"It's not funny," Raiden repeated, staring at Rayla now as he lowered his voice considerably. For some reason, he couldn't seem to get control of the many thoughts running through his head, nor could he stop the trembling in his voice. He was panicking, as if he was afraid Rayla might run off again. He tilted Rayla's head to one side, and then the other, inspecting her for injuries. "Are you okay? You sound awful."

"Am *I* okay?" Rayla demanded. "You're the one who's trembling right now.

"It doesn't matter," Raiden said, sighing shakily. "You're back. As long as you're not hurt … "

"Raiden," Rayla said, gripping his wrists where he was still cupping her face. Her voice was void of all amusement now, and Raiden knew that she was trying to show him that she was serious. "I'm alright."

"But you sound–"

"I know," she said, gently removing his hands. "I got pretty cold and wet from the rain last night."

Raiden recalled the rain shower that he and Macarius had also been forced to endure, as well as the unusually harsh winds.

"Where have you been?" he asked, moving one of his hands back to her face and sliding a single thumb over Rayla's cheek. Rayla sighed.

"It's all a very long story," she admitted. "Can we talk about it later, though?"

Raiden nodded.

"In the meantime, please, Raiden … Please don't touch me."

To his confusion, Rayla moved his hands away again, placing them on his saddle and backing Dóchas away from him.

"What?" he asked, shocked. His heart sank as he wondered what he had done to make her so uncomfortable. He knew that Rayla had always been a relatively independent and closed-off person, but she had never shied away from his touch. At least, not since they were young.

"Just until we know for sure what happened to me. What I–" her voice broke momentarily. "What I did."

Raiden wanted to argue. He wanted to tell Rayla that he trusted her. To tell her that he *knew* her, and knew she would never hurt him. But the deep pain in her eyes stopped him. He gave her a long, sad look before nodding, accepting her decision.

"Thank you," she breathed softly. The pain in her voice made Raiden want to reach out and hug her, but he knew that she would resist. Instead, he changed the subject.

"We should catch up with Sir Macarius and Sir Luca," he said as he turned his horse in their direction. The two men were patiently waiting on them.

As Raiden and Rayla approached, Raiden saw their masters share a glance. He waved the moment aside in his mind, deciding it had been nothing.

"Rayla," Macarius said, smiling at the girl. "I'm so relieved to see you! We were all worried. How do you feel?" Somehow, the bowmaster made his voice sound both concerned and condescending.

Rayla seemed to detect the tone, lowering her head in shame.

"Fine," she said.

Even as she said the word, Rayla began to cough, and Raiden caught Luca shooting the girl a worried glance.

Raiden frowned. Perhaps Rayla felt worse than she was letting on. The idea wasn't absurd. Rayla was known to play tough. Still, the cough ended quickly, and Raiden dismissed the incident.

"You should head back," Macarius said. Luca and Rayla both frowned.

"Don't you mean *we*?" Rayla asked. "And what are you two doing out here, anyway?"

She addressed Raiden when she asked the question. He grimaced. "It's a long story," he said, repeating Rayla's own words from their previous conversation.

"Tell us anyway," she replied. Raiden glanced at Macarius, who took the lead on the conversation.

Careful to leave nothing out, Macarius told Rayla of everything she had missed while she had been gone. Then, once he, Raiden, and Luca had answered all of her questions, Macarius informed both Rayla and Luca of his meeting with his informant, and the uncomfortable position that their group had been left in.

"Raiden and I are headed to the hills now," Macarius concluded. "We want to see what we are up against first-hand."

Luca and Rayla shared a look. The captain of the guard opened his mouth to say something, but Rayla interrupted.

"We're coming with you," she stated. Luca immediately scowled at her.

"That is not what I was going to say," he countered. "I was going to suggest that Raiden takes you back to Castle Riraveth while Macarius and I continue on to the hills."

The group was silent for a few seconds, and Raiden knew that Rayla was about to argue from the look on her face. She pursed her lips.

"I was in those hills a few days ago," she admitted. Raiden's blood ran cold.

"What?" Luca demanded. Rayla grimaced.

"It seemed like the best option at the time," Rayla rushed, defending her actions as best as she could. "I didn't want to be found by anyone, so I couldn't stay in a village. But once I settled down I realized I would have to stay somewhere else. Dóchas and I needed food."

"Rayla," Luca exclaimed. "That was too dangerous! The hills are too close to Riraveth's border with Saodda! Even with the peace treaty, you could have been–"

"I know," Rayla interrupted gently. "And when I heard voices one day, I left immediately. But my point is, I've been there. So I should go back with you now. I know where I heard those voices."

Raiden was shaking his head, but he stopped when he saw the look that Macarius and Luca shared.

"No!" He cried in response to both men before they'd even spoken. "She's not going back there!"

"You're going," Rayla reminded him.

"That's different," he retorted.

"If she wants to come, it's her own decision," Macarius said, shaking his head when Raiden shot him a glare. "But I want to be clear that I'll be giving the orders. No offense to you, Luca," he added, "but I know what we're getting into."

Luca nodded. "No offense taken."

Raiden's nostrils flared as Macarius said, "So it's settled. Let's go."

chapter 31
Raiden

They arrived in the hills by the end of the day. Rayla had led them to the cave she'd stayed in, and they had followed Macarius from there. The sun was now setting as they prepared to make their way over one of the final hills that supposedly led to the valley Macarius had told Raiden about weeks ago.

As they had with the last three hills, Rayla, Luca, and Raiden remained where they were when Macarius held up a hand. He gave his horse's reins to Raiden before crouching low and crawling on his belly to peer over the hill.

Each time he had done this, Macarius had taken roughly one minute to be sure there were no threats beyond before returning to the group and leading them forward.

This time, he remained in his spot for two minutes. Then three. Raiden shifted nervously in his saddle.

Finally, Macarius descended the hill and reached the group. He didn't accept his reins when Raiden moved to hand them back.

"Let's leave the horses here," Macarius suggested, his voice thick. "If we take them to the very top, they might see us."

Raiden's breath caught in his throat.

"You saw them?" He asked. Macarius nodded solemnly.

"How many?" Luca wanted to know. Macarius gave him a weary look.

"You'd better come see for yourself."

They left the horses as Macarius had suggested. As Raiden crawled on his belly beside Rayla, he felt his heart begin to hammer in his chest. He wasn't sure that he wanted to see what was beyond the hill.

The answer was no.

Raiden's jaw dropped as the valley came into view. It was full of troops, separated into even sections that stretched as far as Raiden could see.

"How many are there?" He managed to whisper, his voice trembling.

"At least five-hundred," Macarius said. "Maybe more. And I'm betting most of Saodda's troops haven't even arrived yet."

Raiden's mind began to consider the worst scenarios. If this army reached Maith, would his province have enough protection.

"Sir Luca?" Raiden's voice seemed to shake even more.

"Yes?"

"How many troops does Maith have at hand?"

Luca turned to look at him. His expression said enough, but he answered Raiden nonetheless.

"Two hundred and fifty guards," he said quietly. "Probably an extra hundred if we used the battle school students."

Raiden swallowed.

"So," Rayla clarified in a nervous tone, "even if we enlisted the trainees–"

"We would still be outnumbered nearly two to one," Luca finished.

o o o

That night they camped at the edge of the hills, taking turns keeping watch. The next morning, they set out for Castle Riraveth as soon as the sun began to rise.

"I still can't believe it," Raiden said, more to himself than to the others.

Raiden had to admit, it felt as if it were nearly impossible to comprehend what they had seen. Easily *five* hundred men, and more likely on the way, camped out under one goal; destroying Rathús. The thought made Raiden's head spin.

"Depending on what Carrow has discovered about Lord Dunnman, the lord may need to be informed of this," Macarius thought aloud. "If he turns out to be innocent of any agreement with Kuvira's army, we might as well inform the man of his mistake while we are here."

"His mistake?" Raiden asked. Of course, he despised the lord of Riraveth just as much as Macarius seemed to, but he wasn't sure how Kuvira's army was any mistake of Dunnman's.

"Of course," Macarius growled. "These hills are under his jurisdiction. His discipline. If he had bothered to scout them out even *once* within the last two months, he would have caught this disaster before it had bloomed."

Raiden frowned. That much was true, he supposed. He shook his head, still feeling overwhelmed.

"I just can't believe the size of that army," he said breathily.

"I know," Macarius snapped. "You've said it five times now."

Raiden ignored the man's jibe, still shaking his head.

"What are we going to do?"

"I don't know," Macarius said.

Raiden, noticing the slight change in tone of his master's words, closed his mouth. He could take a hint. Glancing at Rayla, he noticed that she was pale with fear of what they had seen the night before. Raiden couldn't blame her.

"Do you know what I'm still wondering?" Luca thought aloud. Everyone turned to look at him expectantly.

"Why is Saodda risking the current peace between our kingdoms to side with Kuvira's forces?"

Raiden pursed his lips. He hadn't considered the risk Saodda was taking. But Macarius seemed to have thought it through.

"Kuvira promised them a chance at the rest of the Rathús," the man said. "Kuvira only wanted revenge on Lord Hightower. If he had to give away the kingdom, he would have made that bargain."

Raiden listened for a few minutes as Macarius and Luca discussed the matter further. They seemed to be taking turns guessing why Saodda had gotten involved. With nothing to contribute to the conversation, Raiden returned to his own thoughts.

One thought in particular had been bothering him since they had found Rayla. Why had the girl resorted to running away so easily? After years and years of friendship, why hadn't she just talked to him? Even worse, why had he so easily let her go?

Raiden glanced at Rayla. She was staring ahead, but not in a way that made her seem angry. Rather, she seemed to be focusing on something. He followed her line of sight but saw nothing. Glancing back, he caught a quick movement from the girl. She was shivering.

Raiden frowned.

"Are you alright?" he whispered so as not to catch Sir Macarius or Luca's attention. Rayla looked at him in surprise.

"Yes," she replied. "Why wouldn't I be?"

"You're shivering," he pointed out. Rayla shook her head dismissively.

"It's just a head cold," she replied.

Raiden wanted to press Rayla, but at that moment, Dóchas was sent into a fit of shivers as well. Raiden noticed for the first time just how exhausted the mare looked. Her head was drooping considerably. Rayla had noticed as well. Raiden could see the deep concern in his friend's eyes as she considered her horse. He watched as Rayla moved to dismount. It was clear that she was hoping the reduced weight would ease Dóchas's laboring.

Before Raiden could protest, Luca, who had been riding to Rayla's left, grabbed her upper arm firmly and stopped the girl from her dismount.

"Don't," he said forcibly.

Rayla froze, looking to her former master in both fear and desperation. Not fear for herself, Raiden realized with a jolt, but for Luca. She was afraid that she would hurt him. Still, the man didn't waver.

"You are sick and you are exhausted," Luca continued sternly. "You are not walking."

"But, Dóchas–"

"Will have to manage. She will tell you when she absolutely must have a break. And when she does, we can stop. But you *will not* walk. You are not going to collapse on my watch."

Raiden felt both gratitude for Luca keeping Rayla safe, and sympathy for the compassion that his friend felt for her horse. An idea formed in Raiden's head.

"She can ride with me," he suggested. All three of his companions looked at him. He shrugged.

"It would give Dóchas the break she needs and Rayla wouldn't have to walk," he explained.

"Raiden, I don't want to touch–"

"That is an excellent idea," Luca announced, cutting off Rayla's protest.

Raiden watched as Rayla battled her fear and her concern for her horse. The latter apparently won, because she reluctantly allowed Raiden to ease her from her own saddle to the back of his.

"Comfortable?" he asked.

"I suppose so," she replied.

The group rode in silence. Raiden couldn't help but notice the tension in Rayla's body.

"Ray," he whispered so that only she could hear. "Relax. I trust you. You're not going to hurt me."

"You don't know that."

Frustrated, Raiden reached behind his back with both arms, grabbing Rayla's. He pulled her arms around him and clasped them around his waist so that she was forced to have physical contact with him.

To his surprise, she didn't pull away. Instead, she seemed to subconsciously lean into his back. Her hands remained firmly clasped around his stomach. She was quiet for several seconds. Then, Raiden felt her relax.

"Thank you," she whispered softly.

"Always," he replied.

Raiden glanced to his left, where Luca and Macarius were both riding with small smiles on their faces. Raiden frowned. What was so funny?

Behind him, Rayla had begun to lean heavily on his back. Her hands had at some point unclasped themselves so that her arms were hanging limply, resting on his thighs. As he listened, the girl began to snore softly.

Despite the awkwardness that Macarius and Luca had instilled in him, he couldn't help but smile along with them.

chapter 32
Raiden

He wouldn't say that he was worried, exactly. It was clear that Rayla wasn't going to die. But she was obviously sick. Raiden knew how miserable a head cold could make a person, having just gotten over his own. But he had only recovered after a week of rest and warmth in Castle Riraveth's walls. Rayla had gotten no rest or warmth in that time.

Luca had become more and more irritable as Rayla's coughing had increased. It was almost as if the man blamed himself. Raiden considered the idea. It wasn't completely unwarranted. After all, part of the blame fell to all of them for letting Rayla run off in the first place.

The three had each given the girl their blankets. Of course, she had given two of those blankets to Dóchas. Either way, both Dóchas and Rayla had finally stopped shivering, which was good. The action had completely drained Rayla's energy. She had slept the majority of the trip, sometimes behind Raiden and sometimes behind Luca. They had decided to rotate that way so that Dóchas could recuperate as well, with fewer breaks needed.

But Rayla was still pale. She still coughed and sniffled several times within each minute, and it was obvious when she spoke that she didn't feel her best. Her words often slurred together in exhaustion. Again, it wasn't that Raiden was *worried*. There was nothing to be worried about. It was a simple head cold. Still, he didn't like seeing Rayla this way.

"Is she asleep?" Macarius said quietly. Raiden didn't move, afraid that if Rayla was in fact asleep, he would wake her up. Instead, he only muttered a reply.

"Not sure," he said softly.

To his right, Luca leaned back to look.

"She's out," he said, also keeping his voice down. It seemed they all agreed that none of them wanted to disturb her. At this point, sleep was vital for her. Otherwise, she wouldn't recover.

"Good," Macarius mused. Luca nodded.

"How is Dóchas?" Raiden asked. He knew that, were Rayla awake, she would be asking the same question.

"Better," Luca replied. The mare had remained between Raiden and Macarius while Luca had moved to Raiden's right. The new arrangement allowed them to transfer Rayla more easily.

Macarius kept Dóchas's reigns tied firmly to his own pommel, though Rayla had said that the action wasn't necessary. Dóchas would follow them as long as Rayla was with them.

Raiden glanced over to the horse. He had to admit that Dóchas looked much better than she had a few days ago. Her head was no longer drooping. She had stopped shivering. Once, Raiden could have sworn that the mare had even snorted when Macarius had nearly slipped out of his saddle as they had ridden through the night.

"That's good," Raiden replied absent-mindedly.

Behind him, Raiden felt Rayla stir. He quickly reached back to steady her, feeling her slip to one side. *She really must be out cold*, he thought as she remained asleep. Finally, he got her resituated and wrapped her arms back around his waist.

As he moved to regain control of his reins, he felt Rayla stir again. This time, however, she was clearly just moving in her sleep and not slipping off the horse.

As Raiden moved his hands away, one of Rayla's hands caught his. He froze, allowing her to unconsciously lace her fingers through his. Heat rushed to his cheeks. Still, he squeezed her hand in return as she settled against his back.

Hoping that the moment had passed unnoticed, he quickly glanced around. To his embarrassment, both Luca and Macarius were looking at him in amusement.

"I … " Raiden tried, but his voice failed him. He wasn't even sure what he was trying to say.

"It's nothing to be ashamed of, my boy," Macarius said gently. "She's a fine young lady."

"That she is," Luca agreed. "Although, you would certainly have your hands full with her. She won't conform to a typical housewife."

"I don't want her to conform to anything," Raiden said softly. He wasn't sure why he was finally admitting it, especially to these two grown men. Still, their wisdom was somewhat comforting. Besides, it was obvious from their constant looks and grins that they already knew how he felt.

"That's just as well," Macarius chuckled softly. "I'm not sure you could win in a fight against her."

"I don't want to fight her," Raiden replied, clearly not in the mood to joke.

Luca and Macarius shared another look before Luca finally stared at Raiden with wide eyes.

"My heavens," the swordmaster breathed. "You've got it bad, haven't you."

"I believe he does," Macarius agreed.

Raiden felt his heart rate speed up. He wanted to say the words so badly, but they seemed almost silly. Especially when muttered to his former master and to Sir Luca, a renowned soldier.

Still, he had been aware of his feelings for some time now, especially after Rayla had gone missing months ago, in the woods. After she had disappeared the second time, Raiden had decided that it wasn't something he could ignore.

"I… I love her," he said. The words felt odd to say aloud, but to his relief, neither Luca or Macarius ridiculed him. Instead, both men smiled warmly.

"We know," Macarius admitted. "It's obvious. Honestly, I'm not sure how she hasn't noticed."

Raiden felt Macarius and Luca's eyes on him. His cheeks flushed.

"It's that obvious?"

Macarius smiled again. "Yes."

Raiden swallowed. "People don't see the real Rayla," he thought aloud. "I know that she sometimes seems rude, but she isn't. She's just … careful."

"She's been broken," Luca added quietly, but Raiden shook his head.

"She's not broken, she's just her own person. But I love that person. I love how sincere she is when she finally lets you in."

He hadn't meant to say so much, but part of him wanted Macarius, and even Luca, to know how he truly felt. He wanted them to understand the depth of his feelings. He trusted them with his emotions. Better yet, he wanted their advice.

Macarius said nothing. He only stared at Raiden in shock. Raiden turned to look at Luca. To the opposite of Macarius's surprise, Luca smiled in approval.

"Tell her that," he said plainly.

Raiden frowned. "What?"

"You clearly love her with all that you are. You need to tell her that."

"But she has other things on her mind. She has worse things to deal with at the moment. With this new side of her gift, and her fear of not being able to control it–"

"Raiden," Macarius cut in, shaking his head at the boy. "You must tell her. You can't deny her the right to know when she is loved."

"What about the war? This is hardly the time to talk about feelings. Our kingdom is under attack, there's–"

"My boy," Luca said, stopping Raiden mid-sentence. "There will always be plenty of excuses not to tell her. But the one that is ruling them all is your own fear. I know that Rayla is cautious with her trust, but she already trusts you. I know she is careful with her feelings, but she already connects with you deeply. All that is left is to find out if she loves you too."

Raiden blinked, looking at Luca. The man knew Rayla better than anyone else, besides Raiden himself. Raiden knew that he could trust Luca's word. Still, Rayla so rarely spoke of love, and was so clearly unfamiliar with the practice of showing it. What if she didn't return his feelings or he made her feel uncomfortable? What would happen to their friendship?

Raiden's heart lurched as Rayla began to move behind him. This time, he knew that she was waking up, and he was all too aware of their hands still entwined.

"Morning," Luca said casually, clearly trying to drop their previous conversation for Raiden's benefit. Raiden shot the man a look of gratitude.

"Mhm," Rayla mumbled, sounding just as tired as she had been before she had fallen asleep.

Raiden, keeping his arm still so as not to let go of Rayla's hand, turned in his saddle.

"Sleep well?" he asked quietly. His stomach flipped slightly at the sight of his friend. Her eyebrows were pulled together in a way that made her look either confused or upset. She was blinking rapidly, clearly trying to adjust her eyes to the sunlight. Even her lips were pouty.

"I guess," she groaned.

"You sound awful," he admitted.

"Thanks," she huffed. Raiden couldn't help but chuckle. He turned back to face forward. As Rayla continued to shift around, she seemed to realize that her hand was in Raiden's. Both friends tensed with uncertainty before Rayla gently disentangled their fingers. Her hand brushed Raiden's arm as she brought her own arm back to her body. It was a slight touch, but it sent a ray of hope through Raiden.

"Oh," Rayla said, suddenly sounding alert. "How long was I out? Do I need to get down and walk? I feel–"

"No," all three men chorused.

"Fine," she snapped. "But I *do* feel better."

"Good," Luca said. "That means you can resume the normal travel pace when we head home in a few days."

"Or I could start now," Rayla retorted.

"Drop it, Ray," Raiden retorted. Behind him, he heard the girl huff a sigh.

To their right, Luca rolled his eyes to the sky and shook his head.

"I told you," he muttered to Raiden. "Hands. Full."

chapter 33
Raiden

They had done all that they could.

At least, that's what Macarius, Luca, and even Carrow were all saying. Upon their return, Carrow had informed Macarius that, though he didn't believe Lord Dunnman was in league with Kuvira's army, he wasn't unconvinced that the man had accepted money to look the other way when his guards began to disappear. As such, they had elected not to inform the man of the situation in the hills.

There had been an awkward moment in which Carrow had obviously been relieved to see Rayla, but had sensed his unwelcomeness in the group. The scholar had scuttled off quickly to prepare for their journey home.

After a quick reunion, in which Sapphire had shed several tears into Rayla's tunic before proceeding to punch the girl in the arm, the group had been briefed of the situation.

Raiden found himself mulling over everything he had learned in the past week. Tenabris and his troops were in Riraveth province, which was under Lord Dunmann's control. Until they could send word to the king, there was nothing left for them to do. That is, not without starting an unwelcome squabble with Dunmann, who did not seem to believe he needed any help. As things were, they were all helpless until Tenabris himself made a move or the king called for action.

"Who will go to inform the king?" Raiden asked as he, Macarius, and Luca packed their bedrolls and other items in their room.

"Lord Hightower," Luca said shortly. Raiden frowned.

"How will he find time to travel a week and a half away to Rathús Province? He couldn't even afford to come here."

"A lord will be able to get an audience with the king the easiest. Especially on such short notice," Macarius explained. "We will just have to manage without him."

"That seems rather odd," Raiden pointed out. "The king has always been spoken of as understanding and willing to listen to the problems of anyone who comes to him."

"And he is," Luca answered. "But as the king he has many responsibilities, and he can't be expected to drop everything every time a random subject wanders into the castle. If it were a province lord, however, he would most definitely make time to hear what he had to say."

"So who will take over for Lord Hightower in his absence? Surely he will have to plan to be gone for a decent amount of time, and it's not exactly an ideal time to leave the province unattended."

"Carrow will," Macarius replied. "Seeing as how he has no heir, his High Advisor is his next in command."

"We need to head out soon," Luca announced, cutting through the conversation. "The rest of the men should be at the stables by now."

As the three of them left their room, Raiden stopped at Sapphire's door, across from their own.

"Saph," he called, knocking on her door. "Time to go!"

"Coming!" a muffled voice from inside replied. In just a few short moments, the young girl emerged, lugging her bedroll and other supplies through the doorway.

"Here," Raiden offered, taking the bedroll off her shoulder and carrying it for her.

"Thanks."

"Where's Rayla?" Luca asked. The older girl had been placed in Sapphire's room for the night, seeing as how they were the only two female members of the group.

"She's at the stables already," Sapphire replied, a little breathlessly. Clearly, the girl had been rushing to gather her things. "She wanted to check on Dóchas."

"Of course," Luca said. "How silly of me to fail to assume such a thing on my own."

Together, the four of them descended the stairs and made their way to the stables. As Luca had predicted, the rest of the cohort, along with Carrow and Rayla, were gathered around, saddling and packing their horses.

"Is she alright?" Raiden asked as he approached Rayla. The girl was rubbing Dóchas's muzzle affectionately.

"I think so," Rayla said quietly. "But I still think I'm going to walk as much as possible on our trip home."

Raiden didn't like the thought, but he had been expecting as much. Even if Dóchas had been galloping around and bursting with energy, Rayla still would have coddled the animal.

"Are we about ready to leave?" Rayla asked.

Sapphire stepped between the two of them, moving to her horse's stall to prepare the animal for travel. Raiden moved to help his sister saddle the horse.

"I think so," Raiden replied, grunting as he lifted the heavy equipment. "Sir Macarius says we need to travel as quickly as possible. He's anxious to get home, and I can't say I feel any different. We have a lot to do."

Rayla kicked at the dirt under her boots, lowering her voice. "I hate to ask this," she said awkwardly, "but I can't get the thought out of my head."

"What thought?" Raiden asked gently.

Rayla chewed her lip. "What did you all do with … with the body?"

Raiden started in surprise. It hadn't occurred to him that his friend might want to know what they had done with Kuvira's body.

"There's a place behind the castle wall, on the far western side," Raiden explained. "After the guards at the gate *finally* allowed us to show the body to

Lord Dunmann and his men, the Riravethian guards took the body. I assume they buried it there."

Raiden watched Rayla carefully. The girl nodded, clearly disturbed by the thought.

He laid a hand on Sapphire's horse's neck, patting it absently. "I'm sure you didn't … mean to kill him …?" He couldn't help the slight turn in the end of his sentence, asking a silent question.

Rayla caught the tone, sniffing once. "But I still did it," she whispered.

Raiden swallowed. "Have you ever considered that it may not be a bad thing that he is gone?" Realizing how calloused he sounded, he elaborated. "I mean … he didn't deserve to die but … The lack of his leadership for his army could be the one factor that changes this coming war in our favor."

"I suppose," she replied, obviously anxious to drop the subject. Raiden relented.

"Here you go," he said, handing the reins of Sapphire's horse over to his sister. "Do you need help packing your bedroll?"

"No," Sapphire said, grinning. "That I can do for myself. Thanks."

Fifteen minutes later, the group was packed, mounted, and ready to leave. They stood in the same spots as the first time they had traveled. Except, to Raiden's shock, Luca. The swordmaster had replaced Carrow at the front line.

"Where is Carrow?" Raiden asked, attempting to keep his voice neutral.

"He wanted to ride in the back with Rayla," Luca said, clearly trying to calm Raiden down. "He wanted to apologize."

"As well he should," Raiden muttered.

Raiden couldn't help but wonder how the conversation between Carrow and Rayla was going. He had never doubted that Carrow had been worried about Rayla. After all, the man had always been kind and encouraging toward the both of them. Still, Raiden's entire opinion of the scholar had been shaken when he had completely abandoned Rayla without a second thought.

"Raiden," Macarius leaned over to speak directly to the boy. Raiden blinked a few times before turning to look at his master.

"Sir?"

"You must stop worrying," the man insisted. "About everything. About Rayla, because she is safe. About her gift, because Carrow will work with her to find the answer. And about Carrow," Macarius continued quickly, cutting off Raiden's protest. "Because he always has and always will admire and strive to protect Rayla."

"He certainly wasn't trying to protect her when he let her run off on her own."

"He was," Macarius replied.

"How? How is that protecting her, to let her be alone in unknown lands when she was so unstable already?"

"Exactly. She was unstable. If anyone had gone after her, even you, there's no telling what she would or could have done. Not because she would want to, but because she wasn't in control of her gift. Carrow letting her go was exactly what saved her and anyone else from further harm. She had time to calm down and regain control."

Raiden didn't respond. It did make sense. But Raiden despised the thought of admitting that Carrow had done the right thing. He didn't want to let the man off the hook. After all, the blame had to fall on someone, right?

Suddenly, Raiden heard an explosion of noise from behind him. Several voices cried out in alarm. Surprised, he spun in his saddle. His heart stopped.

At least two dozen men, armed and mounted, were rushing from along the castle walls, where they had clearly been hiding out of sight. Nobody had thought to check their surroundings, he realized, mentally kicking himself. Raiden watched in horror as the men crashed into the back row of their group.

The men wore black cloaks.

They were part of Kuvira's troops.

"Rayla!" he called out, much too late. He had turned just in time to see that she had taken a blow to the left arm and then been lost in the chaos. The remaining enemies who hadn't been caught up in a fight already crashed through the Maith ranks. Raiden reared his horse on its hind legs, drawing an arrow as he spun around to face the fight.

He shot as many men as he could, but it was difficult to aim in such close quarters. Men from both sides of the fight were running around on foot or riding around blindly. Some were lying motionless. To his right, he saw a blur of motion and knew immediately that Luca had ridden into the battle.

"Retreat!" Raiden heard Macarius call. The man had remained beside Raiden, also using his bow to pick off as many enemies as possible.

Somewhere within the battle, Luca repeated the order.

Raiden backed his horse up. None of the intruders had reached the front of the lines. Not yet. He stared into the chaos, gasping for breath. Men cried in pain and anger. Too many Maith guards had been taken by surprise and cut down.

"Retreat to the left!" Luca cried, echoing Macarius's orders. Raiden caught sight of the captain of the guard running through the chaos. He must have been dismounted at some point, but that didn't seem to stop him. He was an impenetrable force, plowing through both mounted and unmounted men. The enemy seemed to steer away from him, despite their numbers.

Raiden had lost sight of Rayla, Sapphire, Carrow, and anyone else who wasn't ten meters away from him. He felt guilty, backing away while everyone else was fighting for their lives, trying to retreat as Sir Luca had demanded. Determined to do his part, Raiden drew his sword and kicked his horse's sides, charging back into the battle.

Blow after blow seemed to rain down on him, never deadly but always painful. A cut on the forearm, a slice on the leg, a falling soldier's helmet to the kneecap. He scored a few hits as well, although not enough to do much good. He simply wasn't trained enough with the sword, much less while atop a horse. But his mount was his only advantage. Most of the others had been cut down by now. A few Maith guards and several of the enemies had managed to stay atop their steeds, but not as many as those who had fallen.

"Raiden!" Macarius called in warning. Raiden spun to look behind him, toward the sound of his master's voice. Instead, he saw a man brandishing a broadsword and running toward him. Raiden thrust his own sword out in fear. By sheer luck, Raiden's weapon impaled the enemy before his sword had time to touch Raiden.

The man fell, jerking Raiden's sword out of his hand. Raiden drew his bow as a means of protection now that he had no sword. He turned to thank Macarius.

As his eyes found the man, they widened in horror.

There had been no time to warn the bowmaster. The sword was already coming down, and Macarius was facing the opposite direction of the danger, his bow drawn and aimed somewhere in the distance. Raiden watched the sword tear through Macarius's back. He saw Luca, appearing out of nowhere, strike the enemy down. But he had been a split second too late. Macarius slumped forward, rolling out of his saddle, and Luca caught him.

"No!" Raiden cried.

"Retreat!" Several Maith guards were calling desperately. In shock of what had just happened, Raiden spurred his horse to the left, following where Luca was dragging the injured bowmaster.

"Macarius!" he cried, dismounting before his horse had even stopped.

"Raiden, don't touch him," Luca demanded. "Don't move him."

"Is he–"

"No," Luca cut in. "Not yet, anyway. But we must return to the battle."

"But–"

"He's safer here than he will be anywhere else. We have to go."

Raiden fought to drag his eyes away from his master, who was moaning in pain. Before he could bring himself to leave, Raiden knelt beside the man.

"Don't you *dare*," he threatened. "I'll be back. But don't you *dare* die."

Raiden turned, ready to follow Luca back to the battle, but he stopped dead in his tracks.

There was no battle.

The field in front of Riraveth's gates was covered in bodies. Some were crying out. Some were silent. A few Maith guards stood, walking among the mess and checking for survivors. When one was found, he was dragged over to the side and left as the still standing guards returned to scan the rest of the bodies.

As for the enemies, most of them had vanished. A few remained, lying injured or dead.

Raiden's eyes flew over the scene. His stomach tightened as he realized that two profound figures were missing.

"Where are Rayla and Sapphire?" he said to no one, his voice wavering. He took off, sprinting to the battlefield.

"Rayla!" Luca called, having realized that Raiden was right.

"Sapphire!" Raiden cried immediately after.

"Here!" a female voice returned. Raiden's head snapped to the side and he tackled the girl in a hug.

"Ow," she said weakly, brushing her dark hair out of her face with one hand and holding her abdomen with the other.

"Where is Sapphire?" Raiden asked.

"Don't know," Rayla panted. "It was all so sudden. I heard a noise and then … I lost everyone. I couldn't– I didn't know– Everyone was going in different directions. I'm not even sure I know where *I* am right now."

Beside Raiden, Luca nodded to a nearby Maith guard. "Help the others check the bodies," he ordered. Raiden's heart hammered at the thought of Sapphire being found dead.

"Already done, sir," another approaching guard replied.

"What?" Luca demanded.

"We've checked all the bodies."

"And?"

"The survivors are over there," the man said, pointing to the same spot where Raiden and Luca had laid Macarius. "But there are three that are unaccounted for."

"Who?" Raiden said, filled with dread as he took a step toward the man.

"Nel– er, Nelgev, the younger man who came with us. Also Carrow."

Raiden's heart dropped as the guard finished his account, saying the words that Raiden had been fearing.

"And the girl … Sapphire. They're all missing."

chapter 34
Rayla

When Carrow began riding alongside her as they left the stable yard, Rayla couldn't decide how she felt.

Raiden had hinted at his own disgust with the scholar several times on their journey back from the hills, and she had eventually asked what Carrow had done to lose Raiden's favor. That was when the boy had let on that Carrow had been the reason that he and Luca hadn't gone after her immediately.

Rayla wasn't sure if she should be upset or grateful to the man. She had been so hurt when she had turned to look back at the camp and saw that nobody was moving to stop her from leaving. Still, looking back on the incident, she was sure of only one thing. She hadn't felt like herself at that moment. If anyone had come after her, she would have lost control out of fear. Perhaps Carrow had done her, and everyone else, a favor.

She had noticed that Carrow gave her a disapproving look, which she ignored, as she slipped her metal breastplate off. The metal had been cold, and she didn't need any help feeling cold in the autumn wind.

They began moving out of the castle walls. Sapphire slipped into line beside Rayla, but she didn't seem to be in the mood for talking. Rayla decided to give the girl some time to cope with everything their group had been through.

"I'll be taking Luca's spot on the way home," Carrow said as he approached, taking his place on Rayla's other side.

"Okay," Rayla replied. She wasn't sure what else to say.

"Rayla," Carrow said, his voice cautious. The scholar leaned over and placed a hand on Rayla's arm.

Immediately, she flinched away. Carrow froze, and Rayla could tell by the pain in his eyes that he had misread her reason for pulling away. She opened her mouth to explain, but Carrow interrupted.

"I'm sorry," he said softly. Rayla's heart ached at the pain in his voice. "I didn't want to let you go, you must understand. But I had to. You were unstable, you–"

"Could have hurt anyone," Rayla finished. "I know." She dropped her eyes to her saddle. "I believe you. And thank you. You were just protecting me."

"I was," Carrow agreed, clearly relieved that Rayla understood.

"And that's why I still think that you and anyone else have to keep a distance from me," Rayla pressed, urging Carrow to see the reason behind her words. "No one can touch me. I don't know what happened, and I don't want to do it again. Especially not to any of you."

"I think I know what happened."

"What?" Rayla whirled in her saddle to look at Carrow in shock. "You do?"

"I think," the scholar repeated slowly. "The legend of your gift places heavy emphasis on the concept of balance."

Rayla frowned. "Balance?"

Macarius nodded. "I'll look into it more when we are home, but think of it this way. If your gift has to be balanced, then the holder must stay *emotionally* balanced. What can be used to heal can also be used to hurt. That would explain why you can both heal and harm people with your gift."

They passed through the gates and the field opened around them. Rayla looked forward, still in shock.

"But that still wouldn't explain *how* I did what I did," she pointed out.

"Yes," Carrow insisted. "It does. What's the opposite of love, Rayla?"

"Love? What's that got to do with anything?"

"Surely by now you've realized your healing gift isn't *just* from good memories. You can only heal those that you have a strong emotional connection to – you can only heal those you love."

It felt as if the breath had been knocked out of her lungs. She felt her mouth drop open slightly.

Love was something she'd never had. Rather, it was something she had never thought she'd had. But she had healed Raiden. Did that mean she loved Raiden?

Rayla gasped. She recalled the feeling that went through her as she conjured memories when healing her friend. The warm feeling wasn't just from the power inside of her blood. It was from her own mind.

She *did* love Raiden.

"And the opposite of love," Carrow continued. She hadn't realized he was still speaking. "Is hate. You heal when you love, but when you hate with a certain passion, you can kill somebody. You had plenty of motive to hate Kuvira. And so you killed him not by brute strength, but by the pure hatred in your heart."

Rayla recalled the memories that had flashed through her mind as she had grabbed Kuvira's arm that night. She had seen images of him whipping her, of him laughing over Finn's dead body. She *had* hated the man. And she had used those memories and that hatred to kill him.

"Bloodcry," she whispered.

"What?" Carrow asked.

"The awful noise that came out of my mouth when I killed him." Even as she said it, she wasn't sure how she knew it. But she did. "It's called a bloodcry, isn't it?"

Carrow frowned. "I faintly recall seeing the word somewhere, but I'm not sure–"

A roar from behind them cut Carrow off. Before she realized what was happening, Rayla felt an intense stinging sensation on her left forearm. She jerked the limb toward her body, immediately aware of the warm blood that had seeped through her clothes.

"Rayla!" She heard a voice call from somewhere in front of her. She turned to look, but her line of sight was cut off. Already, several mounted men had crashed through the ranks and were cutting the Maith men off their horses. Rayla glanced around in confusion, but all she could see was mounted men rushing from behind the group. Then she caught sight of the clothes that their attackers wore. Black cloaks. Kuvira's – now Tenabris's – men. Her heart plummeted as she realized what must have happened. The spy that had escaped when Macarius had arrested his informant had sent word to Tenabris, and now Kuvira's men had found them.

"Saph!" she called, drawing her sword. She fought off any men that dared to come near her. She turned in her saddle to look for the young girl, but too many men began to swing their weapons at her.

Rayla felt her training kick in. She wanted to find Raiden or Sapphire or Luca. Even Nel, who had been silently allowing her to speak with Carrow only a moment earlier, would have been a comforting sight. But the battle stole all of Rayla's attention. She had no time to search for her friends.

She was too busy fighting for her life.

Several cuts and bruises found their way onto Rayla's body. Once, she received a blow to the stomach. Luckily, her thick winter clothes saved her, and all that remained was a thick gash in her tunic. Still, the close call had been enough to refocus her mind on the task at hand, and she momentarily ignored the worry she felt for her friends.

"Retreat!" Rayla heard someone call. She thought it sounded like Luca, but she couldn't be sure.

"Retreat to the left!"

Rayla whirled around in panic. She couldn't retreat to the left. She didn't know which way *was* left.

With no other option but to continue fighting, Rayla defended herself until, with no explanation, the enemy seemed to turn and disappear back the way they had come. Some of Maith's men tried to go after them, but Luca called them off. There were too many injured men for the remaining guards to give chase.

With the immediate threat to her life now gone, she remembered her friends.

"Saph!" she called. There was no answer.

Rayla turned to find a man brandishing a large broadsword charging toward her, apparently late to follow the other men in their retreat. Rayla pressed her heel to Dóchas's side and the mare sidestepped his attack at the last minute. Rayla slammed the pommel of her own sword into the back of the man's skull, sending him down to the ground with a sickening crunch.

"Carrow!" she tried again.

Even the scholar who had been right beside her a moment ago was completely out of sight. Gasping and grimacing, she turned Dóchas in a full circle. No Sapphire. No Carrow. No Nel. No Raiden. No Luca.

"Rayla!" a voice called. Rayla turned to the sound and found a familiar figure running back to the battle scene. To her relief, Raiden was directly beside Luca, the former calling for Sapphire. She dismounted and held Dóchas's reins in her hand.

"Here!" she called. Raiden's head snapped to her and he ran to her immediately. Before she could protest, he wrapped her into a hug. She felt her cuts and aches protesting and her gut sent a wave of nausea through her body at the sensation.

"Ow," she managed.

"Where is Sapphire?" Raiden asked, pulling back to look at her. She tried to catch her breath.

"I don't know," she admitted, her voice wavering. "Everything was so sudden. I heard a noise and then … I lost everyone. I couldn't– I didn't know–" She paused, trying to gather her scattered thoughts. "Everyone was going in different directions. I'm not even sure I know where *I* am right now."

It was true. The field still seemed to be spinning around.

"Help the others check the bodies," Luca said, approaching to check Rayla for injuries. But before he could reach her, a voice stopped them all in their tracks.

"Already done, sir."

Rayla turned to see an older guard approaching.

"What?" Luca demanded.

"We've checked all the bodies," the man said.

"And?" Luca replied.

"The survivors are over there," the man reported, pointing to the left. Rayla glanced over to see only a small portion of the Maith men. Her heart dropped.

"But there are three that are unaccounted for," the guard continued.

"Who?" Raiden said. Rayla felt the fear in her friend's voice seep into her own heart.

"Nel ... Er ... Nelgev, the younger man who came with us, and also Carrow."

Rayla covered her mouth with her hand. She felt tears spring to her eyes as the man finished his sentence.

"And the girl, Sapphire. They are all missing."

chapter 35
Rayla

They had all rendezvoused on the far east of the field, nearly beside the castle wall. Luca hadn't wanted to move some of the injured too far, Macarius included.

She had obeyed the order immediately, completely in shock. She felt nothing, both physically and mentally. Her limbs felt numb, even when she walked over to the grassy area where the injured and surviving Maith guards lay. Her head was buzzing. Not even the disappearance of Sapphire had seemed to sink in yet.

One thing seemed to stick out in her mind more clearly than anything else, and it was an odd thing to notice in such chaos. Not one soldier or citizen from inside Riraveth's walls had come to their aid. After all, the attack had happened right outside their gates. And yet, they had done nothing to help.

Perhaps Carrow had been wrong. Perhaps Lord Dunnman was helping Kuvira's army after all.

A warm breath on her neck sent a chill down Rayla's spine. She turned to see Dóchas, bumping her muzzle against Rayla's shoulder.

"I'm alright," she assured the mare, moving to tie her reins to a peg that she placed in the ground. "You stay here while I find the others."

Quickly, she spotted Luca and Raiden across from her and made her way to them. Raiden, she noticed, was pale in the face. Rayla's heart stumbled as she recognized the figure that he and Luca were kneeling beside. It was Macarius.

She stepped closer, careful to keep a respectful distance. There were several cuts and bruises on the man's body, and he was lying on his stomach. Worst of all was a deep, sickening gash across the man's back.

Not wanting to focus on the horrible sight, Rayla glanced over Raiden's body. He had several cuts as well, and a bloody gash on his jaw, but nothing that looked too serious. Luca had a gash on his right bicep, but seemed otherwise healthy from what she could see.

Rayla turned in a circle, examining their camp. Nine Maith guards were left, and they were all wounded in some way. Rayla remembered with a small amount of relief that Macarius had sent two guards ahead of them to warn Lord Hightower of their new information. Still, that meant that eight guards were dead and one was missing, as were Carrow and Sapphire.

Behind Rayla, a groan of pain cut through the eerie silence. She turned to see Luca ripping open Macarius's shirt.

"Raiden, give me a piece of cloth," Luca ordered. Quickly, the boy scrambled around before finally deciding to rip a piece from the bottom of his tunic. He returned, handing the cloth to Luca.

Rayla winced in sympathy as she watched Luca soak the cloth in some water from his canteen before bring it down onto Macarius's back. The man cried out. Rayla couldn't help but remember the whiplashes she had endured months ago.

"Will he ... " she tried to ask, but her voice caught in her throat. Both Raiden and Luca were too busy with their work to hear her anyway.

It occurred to Rayla that she could help, but she wasn't sure if she had any memories of Macarius to heal the man. It wasn't that she disliked him, but now that she knew the truth of how her gift worked, she wasn't sure if she could use them on the bowmaster. She had only just realized that she loved Raiden. She wasn't sure that she felt that level of emotion toward Macarius.

Still, she felt as if she had to try.

"Let me," she said, moving to kneel beside Raiden. She closed her eyes and recalled any small memory that she could. Nothing happened.

Frustrated, she decided to try a new tactic.

I may not love this man, she told herself. *But Raiden does. And I love Raiden. So for heaven's sake, WORK!*

It was by no means the same type of power she felt when she healed Raiden. Instead of a warm stream of memories and energy, she felt her gift sputtering. Even the golden light seemed to be flickering from beyond her eyelids. She opened her eyes and stared at Macarius's back.

It wasn't healed, but it did seem to have stopped bleeding.

"I … " her voice trailed off. Raiden placed a hand on her shoulder.

"Thank you," he said.

She nodded, standing and backing away. The action made her head spin, and her heart felt like it was skipping beats irregularly. She shook it off.

She had done all she could, but it wasn't enough.

Finally, after several minutes of excruciating anticipation from the others, Macarius ceased his cries of pain. Luca had finished cleaning the wound and was now using strips of Macarius's extra shirt, which Luca had asked a guard to bring over at some point, to bandage Macarius's wounds. Raiden, loyal as he was, had kept a firm and comforting hand on Macarius's own the entire time.

"He needs to rest," Luca announced, sighing as he leaned back on his heels.

Rayla, still standing off to the side, sighed as well. She was relieved to see that they wouldn't be losing another member of the group. At least, not today.

She glanced around, all too aware of the fact that there was nothing for her to do at the moment. She felt useless. Sapphire was gone. She could now admit that much to herself. Rayla began to tremble. She could do nothing to get the young girl back.

Thoughts of what she had endured while in Kuvira's camp came flooding into her mind. The idea of Sapphire, or Nel and Carrow, going through such a thing – being whipped raw, spat on, and beaten – made Rayla's stomach ache.

Suddenly Rayla found herself praying that Tenabris was less cruel than his father.

At least Sapphire would have Nel, she reminded herself. And Carrow. Unless they were all dead.

"Rayla, what's wrong?" Luca asked, pulling Rayla from her thoughts. Raiden's head snapped up from his master, looking to her in concern.

"Are you hurt?" he demanded.

Rayla opened her mouth to reply, but couldn't. She wasn't sure what to say, or how to say it. She didn't want to put the thought of Sapphire being tortured in Raiden's mind. Not when he was already so worried about Macarius as it was.

"Rayla?" Luca repeated. She looked at him. His face was white. "Why are you holding your stomach?"

Rayla looked down. She hadn't realized it, but Luca was right. Her right arm was clutched over her abdomen. *Probably from the nausea of thinking about Sapphire,* she reasoned.

She looked back to her master and shrugged, removing her hand. As the pressure from her hand left her stomach, she felt a strange and uncomfortable feeling go through her body.

Before she could say anything, Luca and Raiden both scrambled to their feet and ran to her. In seconds, they were on either side of her, holding her arms to keep her steady.

"What's wrong?" she asked, though her voice sounded more like a buzz in her head.

"Please ... No," Raiden whispered.

"Rayla?" Luca said in a strained voice. The girl frowned. Why were they acting so strange?

She looked to her master in wonder. Why was everything moving so slow? She blinked. Luca, she noticed, had fear in his eyes.

Confused, she turned to look at Raiden. His eyes were also filled with horror.

"What is going on?" she asked again.

"Raiden," Luca said in a rushed voice. "We need to lower her to the ground. Now."

"But what–" she tried as the men gently laid her down.

"Shh," Luca interrupted gently. "Don't worry, Rayla."

"But I–"

"Raiden, prop her head up."

She felt Raiden do as he was told.

"I don't understand–"

"Distract her," Luca said. Rayla tilted her head up to look at Raiden, who was trying to cover his fear. He cradled her head in his lap and smiled down at her. It was clearly a forced smile.

"What's wrong?" she managed, but Raiden only shook his head.

"What's your favorite thing about Dóchas?" he asked instead.

Rayla frowned. Why was he asking about Dóchas?

A little annoyed, she decided to humor her friend. She thought about her mare. She liked Dóchas's markings on her dark brown coat, and her intelligent eyes.

Rayla frowned. It was a hard question, but she thought she knew the answer. More than anything, she loved Dóchas's gentle nature.

She moved her mouth to convey her answer.

"Why are there stars on your face?" she asked instead.

Rayla blinked several times, but the stars wouldn't go away. She had also lost the feeling in her tongue, she noticed. How strange. Her eyes and body felt heavy, and she was using an unusual amount of energy to keep herself awake.

"Rayla?" she heard Raiden call. She couldn't respond.

"Rayla, stay awake!" Luca demanded. "Open your eyes! Rayla!"

But she couldn't open her eyes. She couldn't move her body. She couldn't stay awake. And so she let the stars overtake her.

chapter 36
Raiden

He hadn't moved at all. Rayla's head had remained on his lap since she had lost consciousness. At some point in the night, he had laid on his back to catch what little sleep he could. Then, when the sun had risen, he had sat back up and stroked Rayla's hair.

Sapphire wasn't here, taken away by whoever had attacked them. Almost definitely, they had been sent by Tenabris.

But with Sapphire currently missing, Raiden only clung more desperately to Rayla. He couldn't lose her too.

He couldn't.

Macarius had awoken in the night and gone through more treatments with Luca. The swordmaster seemed to care deeply for Macarius. It made sense, Raiden reasoned. The two had been friends for a number of years.

Today, Luca had seemed a bit more relaxed, which told Raiden that Macarius was out of immediate danger.

Both Macarius and Rayla had suffered deep, possibly life-threatening wounds. Macarius had taken a blow to the back that had cut through his muscles. Luckily, Luca had informed Raiden, the sword had missed his spine, judging by Macarius's ability to move his legs.

Rayla's however, had been an even stranger wound. She had been standing, and had even knelt to heal Macarius, without realizing that she was injured.

Luca had explained that, to some degree, Rayla had known. She had been holding her stomach, after all. But her conscious state seemed to be able to cope with that pain after the chaos and adrenaline of the battle.

Throughout the night, Rayla had regained semi-consciousness, muttering about things that didn't make any sense. Each time, Raiden had stroked her hair or whispered to her in an attempt to calm her down.

Now, it was midmorning, a full day after the ambush. Still, no one from inside Riraveth's walls had come out to check on them or help them. Luca had sent one of the few standing guards inside to inform the Riravethian guards, but the man had returned with no promise of aid. The guards had simply turned him away.

The thought made Raiden livid. They were such hateful people. They had sat idly by while his entire life had been flipped upside down. While his sister had been taken hostage, at best, and killed at worst, and while both his master and best friend had nearly been killed.

It had been too risky to move either Macarius or Rayla, as well as a few of the other guards that had been severely injured. They couldn't even travel back into the gates. Not that Raiden would want to if they could.

They had simply stayed outside, camping out along the eastern castle wall. Those who were able to had taken turns keeping watch. Raiden had helped as well, although he did so from his current position. Luca had offered to relieve him for a few hours' rest, but Raiden had refused.

"Has she woken up?" a familiar voice asked. Raiden looked up to see Luca approaching.

"No," he replied. His voice was hoarse from both lack of use and sleep deprivation. Luca sat down by Rayla's feet, looking at the girl in concern.

"Any change at all?"

"No," Raiden said. "She stirred a little last night, but never woke up."

Luca nodded and moved to kneel beside Rayla's body.

"I'm going to change her bandages," the swordmaster said. "You might want to take this chance to go see Macarius while–"

"No."

Luca froze at the harshness in Raden's voice. He hadn't intended to sound so calloused, but he was so worried about Rayla, and exhausted on top of that. Not to mention Sapphire …

"Raiden," Luca tried, but the boy looked at him with cold eyes.

"I'm not leaving her."

Luca's eyes flashed with something like annoyance. "I'm going to take care of her. Macarius is in just as bad a shape."

"I don't care."

This time, Luca's eyes flared. Only briefly, but the anger was there.

"He is your master."

"Yes, he was," Raiden corrected subtly, never taking his eyes off of Rayla's sleeping face. "But Rayla needs me more."

"Macarius needs you as well."

"I don't care!"

Raiden felt himself trembling, and suddenly he couldn't control his breathing. It was too much for him. He had spent days under too much stress as they had frantically searched for Rayla, not to mention the war they were now preparing for. For a fleeting moment, he had experienced some relief as they had been reunited with Rayla. But that had been taken away in moments, replaced by worry for Sapphire, Rayla, and Macarius.

Raiden felt as if he had experienced emotional whiplash, and he was tired of it. He needed a break. But even as he thought these things, he remembered the words of Sir Macarius on the day of Rayla's ceremony, when the man had offered advice to Raiden for dealing with hardships.

It's okay to feel overwhelmed, Macarius's voice echoed in his head. *But don't let it consume you.*

But that was before Macarius and Rayla had nearly been killed, and Sapphire had been captured.

Slowly, Raiden looked up to glare at Luca.

Although Luca's expression clearly showed that he did not approve of Raiden's outburst, the captain of the guard did not reply.

Instead, he began to clean and rebandage Rayla's wound.

Raiden looked away. The sight of Rayla's bloody body was too much, even with her blood trying to self-heal the terrible wound. He decided instead to focus on Rayla's sleeping face. At one point, her eyebrows drew together, and Raiden assumed that something had hurt her.

Without taking his eyes off Rayla's face, Raiden asked the question that had been bothering him most.

"Is it a bad sign that she hasn't woken up?"

For several seconds, Luca didn't reply. Raiden's thoughts began to run rampant. What if she never woke up? What if he woke up one day and she was cold, like Sapphire had with her sister? What if she kept getting worse and worse and he had to watch her slowly die?

"It's hard to tell," Luca finally admitted. The answer didn't ease Raiden's worry. "She lost a lot of blood. And I'm sure trying to heal Macarius only made things worse. She needs lots of rest."

Raiden couldn't stand to look at her face as Luca spoke. He squeezed his eyes shut. A tear fell from the corner of his eye and traced its way down his cheek.

"But if she doesn't wake by nightfall," Luca continued gravely, "it likely means that things are much worse than we thought."

Raiden didn't know what to say.

"What are we going to do tonight?" he asked, looking at Luca. The man sighed.

"I don't know," he admitted. "I considered traveling home, but too many of us are in no shape. So, I suppose we will have to stay here."

"Staying here is hardly safe," Raiden said, wishing the words weren't true. He wanted to find Sapphire, not leave her behind.

"We won't be able to do anything until Rayla improves. And significantly so," Luca stated. "After that, we will probably travel home."

Raiden's nostrils flared.

"We weren't going to leave without Rayla," he reminded Luca. "Why are you leaving without Sapphire? Or Nel, or Carrow?"

Luca grimace.

"Sir Macarius promised me that you would never leave a man behind," Raiden accused. "But it sounds like he was wrong."

"Raiden," the captain's voice cut across Raiden's protests firmly, but there was understanding in his eyes. "I know that you are angry. But I'm the authority figure left in this cohort. Macarius is out of commission, and Carrow is missing."

"But you're proposing that we leave–"

"Who do you think attacked us?"

The question caught Raiden off guard.

"I– I assumed they were from the hills," he answered slowly. Luca nodded.

"Tenabris sent them. Did you notice their cloaks?"

Raiden nodded.

"And that means that, if they were taken as hostage, our friends will be in the hills," Luca explained. "We don't have enough healthy men to attack the group that retreated, and we certainly don't have enough to sneak into the hills. Unless you have another suggestion, we need to go home and regroup."

Raiden felt his throat closed up as he realized that Luca was right.

"So what do we do?" He asked in a broken voice.

Luca sighed. "Once we are home, we can inform Lord Hightower of what has happened and gather troops for a search and rescue."

Raiden was silent for several minutes. There was another question that he wanted to ask, but he wasn't sure if he should. There was no way of knowing how Luca would take it.

Rayla trusts him, Raiden told himself. *That means I can, too.*

"Why do I feel nothing?" he blurted before he could change his mind. "Why don't I feel the same way as I did when Rayla was captured in the woods? Or even when she ran off after killing Kuvira? Why don't I feel this overwhelming desire to ride after Sapphire? Am I a terrible brother? What's wrong with me?"

Luca, to Raiden's surprise, didn't look shocked. Rather, the man appeared as though the question was normal.

"Nothing is wrong with you, Raiden," Luca consoled, adding the finishing touches to Rayla's bandages. "There are numerous reasons that you feel numb. The first and probably the biggest reason is that you've been forced to deal with so many issues at once – processing everything we've been through in the last two weeks, watching your master and your closest friend fight for their lives, losing your sister.

"You could also still be in shock," Luca continued. "And let's not forget that it's possible that you are starting to learn that the impulsive thing isn't always the smartest thing. Perhaps you know that Sapphire is strong, and that she can take care of herself until you can arrive with a means of rescue."

Though his face didn't show it, Raiden was surprised at how much better Luca's words made him feel. He nodded his thanks. Luca stood, laying a hand on Raiden's shoulder.

"Keep an eye on her," the man advised. "She's stubborn enough to surprise us with an unexpected turn of events."

"That's the truth," Raiden muttered as Luca walked away.

He looked down at Rayla's face again. She looked peaceful, despite her paleness. Raiden noted the stray strands of her red-brown hair that blew into her face. He glanced over her determined eyebrows, her thick eyelashes, and her small nose that somehow made her look as if she was always regarding someone or something with skepticism. Her thin lips were parted slightly as she breathed deeply.

A sudden protective urge came over Raiden. He leaned down, planting a soft kiss on Rayla's forehead.

"Hurry up and get better," he whispered into the girl's ear. "We have to go get my sister."